Ravensdene Court

By
J.S. Fletcher

We are pleased to present this easier-to-read,
specially formatted Classic Mystery Story,
Ravensdene Court, by J.S. Fletcher
For your Reading Pleasure

Originally Published in 1922
This Edition Published in 2022

ISBN: 9798371756756

Chapter 1

According to an entry in my book of engagements, I left London for Ravensdene Court on March 8th, 1912. Until about a fortnight earlier I had never heard of the place, but there was nothing remarkable in my ignorance of it, seeing that it stands on a remote part of the Northumbrian coast, and at least three hundred miles from my usual haunts. But then, towards the end of February, I received the following letter which I may as well print in full: it serves as a fitting and an explanatory introduction to a series of adventures, so extraordinary, mysterious, and fraught with danger, that I am still wondering how I, until then a man of peaceful and even dull life, ever came safely through them.

Dear Sir,

I am told by my friend Mr. Gervase Witherby of Monks Welborough, with whom I understand you to be well acquainted, you are one of our leading experts in matters relating to old books, documents, and the like, and the very man to inspect, value, and generally criticize the contents of an ancient library. Accordingly, I should be very glad to secure your valuable services. I have recently entered into possession of this place, a very old manor-house on the Northumbrian coast, wherein the senior branch of my family has been settled for some four hundred years. There are here many thousands of volumes, the majority of considerable age.

There are also large collections of pamphlets, manuscripts, and broadsheets. My immediate predecessor, my uncle, John Christopher Raven, was a great collector; but, from what I have seen of his collection up to now, I cannot say that he was a great exponent of the art of order, or a devotee of system, for an entire wing on this house is neither more nor less than a museum, into which books, papers, antiques, and similar things appear to have been dumped without regard to classification or arrangement. I am not a book-man, nor an antiquary; my life until recently has been spent in far different

5

fashion, as a Financial Commissioner in India. I am, however, sincerely anxious that these new possessions of mine should be properly cared for, and I should like an expert to examine everything that is here, and to advise me as to proper arrangement and provision for the future. I should accordingly be greatly obliged to you if you could make it convenient to come here as my guest, give me the benefit of your expert knowledge, and charge me whatever fee seems good to you.

I cannot promise you anything very lively in the way of amusement in your hours of relaxation, for this is a lonely place, and my family consists of nothing but myself and my niece, a girl of nineteen, just released from the schoolroom; but you may find some more congenial society in another guest of mine, Mr. Septimus Cazalette, the eminent authority on numismatics, who is here for the purpose of examining the vast collection of coins and medals formed by the kinsman I have just referred to. I can also promise you the advantages of a particularly bracing climate, and assure you of a warm welcome and every possible provision for your comfort. In the hope that you will be able to come to me at an early date,
I am, dear sir,
Yours truly,
Francis Raven
Leonard Middlebrook, Esq.,
35M, Old Buildings, Lincoln's Inn, W. C.

Several matters referred to in this letter inclined me towards going to Ravensdene Court...the old family mansion... the thousands of ancient volumes...the prospect of unearthing something of real note...the chance of examining a collector's harvest and perhaps more than anything, the genuinely courteous and polite tone of my invitation. I was not particularly busy at that time, nor had I been out of London for more than a few days now and then for several years: a change to the far-different North had its attractions. And after a brief correspondence with him, I arranged to go down to Mr. Raven early in March, and remain under his roof until I had completed the task which he desired me to undertake. As I have said already, I left London on the 8th of March, journeying to Newcastle by the afternoon express from King's Cross. I spent that night at Newcastle and went forward next morning to Alnmouth, which according to a map with which I had provided myself, was the nearest station to Ravensdene Court. And soon after arriving at Alnmouth the first chapter of my adventures opened, and came about by sheer luck. It was a particularly fine, bright, sharply-bracing morning, and as I was under no particular obligation to present myself at Ravensdene Court at any fixed time, I determined to walk thither by way of the coast. The distance, according to my map, was about nine or ten miles. Accordingly, sending on my luggage by a conveyance, with a message to Mr. Raven that I should arrive during the afternoon, I made through the village of Lesbury toward the sea, and before long came in sight of it...a glorious stretch of blue, smooth that day as an island lake and shining like polished steel in the light of the sun. There was not a sail in sight, north or south or due east, nor a wisp of trailing smoke from any passing steamer. I got an impression of silent, unbroken immensity which seemed a fitting prelude to the solitudes into which my mission had brought me.

I was at that time just thirty years of age, and though I had been closely kept to London of late years, my youth had been spent in lonely places, and had an innate love of solitudes and wide spaces. I saw at once that I should fall in love with this Northumbrian coast, and once on its headlands I took my time, sauntering along at my leisure.

Mr. Raven, in one of his letters, had mentioned seven as his dinner hour: therefore, I had the whole day before me. By noon the sun had grown warm, even summer-like; warm enough, at any rate, to warrant me in sitting down on a ledge of the cliffs while I smoked a pipe of tobacco and stared lazily at the mighty stretch of water across which, once upon a time, the Vikings had swarmed from Norway.

I must have become absorbed in my meditations... certainly it was with a start of surprise that I suddenly realized somebody was near me, and looked up to see, standing close by and eyeing me furtively, a man. It was, perhaps, the utter loneliness of my immediate surroundings just then that made me wonder to see any living thing so near. At that point there was neither a sail on the sea, nor a human habitation on the land; there was not even a sheep cropping the herbage of the headlands. I think there were birds calling about the pinnacles of the cliffs...yet it seemed to me the man broke a complete stillness when he spoke, as he quietly wished me a good morning. The sound of his voice startled me; also, it brought me out of a reverie and sharpened my wits, and as I replied to him, I took him in from head to foot. A thick-set middle-aged man, tidily dressed in a blue serge suit of nautical cut, the sort of thing they sell, ready-made, in sea-ports and naval stations. His clothes went with his dark skin and grizzled hair and beard, and with the gold rings which he wore in his ears. And there was that about him which suggested that he was for that time an idler, lounging.

"A fine morning," I remarked, not at all averse to entering into conversation, and already somewhat curious about him.

"A fine morning it is, master, and good weather, and likely to keep so," he answered, glancing around at sea and sky. Then he looked significantly at my knickerbockers and at a small satchel which I carried over my shoulders. "The right sort of weather," he added, "for gentlemen walking about the country pleasuring."

"You know these parts," I suggested.

"No!" he said, with a decisive shake of his head. "I don't, and that's a fact. I'm from the south, I am...never been up this way before, and, queerly enough, for I've seen most of the world in my time, never sailed this here sea as lies before us. But I've a sort of connection with this bit of country...mother's side came from hereabouts. And me having nothing particular to do, I came down here to take a cast round, like, seeing places as I've heard of...heard of, you understand, but never seen."

"Then you're staying in the neighborhood?" I asked. He raised one of his brown, hairy hands, and jerked a thumb landwards.

"Stopped last night in a little place, inland," he answered. "Name of Lesbury...a riverside spot. But that's not what I want...what I want is a churchyard, or it might be two, or it might be three, where there's gravestones what bears a name. Only I don't know where that churchyard or, again, there may be more than one...is. Except...somewhere between Alnmouth one way and Brandnell Bay, the other."

"I have a good map, if it's any use to you," I said. He took the map with a word of thanks, and after spreading it out, traced places with the end of his thick forefinger.

"Hereabouts we are, at this present," he said, "and here and there is, to be sure, villages...mostly inland. And it will have graveyards to them...folks must be laid away somewhere. And in one of them graveyards there'll be a name, and if I see that name, I'll know where I am, and I can ask further, aiming at to find out if any of that name is still flourishing hereabouts. But till I get that name, I'm clear off my course, so to speak."

"What is the name?" I asked him.

"Name of Netherfield," he answered, slowly. "Netherfield. Mother's people...long since. So I've been told. And seen it...in old books, what I have far away in Devonport. That's the name, right enough, only I don't know where to look for it. You've never seen it, in your wanderings round these parts?"

"I've only come into these parts this morning," I replied. "But if you look closely at that map, you'll observe there aren't many villages along the coast, so your search ought not to be a lengthy one. I should question if you'll find more than two or three churchyards between here and Brandell Bay judging by the map."

"Aye, well, Netherfield is the name," he repeated. "Netherfield, mother's side. In some churchyards hereabouts. And there may be some of them left and again there mayn't be. My name being Quick...Salter Quick. Of Devonport when on land."

He folded up and handed back the map, with an old-fashioned bow. I rose from the ledge of rock on which I had been resting, and made to go forward.

"I hope you'll come across what you're seeking, Mr. Quick," I said. "But I should say you won't have much difficulty. There can't be many churchyards in this quarter, and not many gravestones in any of them."

"I found nothing in that one behind," he answered, jerking his thumb towards Lesbury. "And it's a long time since my mother left these parts. But here I am...for the purpose. Time's no object...nor yet expense. A man must take a bit of a holiday some day or other. Never had one...me for thirty odd year."

We walked forward, northing our course, along the headlands. And rounding a sharp corner, we suddenly came in sight of a little settlement that lay half-way down the cliff.

There was a bit of a cottage or two, two or three boats drawn up on a strip of yellow sand, a crumbling smithy, and above these things, on a shelf of rock, a low-roofed, long-fronted inn, by the gable of which rose a mast, where floated a battered flag. At the sight of this I saw a gleam come into my companion's eye, and I was quick to understand it's meaning.

"Do you feel disposed to a glass of ale?" I asked. "I should say we could get one down there."

"Rum," he replied, laconically. "Rum is my drink, master. Used to that...I'm used to ale. Cold stuff! Give me something that warms a man."

"It's poor ale that won't warm a man's belly," I said with a laugh. "But every man to his taste. Come on, then."

He followed in silence down the path to the lonely inn; once, looking back, I saw that he was turning a sharp eye round and about the new stretch of country that had just opened before us. From the inn and its surroundings a winding track, a merely rough cartway, wound off and upward into the land; in the distance I saw the tower of a church. Salter Quick saw it, too, and nodded significantly in its direction.

"That'll be where I'll make next," he observed. "But first...meat and drink. I ate my breakfast before seven this morning, and this walking about on dry land makes a man hungry."

"Drink you'll get here, no doubt," I said. "But as to meat...doubtful."

His reply to that was to point to the sign above the inn door, to which we were now close. He read its announcement aloud, slowly.

"The Mariner's Joy. By Hildebrand Claigue. Good Entertainment for Man and Beast," he pronounced. "Entertainment...that means eating...meat for man; hay for cattle. Not that there's much sign of either in these parts, I think."

We walked into the Mariner's Joy side by side, turning into a low-ceilinged, darkish room, neat and clean enough, wherein there was a table, chairs, the model of a ship in a glass case on the mantelpiece, and a small bar, furnished with bottles and glasses, behind which stood a tall, middle-aged man, clean-shaven, spectacle, reading a newspaper. He bade us good morning, with no sign of surprise at the presence of strangers, and looked expectantly from one to the other. I turned to my companion.

"Well?" I said. "You'll drink with me? What is it...rum?"

"Rum it is, thanking you," he replied. "But food, too, is what I want." He glanced knowingly at the landlord. "You haven't got such a thing as a plateful...a good plateful of cold beef, with a pickle...onion or walnut? And bread...a loaf of real home-baked? And a morsel of cheese?"

The landlord smiled as he reached for the rum bottle.

"I daresay we can fit you up, my lad," he answered. "Got a nice round of boiled beef on go...as it happens. Drop of rum first, eh? And...yours sir?"

"A glass of ale if you please," I said. "And as I'm not quite as hungry as our friend here, a crust of bread and a piece of cheese."

The landlord satisfied our demands, and then vanished through a door at the back of his bar. And when he had expressed his wishes for my good health, Salter Quick tasted the rum, smacked his lips over it, and looked about him with evident approval.

"Sort of port that a vessel might put into with security and comfort for a day or two," he observed. "I reckon I'll put myself up here, while I'm looking round...this will do me very well. And doubtless there'll be them coming in here, night-time that will know the neighborhood, and be able to give a man points as to his bearings."

"I daresay you'll be very comfortable here," I assented. "It's not exactly a desert island."

"Aye, well, and Salter Quick's been in quarters of that sort in his time," he observed, with a glance that suggested infinite meaning. "He has, so! But this isn't no desert island, master. I can see they're not short of good grub and sound liquor here!"

He made his usual jerk of the thumb...this time in the direction of the landlord, who just then came back with a well-filled tray. And presently, first removing his cap and saying his grace in a devout fashion, he sat down and began to eat with an evidently sharp-set appetite. Trifling with my bread and cheese, I turned to the landlord.

"This is a very lonely spot," I said. "I was surprised to see a licensed house here. Where do you get your customers?"

"Ah, you wouldn't see it as you came along," replied the landlord. "I saw you coming...you came from Alnmouth way. There's a village just behind here it would be hidden from you by this headland at back of the house a good sized place. Plenty of custom from that, of nights. And of course there's folks going along, north and south."

Quick, his weather-stained cheeks bulging with his food, looked up sharply.

"A village, says you!" he exclaimed. "Then if a village, a church. And if a church, a churchyard. There is a churchyard, isn't there?"

"Why, there is a church, and there's a churchyard to it," replied the landlord. "What of that?"

Quick nodded at me.

"As I been explaining to this gentleman," he said, "churchyards is what I'm looking for. Graves in them, you understand. And on them graves, a name. Name of Netherfield. Now I asks you, friendly...have you ever seen that name in your churchyard? Because if so I'm at anchor. For the time being."

"Well, I haven't," answered the landlord. "But our churchyard...Lord bless you, there's scores of them flat stones in it that's covered with long grass. There might be that name on some of them, for anything I know. I've never looked them over, I'm sure. But..."

Just then there came into the parlor a man, who from his rough dress, appeared to be a cattle-drover or a shepherd. Claigue turned to him with a glance that seemed to indicate him as authority.

"Here's one as lives by that churchyard," he observed. "Jim! have you ever noticed the name of Netherfield on any of them old gravestones up yonder? This gentleman's asking after it, and I know you mow that churchyard grass time and again."

"Never seen it!" answered Jim. "But...strange things! There was a man come up to me the other night, this side of Lesbury, and asked that very question...not of these parts, he wasn't. But..."

He stopped at that. Salter Quick dropped his knife and fork with a clatter, and held up his right hand.

12

Chapter 2

It was very evident to Claigue and myself, interested spectators, Jim's announcement, sudden and unexpected as it was, had the instantaneous effect of making Quick forget his beef and his rum. Indeed, although he was only half-way through its contents, he pushed his plate away from him as if food were just then nauseous to him. His right hand lifted itself in an arresting, commanding gesture, and he turned a startled eye on the speaker, looking him through and through as if in angry doubt of what he had just said.

"What's that?" he snapped out. "What says you? Say it again...no, I'll say it for you...to make sure that my ears are not deceiving me! You met a man...hereabouts...what asked you if you knew where there was graves with a certain name on them? And that name was...Netherfield? Did you say that? I asks you serious?"

The drover, or shepherd, or whatever he was, looked from Quick to me and then to Claigue, and smiled, as if he wondered at Quick's intensity of manner.

"You've got it all right, mister," he answered. "That's just what I did say. A stranger chap, he was...never seen him in these parts before."

Quick took up his glass and drank. There was no doubt about his being upset, for his big hand trembled.

"Where was this here?" he demanded. "Recent?"

"Two nights ago," replied the man readily. "I was coming home, late, from Almwick, and met with this here chap a bit this side of Lesbury. We walked a piece of the road together, talking. And he asked me what I've told you. Did I know these parts? Was I a native hereabouts? Did I know any churchyards with the name Netherfield on gravestones? And I said I didn't, but there was such-like places in our parts where you couldn't see the gravestones for the grass, and these might be what he was asking after. And when we came to them cross-roads, where it goes to Denwick one direction and Boulmer the other, he left me, and I haven't seen anything of him since. Nor heard."

Quick pushed his empty glass across the table, with a sign to Claigue to refill it; at the same time he pointed silently to his informant, signifying that he was to be served at his expense. He was evidently deep in thought by that time, and for a moment or two he sat staring at the window and the blue sea beyond, abstracted and pondering. Suddenly he turned again on his informant.

"What like was this here man?" he demanded.

"I couldn't tell you, mister," Jim replied. "It was well after dark and I never saw his face. But, for the build of him, a strong-set man, like myself, and just about your height. And now I come to think of it, spoke in your way...not as we do in these quarters. A stranger...like yourself. Seafaring man, I took him for."

"And you never heard of his being about?" asked Quick.

"Not a word, mister," affirmed Jim. "He went Denwick way when he left me. That's going inland."

Quick turned to me.

"I would like to see that map of yours again, master, if you please," he said. "I ought to have provided myself with one before I came here." He spread the map out before him, and after taking another gulp of his rum, proceeded to trace roads and places with the point of his finger. "Denwick?" he muttered. "Aye I see that. And these places where there's a little cross? That'll mean there's a church there?"

I nodded an affirmative, silently watching him, and wondering what this desire on the part of two men to find the graves of the Netherfields might mean. And the landlord evidently shared my wonder, for presently he plumped his customer with a direct question.

"You seem very anxious to find these Netherfield gravestones," he remarked, with good-humored inquisitiveness. "And so, apparently, does another man. Now, I've been in these parts a good many years, and I've never heard of them; never even heard the name."

"Nor me!" said the other man. "There's none of that name in these parts between Alnmouth Bay and Budle Point. I never heard it!"

"And he's a native," declared the landlord. "Born and

bred and brought up here. Wasn't you, Jim?"

"Never been away from it," assented Jim, with a short laugh. "Never been farther north than Belford, south than Warkworth, west than Whittingham. And as for east, I reckon you can't get much further that way than where we are now."

"Not unless you take to the water, you can't," said Claigue. "No...we never heard of no Netherfields hereabouts."

Quick seemed indifferent to these remarks. He suddenly folded up the map, returned it to me with a word of thanks, and plunging a hand in his trousers pocket, produced a fistful of gold coins. "What's to pay?" he demanded. "Take it out of that...all we've had, and do you help yourself to a glass and a cigar." He flung a sovereign on the table, and rose to his feet. "I must be stepping along," he continued, looking at me. "If so be as there's another man seeking for..."

But at that he checked himself, remaining silent until Claigue counted out and handed over his change; silently, too, he pocketed it, and turned to the door. Claigue stopped him with an arresting word and motion of his hand.

"I say!" he said. "No business of mine, to be sure, but... don't you show that money of yours over readily hereabouts... in places like this, I mean. There's folk up and down these roads that would track you for miles on the chance of...eh, Jim?"

"Aye and farther!" assented Jim. "Keep it close."

Quick listened quietly...just as quietly he slipped a hand to his hip pocket, brought it back to the front and showed a revolver.

"That and me, together...eh?" he said significantly. "Bad look out for anybody that came between us and the light."

"They might come between you and the dark," retorted Claigue. "Take care of yourself! It isn't a wise thing to flash a handful of gold about, my lad."

Quick made no remark. He walked out on to the cobbled pavement in front of the inn, and when I had paid Claigue for my modest lunch, and asked how far it was to Ravensdene Court, I followed him. He was still in a brown study, and stood staring about him with moody eyes.

"Well?" I said, still inquisitive about this apparently mysterious man. "What next? Are you going on with your search?"

15

He scraped the point of a boot on the cobble-stones for a while, gazing downwards almost as if he expected to unearth something; suddenly he raised his eyes and gave me a franker look than I had so far had from him.

"Mister," he said, in a low voice, and with a side glance at the open door of the inn, "I'll tell you a bit more than I've said before...you're a gentleman, I can see, and such keeps counsel. I've an object and a particular object...in finding them graves. That's why I've travelled all this way...as you might say, from one end of England to the other. And now, arriving where they ought to be, I find...another man after what I'm after! Another man!"

"Have you any idea who he may be?" I asked.

He hesitated and then suddenly shook his head.

"I haven't!" he answered. "No, I haven't, and that's a fact. For a minute or two, in there, I thought maybe I did know, or, at any rate, had a notion; but it's a fact, I haven't. All the same, I'm going Denwick way, to see if I can come across whoever it is, or get news of him. Is that your road?"

"No," I replied. "I'm going some way farther along the headlands. Well...I hope you'll be successful in your search for the family gravestones."

He nodded, very seriously.

"I'm not going out of this country till I've found them!" he asserted determinedly. "It's what I've come three hundred miles for. Good day."

He turned off by the track that led over the top of the headlands, and as long as I watched him went steadily forward without even looking back, or to the right or left of him. And presently I, too, went on my way, and rounding another corner of the cliff left the lonely inn behind me. But as I went along, following the line of the headlands, I wondered a good deal about Salter Quick and the conversation at the Mariner's Joy. What was it that this hard-bitten, travel-worn man, one who had seen, evidently, much of wind and wave, was really after? I gave no credence to his story of the family relationship. It was not at all likely that a man would travel all the way from Devonshire to Northumberland to find the graves of his mother's ancestors. There was something beyond that...but what? It was very certain that Quick wanted to come across the tombs of the dead and gone Netherfields, however, for whatever purpose...certain, too, there was another man who had the same wish. That complicated matters, and it deepened the mystery. Why did two men...seafaring men, both of them arrive in this out-of-the-way spot about the same time, unknown to each other, but each apparently bent on the same object? And what would happen if, as seemed likely, they met? It was impossible to find an answer to these questions; but the mystery was there, all the same.

The afternoon remained fine, and, for the time of year, warm, and I took advantage of it by dawdling along that glorious stretch of sea-coast, taking in to the full its rich stores of romantic scenery and suggestion of long-past ages. Sometimes I sat for a long time, smoking my pipe on the edge of the headlands, staring at the blue of the water, the curl of the waves on the brown sands, conscious most of the compelling silence, and only dimly aware of the calling of the sea-birds on the cliffs. Altogether, the afternoon was drawing to its close when, rounding a bluff that had been in view before me for some time, I came in sight of what I felt sure to be Ravensdene Court, a grey-walled, stone-roofed Tudor mansion that stood at the head of a narrow valley or ravine...dene they call it in those parts, though it is really a tract of sand, while these breaks in the land are green and thickly treed...through which a narrow, rock-encumbered stream ran murmuring to the sea. Very picturesque in its old world it looked in the mellowing light; the very place, I thought, which a book-man and an antiquary, such as I had heard the late owner to be, would delight to store with his collections.

A path that led inland from the edge of the cliffs took me after a few minutes walking to a rustic gate which was set in the boundary wall of a small park; within the wall rose a belt of trees, mostly oak and beech, their trunks obscured by a thick undergrowth. Passing through this, I came out on the park itself, at a point where, on a well-kept green, a girl, whom I immediately took to be the niece, recently released from the schoolroom, of whom Mr. Raven had spoken in his letter, was studying the lie of a golf ball. Behind her, carrying a bag of sticks, stood a small boy, chiefly remarkable for his large boots and huge tam-o'-shanter bonnet, who, as I appeared on the scene, was intently watching his young mistress's putter, wavering uncertainly in her slender hands before she ventured on what was evidently a critical stroke. But before the stroke was made the girl caught sight of me, paused, seemed to remember something, and then, swinging her club, came lightly in my direction....a tall, elastic-limber girl, not exactly pretty, but full of attraction because of her clear eyes, healthy skin, and general atmosphere of life and vivacity. Recently released from the schoolroom though she might be, she showed neither embarrassment nor shyness on meeting a stranger. Her hand went out to me with ready frankness.

"Mr. Middlebrook?" she said inquiringly. "Yes, of course...I might have known you'd come along the cliffs. Your luggage came this morning, and we got your message. But you must be tired after all those miles? I'll take you up to the house and give you some tea."

"I'm not at all tired, thank you," I answered. "I came along very leisurely, enjoying the walk. Don't let me take you from your game."

"Oh, that's all right," she said carelessly, throwing her putter to the boy. "I've had quite enough; besides, it's getting towards dusk, and once the sun sets, it's soon dark in these regions. You've never seen Ravensdene Court before?"

"Never," I replied, glancing at the house, which stood some two or three hundred yards before us. "It seems to be a very romantically-situated, picturesque old place. I suppose you know all its nooks and corners?"

She gave her shoulders...squarely-set, well-developed ones...a little shrug, and shook her head.

"No, I don't," she answered. "I never saw it before last month. It's all that you say...picturesque and romantic enough. And queer! I believe it's haunted."

"That adds to its charm," I remarked with a laugh. "I hope I shall have the pleasure of seeing the ghost."

"I don't!" she said. "That is, I hope I shan't. The house is odd enough without that! But...you wouldn't be afraid?"

"Would you?" I asked, looking more closely at her.

"I don't know," she replied. "You'll understand more when you see the place. There's a very odd atmosphere about it. I think something must have happened there, some time. I'm not a coward, but, really, after the daylight's gone..."

"You're adding to its charms!" I interrupted. "Everything sounds delightful!"

She looked at me half-inquiringly, and then smiled a little.

"I believe you're pulling my leg," she said. "However, we'll see. But you don't look as if you would be afraid and you're not a bit like what I thought you'd be, either."

"What did you think I should be?" I asked, amused at her candor.

"Oh, I don't know...a queer, snuffy, bald-pated old man, like Mr. Cazalette," she replied. "Booky, and papery, and that sort of thing. And you're quite...something else and young!"

"The frost of thirty winters have settled on me," I remarked with mock seriousness.

"They must have been black frosts, then!" she retorted. "No! You're a surprise. I'm sure Uncle Francis is expecting a venerable, dry-as-dust sort of man."

"I hope he won't be disappointed," I said. "But I never told him I was dry as dust, or snuffy, or bald..."

"It's your reputation," she said quickly. "People don't expect to find such learning in ordinary young men in tweed suits."

"Am I an ordinary young man, then?" I demanded. "Really..."

"Oh, well, you know what I mean!" she said hastily. "You can call me a very ordinary young woman, if you like."

"I shall do nothing of the sort!" I said. "I have a habit of always calling things by their right names, and I can see already you are very far from being an ordinary young woman."

"So you begin by paying me compliments?" she retorted with a laugh. "Very well...I've no objection, which shows that I'm human, anyhow. But here is my uncle."

I had already seen Mr. Francis Raven advancing to meet us; a tall, somewhat stooping man with all the marks of the Anglo-Indian about him: a kindly face burnt brown by equatorial suns, old-fashioned, grizzled mustache and whiskers; the sort of man I had seen more than once coming off big liners at Tilbury and Southampton, looking as if England, seen again after many years of absence, were a strange country to their rather weary, wondering eyes. He came up with outstretched hands; I saw at once he was a man of shy, nervous temperament.

19

"Welcome to Ravensdene Court, Mr. Middlebrook!" he exclaimed in quick, almost deprecating fashion. "A very dull and out-of-the-way place to which to bring one used to London; but we'll do our best...you've had a convoy across the park, I see," he added with a glance at his niece. "That's right!"

"As charming a one as her surroundings are delightful, Mr. Raven," I said, assuming an intentionally old-fashioned manner. "If I am treated with the same consideration I have already received, I shall be loath to bring my task to an end!"

"Mr. Middlebrook is a bit of a tease, Uncle Francis," said my guide. "I've found that out already. He's not the paper-and-parchment person you expected."

"Oh, dear me, I didn't expect anything of the sort!" protested Mr. Raven. He looked from his niece to me, and laughed, shaking his head. "These modern young ladies...ah!" he exclaimed. "But come I'll show Mr. Middlebrook his rooms."

He led the way into the house and up the great stair of the hall to a couple of apartments which overlooked the park. I had a general sense of big spaces, ancient things, mysterious nooks and corners; my own rooms, a bed-chamber and a parlor, were delightful. My host was almost painfully anxious to assure himself that I had everything in them I was likely to want, and fussed about from one room to the other, seeing to details that I should never have thought of.

"You'll be able to find your way down?" he said at last, as he made for the door. "We dine at seven...perhaps there'll be time to take a little look round before then, after we've dressed. And I must introduce Mr. Cazalette...you don't know him personally? Oh, a remarkable man, a very remarkable man indeed...yes!"

I did not waste much time over my toilet, nor, apparently did Miss Marcia Raven, for I found her, in a smart gown, in the hall when I went down at half-past-six. And she and I had taken a look at its multifarious objects before Mr. Raven appeared on the scene, followed by Mr. Cazalette. One glance at this gentleman assured me that our host had been quite right when he spoke of him as remarkable...he was not merely remarkable, but so extraordinary in outward appearance that I felt it difficult to keep my eyes off him.

Chapter 3

Miss Raven had already described Mr. Cazalette to me, by inference, as a queer, snuffy bald-pated old man, but this summary synopsis of his exterior features failed to do justice to a remarkable original. There was something supremely odd about him. I thought, at first, my impression of oddity might be derived from his clothes. He wore a strangely-cut dress-coat of blue cloth, with gold buttons, a buff waistcoat, and a frilled shirt...but I soon came to the conclusion he would be queer and uncommon in any garments. About Mr. Cazalette there was an atmosphere and it was decidedly one of mystery. First and last, he looked uncanny.

Mr. Raven introduced us with a sort of old-world formality I soon discovered, as regards him, that he was so far unaware that a vast gulf lay between the manners and customs of society as they are nowadays and as they were when he left England for India in the seventies. He was essentially mid-Victorian and in order to keep up to it, I saluted Mr. Cazalette with great respect and expressed myself as feeling highly honored by meeting one so famous as my fellow-guest. Somewhat to my surprise, Mr. Cazalette's tightly-locked lips relaxed into what was plainly a humorous smile, and he favored me with a knowing look that was almost a wink.

"Aye, well," he said, "you're just about as well known in your own line, Middlebrook, as I am in mine, and between the pair of us I've no doubt we'll be able to reduce chaos into order. But we'll not talk shop at this hour of the day...there's more welcome matters at hand."

He put his snuff box and his gaudy handkerchief out of sight, and looked at his host and hostess with another knowing glance, reminding me somehow of a wicked old condor which I had sometimes seen at the Zoological Gardens, eyeing the keeper who approached with its meal.

"Mr. Cazalette," remarked Miss Raven, with an informing glance at me, "never, on principle, touches bite or sup between breakfast and dinner and he has no great love of breakfast."

"I'm a disciple of the justly famed and great man, Abernethy," observed Mr. Cazalette. "I'd never have lived to my age nor kept my energy at what, thank Heaven, it is, if I hadn't been. Do you know how old I am, Middlebrook?"

"I really don't, Mr. Cazalette," I replied.

"Well I'm eighty years of age," he answered with a grin. "And I'm intending to be a hundred! And on my hundredth birthday, I'll give a party, and I'll dance with the sprightliest lassie that's there, and if I'm not as lively as she is I'll be sore out of my calculations."

"A truly wonderful young man!" exclaimed Mr. Raven. "I veritably believe he feels and is younger than myself and I'm twenty years his junior."

So I had now discovered certain facts about Mr. Cazalette. He was an octogenarian. He was uncannily active. He had an almost imp-like desire to live and to dance when he ought to have been wrapped in blankets and saying his last prayers. And a few minutes later, when we were seated round our host's table, I discovered another fact...Mr. Cazalette was one of those men to whom dinner is the event of the day, and who regard conversation...on their own part, at any rate as a wicked disturbance of sacred rites.

As the meal progressed and Mr. Raven's cook proved to be an unusually clever and good one, I was astonished at Mr. Cazalette's gastronomic powers and at his love of mad dishes: indeed, I never saw a man eat so much, nor with such hearty appreciation of his food, nor in such a concentrated silence. Nevertheless, he kept his ears wide open to what was being said around him, I soon discovered. I was telling Mr. Raven and his niece of my adventure of the afternoon, and suddenly I observed Mr. Cazalette, on the other side of the round table at which we sat, had stopped eating, and the knife and fork still in his queer, claw-like hands, he was peering at me under the shaded lamps, his black, burning eyes full of a strange, absorbed interest. I paused...involuntarily.

"Go on!" said he. "Did you mention the name Netherfield just then?"

"I did," I said. "Netherfield."

"Well, continue with your tale," he said. "I'm listening.

I'm a silent man when I'm busy with my meat and drink, but I've a fine pair of ears."

He began to ply knife and fork again, and I went on with my story, continuing it until the parting with Salter Quick. When I came to that, the footman who stood behind Mr. Cazalette's chair was just removing his last plate, and the old man leaned back a little and favored the three of us with a look.

"Aye, well," he said, "and that's an interesting story, Middlebrook, and it tempts me to break my rule and talk a bit. It was some churchyard this fellow was seeking?"

"A churchyard in this neighborhood," I replied. "Or churchyards."

"Where there were graves with the name Netherfield on their stones or slabs or monuments," he continued.

"Aye...just so. And those men he foregathered with at the inn, they'd never heard of anything at that point, nor elsewhere?"

"Neither there nor elsewhere," I assented.

"Then if there is such a place," he said, "it'll be one of those disused burial-grounds of which there are examples here in the north, and not a few."

"You know of some?" suggested Mr. Raven.

"I've seen such places," answered Mr. Cazalette. "Betwixt here...the sea-coast and the Cheviots, westward, there's a good many spots that Goldsmith might have drawn upon for his deserted village. The folks go...the bit of a church falls into ruins...its graveyard gets choked with weeds...the stones are covered with moss and lichen...the monuments fall and are obscured by the grass....underneath the grass and the weed many an old family name lies hidden. And what'll that man be wanting to find any name at all for, I'd like to know!"

"The queer thing to me," observed Mr. Raven, "is that two men should be wanting to find it at the same time."

"That looks as if there were some very good reason why it should be found, doesn't it?" remarked his niece. "Anyway, it all sounds very queer...you've brought mystery with you, Mr. Middlebrook! Can't you suggest anything, Mr. Cazalette? I'm sure you're good at solving problems."

But just then Mr. Cazalette's particular servant put a fresh dish in front of him...a curry, the peculiar aroma of which evidently aroused his epicurean instinct. Instead of responding to Miss Raven's invitation he relapsed into silence, and picked up another fork. When dinner was over I excused myself from sitting with the two elder men over their wine...Mr. Cazalette, whom by that time I, of course, knew for a Scotchman, turned out to have an old-fashioned taste for claret and joined Miss Raven in the hall, a great, roomy, shadowy place which was evidently popular. There was a great fire in its big hearth-place with deep and comfortable chairs set about it; in one of these I found her sitting, a book in her hand. She dropped it as I approached and pointed to a chair at her side.

"What do you think of that queer old man?" Marcia asked in a low voice as I sat down. "Isn't there something almost...what is it? Uncanny about him?"

"You might call him that," I assented. "Yes...I think uncanny would fit him. A very marvelous man, though, at his age."

"Aye!" Marcia exclaimed, under her breath. "If I could live to see it, it wouldn't surprise me if he lived to be four hundred. He's so queer. Do you know that he actually goes out early...very early in the morning and swims in the open sea?"

"Any weather?" I suggested.

"No matter what the weather is," Marcia replied. "He's been here three weeks now, and he has never missed that morning swim. And sometimes the mornings have been Arctic...more than I could stand, anyway, and I'm pretty well hardened."

"A decided character!" I said musingly. "And somehow, he seems to fit in with his present surroundings. From what I have seen of it, Mr. Raven was quite right in telling me this house was a museum."

I was looking about me as I spoke. The big, high-roofed hall, like every room I had so far seen, was filled from floor to ceiling with books, pictures, statuary, armor, curiosities of every sort and of many ages. The prodigious numbers of the books alone showed me that I had no light task in prospect. But Marcia shook her head.

"Museum!" Marcia exclaimed. "I should think so! But you've seen nothing...wait till you see the north wing. Every room in that is crammed with things. I think my great-uncle, who left all this to Uncle Francis recently, must have done

24

nothing whatever but buy, and buy, and buy things, and then, when he got them home, have just dumped them down anywhere! There's some order here," she added, looking round, "but across there, in the north wing, it's confusion."

"Did you know your great-uncle?" I asked.

"I? No!" Marcia replied. "Oh, dear me, no! I'd never been in the north until Uncle Francis came home from India some months ago and fetched me from the school where I'd been ever since my father and mother died...that was when I was twelve. No, except my father, I never knew any of the Raven family. I believe Uncle Francis and myself are the very last."

"You must like living under the old family roof?" I suggested.

She gave me a somewhat undecided look.

"I'm not quite sure," Marcia answered. "Uncle Francis is the very soul of kindness. I think he's the very kindest person, man or woman, I ever came across, but...I don't know."

"Don't know...what?" I asked.

"Don't know if I really like this place," Marcia said. "As I said to you this afternoon, this is a very odd house altogether, and there's a strange atmosphere about it, and I think something must have happened here. I...well, personally, I feel as if I were something so very small and insignificant, shut up in immensity."

"That's because it's a little strange, even now," I suggested. "You'll get used to it. And I suppose there's society."

"Uncle Francis is a good deal of a recluse," Marcia answered. "It's really a very good thing I'm fond of outdoor life, and I take an interest in books, too. But I'm very deficient in knowledge in book matters...do teach me something while you're here! I'd like to know a good deal about all these folios and quartos and so on."

I made haste to reply I should be only too happy to put my knowledge at her disposal, and she responded by saying she would like to help me in classifying and inspecting the various volumes which the dead-and-gone great-uncle had collected. We got on very well together, and I was a little sorry when my host came in with his other guest...who, a loop-hole being given him, proceeded to give us a learned dissertation on the evidences of Roman occupation of the North of England as evidenced by recent and former discoveries of coins between Trent and Tweed: it was doubtless very interesting, and a striking proof of Mr. Cazalette's deep and profound knowledge of his special subject, and at another time I should have listened to it gladly.

But...somehow I should just then have preferred to chat quietly in the corner of the hearth with Miss Raven. We all retire early, Mr. Raven informed me with a shy laugh, as if he were confessing a failing, was the custom of the house. But, he added, I should find a fire in my sitting-room, so if I wanted to read or write, I should be comfortable in my retirement. On hearing that, I begged him to countermand any such luxuries on my account in future; it was my invariable habit, I assured him, to retire to bed at ten o'clock, wherever I was...reading or writing at night, I said, were practices which I rigidly tabooed. Mr. Cazalette, who stood by, grimly listening, nodded approval.

"Wise lad!" he said. "That's another reason why I'm what I am. Don't let any mistake be made about it! The old saw, much despised and laughed at though it is, has more in it than anybody thinks for. Get to your pillow early, and leave it early...that's the sure thing."

"I don't think I should like to get up as early as you do, though," remarked Mr. Raven. "You certainly don't give the worms much chance!"

"Aye, and I've caught a few in my time," assented the old gentleman, complacently. "And I hope to catch a few more yet. You folk who don't get up till the morning's half over don't know what you miss."

I slept soundly that night...a strange bed and unfamiliar surroundings affect me not at all. Just as suddenly as I had dropped asleep, I woke. My windows face due east. I was instantly aware the sun had either risen or was just about to rise. Springing out of bed and drawing up the blind of one of the three tall, narrow windows of my room, I saw him mounting behind a belt of pine and fir which stretched along a bluff of land that ran down to the open sea.

And I saw, too, that it was high tide...the sea had stolen up the creek which ran right to the foot of the park, and the wide expanse of water glittered and coruscated in the brilliance of the morning glory. My watch lay on the dressing-table close by; glancing at it, I saw that the time was twenty-five minutes to seven. I had been told that the family breakfasted at nine, so I had nearly two-and-a-half hours of leisure. Of course, I would go out, and enjoy the freshness of the morning. I turned to the window again, just to take another view of the scenery in front of the house, and to decide in which direction I would go.

And there, emerging from a wicket-gate that opened out of an adjacent plantation, I caught sight of Mr. Cazalette. It was evident that this robust octogenarian had been taking a morning swim Miss Raven had told me the previous evening. He was muffled up in an old pea-jacket; various towels were festooned about his shoulders; his bald head shone in the rising sun. I watched him curiously as he came along the borders of a thick yew hedge at the side of the gardens. Suddenly, at a particular point, he stopped, and drawing something out of his towels, thrust it, at the full length of his arm, into the closely interwoven mass of twig and foliage at his side. Then he moved forward towards the house; a bushy clump of rhododendron hid him from my sight. Two or three minutes later I heard a door close somewhere near my own; Mr. Cazalette had evidently re-entered his own apartment. I was bathed, shaved, and dressed by a quarter past seven, and finding my way out of the house went across the garden towards the wicket-gate through which I had seen Mr. Cazalette emerge...as he had come from the sea that way, it was, I concluded, the nearest way to it.

My path led by the yew-hedge which I have just mentioned, and I suddenly saw the place where Mr. Cazalette had stood when he thrust his arm into it; there on the ground was soft, mossy, damp. The marks of his shoes were plain. Out of mere curiosity, I stood where he had stood, and slightly parting the thick, clinging twigs, peeped into the obscurity behind. And there, thrust right in among the yew, I saw something white, a crumpled, crushed-up lump of linen, perhaps a man's full-sized pocket-handkerchief, where I could make out, even in that obscurity and nothing in the way of hedges can be thicker or darker than one of old, carefully-trimmed yew brown stains and red stains, as if from contact with soil or clay in one case, with blood in the other. I went onward, considerably mystified. But most people, chancing upon anything mysterious try to explain it to their own

27

satisfaction. I came to the conclusion Mr. Cazalette, during his morning swim...no doubt in very shallow waters had cut hand or foot against some sharp pebble or bit of rock, and had used his handkerchief as a bandage until the bleeding stopped. Yet... why thrust it away into the yew-hedge, close to the house? Why carry it from the shore at all, if he meant to get rid of it? And why not have consigned it to his dirty-linen basket and have it washed?

"Decidedly an odd character," I mused. "A man of mystery!"

Then I dismissed him from my thoughts, my mind becoming engrossed by the charm of my surroundings. I made my way down to the creek, passed through the belt of pine and fir over which I had seen the sun rise, and came out on a little, rock-bound cove, desolate and wild. Here one was shut out from everything but the sea in front: Ravensdene Court was no longer visible; here, amongst great masses of fallen cliff and limpet-encrusted rock, round which the full strength of the tide was washing, one seemed to be completely alone with sky and strand. But the place was tenanted. I had not taken twenty paces along the foot of the overhanging cliff before I pulled myself sharply to a halt. There, on the sand before me, his face turned to the sky, his arms helplessly stretched, lay Salter Quick. I knew he was dead in my first horrified glance. And for the second time that morning, I saw blood...red, vivid, staining the shining particles in the yellow, sun-lighted beach.

Chapter 4

My first feeling of almost stupefied horror at seeing a man whom I had met only the day before in the full tide of life and vigor lying there in that lonely place, literally weltering in his own blood and obviously the victim of a foul murder speedily changed to one of angry curiosity. Who had wrought this crime? Crime it undoubtedly was...the man's attitude, the trickle of blood from his slightly parted lips across the stubble of his chin, the crimson stain on the sand at his side, the whole attitude of his helpless figure, showed me that he had been attacked from the rear and probably stricken down by a deadly knife thrust through his shoulders. This was murder...black murder. And my thoughts flew to what Claigue, the landlord, had said, warningly, the previous afternoon, about the foolishness of showing so much gold.

Had Salter Quick disregarded that warning, flashed his money about in some other public house, been followed to this out of the way spot and run through the heart for the sake of his fistful of sovereigns? It looked like it. But then that thought fled, and another took its place...the recollection of the blood-stained linen, rag, bandage, or handkerchief, which that queer man Mr. Cazalette had pushed into hiding in the yew-hedge. Had Cazalette anything to do with this crime?

The instinctive desire to get an answer to this last question made me suddenly stoop down and lay my fingers on the dead man's open palm. I was conscious as I did so of the extraordinary, appealing helplessness of his hands...instead of being clenched in a death agony as I should have expected they were stretched wide; they looked nerveless, limp, effortless. But when my fingers came to the nearest one...the right hand... I found it was stiff, rigid, stone-cold. I knew then Salter Quick had been dead for several hours; had probably been lying there, murdered, all through the darkness of the night. There were no signs of any struggle. At this point the sands were unusually firm and for the most part, all round and about the body, they remained unbroken. Yet there were footprints, very faint indeed, yet traceable, and I saw at once that they did not extend beyond this spot. There were two distinct marks; one there of boots with nails in the heels; these were certainly made by the dead man; the other indicated a smaller, very light-soled boot, perhaps a slipper. A yard or so behind the body these marks were mingled; that had evidently been done when the murderer stole close up to his victim, preparatory to dealing the fatal thrust.

Carefully, slowly, I traced these footsteps. They were plainly traceable, faint though they were, to the edge of the low cliff, there a gentle slope of some twelve or fifteen feet in height; I traced them up its incline. But from the very edge of the cliff the land was covered by a thick wire-like turf; you could have run a heavy gun over it without leaving any impression. Yet it was clear two men had come across it to that point, had then descended the cliff to the sand, walked a few yards along the beach, and then...one had murdered the other.

Standing there, staring around me, I was suddenly startled by the explosion of a gun, close at hand. And then, from a coppice, some thirty yards away, a man emerged, whom I took, from his general appearance, to be a gamekeeper. Unconscious of my presence he walked forward in my direction, picked up a bird which his shot had brought down, and was thrusting it into a bag that hung at his hip, when I called to him. He looked round sharply, caught sight of me, and came slowly in my direction, wondering, I could see, who I was. I made towards him. He was a middle-aged, big-framed man, dark of skin and hair, sharp-eyed.

"Are you Mr. Raven's gamekeeper?" I asked, as I got within speaking distance. "Just so...I am staying with Mr. Raven. And I've just made a terrible discovery. There is a man lying behind the cliff there...dead."

"Dead, sir?" he exclaimed. "What...washed up by the tide, likely."

"No," I said. "He's been murdered. Stabbed to death!"

He let out a short, sibilant breath, looking at me with rapidly dilating eyes: they ran me all over, as if he wondered whether I were romancing.

"Come this way," I continued, leading him to the edge of the cliff. "And mind how you walk on the sand...there are foot-mark's there, and I don't want them interfered with till the police have examined them. There!" I continued, as we reached the edge of the turf and came in view of the beach. "You see?"

He gave another exclamation of surprise: then carefully followed me to the dead man's side where he stood staring wonderingly at the stains on the sand.

"He must have been dead for some hours," I whispered. "He's stone cold and rigid. Now, this is murder! You live about here, no doubt? Did you see or hear anything of this man in the neighborhood last night or in the afternoon or evening?"

"I, sir?" he exclaimed. "No, sir...nothing!"

"I met him yesterday afternoon on the headlands between this and Alnmouth," I remarked. "I was with him for a while at the Mariner's Joy. He pulled out a big handful of gold there, to pay for his lunch. The landlord warned him against showing so much money. Now, before we do more, I'd like to know if he's been murdered for the sake of robbery. You're doubtless quicker of hand than I am...just slip your hand into that right-hand pocket of his trousers, and see if you feel money there."

He took my meaning on the instant, and bending down, did what I suggested. A smothered exclamation came from him.

"Money?" he said. "His pocket's full of money!"

"Bring it out," I commanded.

He withdrew his hand; opened it; the palm was full of gold. The light of the morning sun flashed on those coins as if in mockery. We both looked at them and then at each other with a sudden mutual intelligence.

"Then it wasn't robbery!" I exclaimed. "So..."

He thrust back the gold, and pulling at a thick chain of steel which lay across Quick's waistcoat, drew out a fine watch.

"Gold again, sir!" he said. "And a good one that's never been bought for less than thirty pound. No, it's not been robbery."

"No," I agreed, "and that makes it all the more mysterious. What's your name?"

"Tarver, sir, at your service," he answered, as he rose from the dead man's side. "Been on this estate a many years, sir."

"Well, Tarver," I said, "the only thing to be done is that I

31

must go back to the house and tell Mr. Raven what's happened, and send for the police. Do you stay here and if anybody comes along, be very careful to keep them off those foot-mark's."

"Not likely there'll be anybody, sir," Tarver remarked. "As lonely a bit of coast, as there is, hereabouts. What beats me," he added, "is what was he and the man as did it...doing, here? There's nothing to come here for. And it must have happened in the night, judging by the looks of him."

"The whole thing's a profound mystery," I answered. "We shall hear a lot more of it."

I left him standing by the dead man and went hurriedly away towards Ravensdene Court. Glancing at my watch as I passed through the belt of pine, I saw that it was already getting on to nine o'clock and breakfast time. But this news of mine would have to be told. This was no time for waiting or for ceremony. I must get Mr. Raven aside, at once, and we must send for the nearest police officer. Just then, fifty yards in front of me, I saw Mr. Cazalette vanishing round the corner of the long yew-hedge, at the end nearest to the house.

So...he had evidently been back to the place whereat he had hidden the stained linen, whatever it was? Coming up to that place a moment later, and making sure that I was not observed, I looked in among the twigs and foliage. The thing was gone. This deepened the growing mystery more than ever. I began, against my will, to piece things together.

Mr. Cazalette, returning from the beach, hides a blood-stained rag. I, going to the beach, find a murdered man and coming back, I ascertain Mr. Cazalette has already removed what he had previously hidden. What connection was there...if any between Mr. Cazalette's actions and my discovery? To say the least of it, the whole thing was queer, strange, and even suspicious. Then I caught sight of Mr. Cazalette again. He was on the terrace, in front of the house, with Mr. Raven. They were strolling up and down, before the open window of the morning room, chatting. And I was thankful Miss Raven was not with them, and I saw no sign of her near presence. I determined to tell my gruesome news straight out...Mr. Raven, I felt sure, was not the man to be startled by tidings of sudden death, and I wanted, of set purpose, to see how his companion would take the announcement.

So, as I walked up the steps of the terrace, I loudly

called my host's name. He turned, saw from my expression something had happened, and hurried toward me, Cazalette trotting in his rear. I gave a warning look in in the direction of the house and its open windows.

"I don't want to alarm Miss Raven," I said in a low voice, which I purposely kept as matter-of-fact as possible. "Something has happened. You know the man I was telling you of last night...Salter Quick? I found his dead body, half-an-hour ago, on your beach. He has been murdered...stabbed to the heart. Your gamekeeper, Tarver, is with him. Had you not better send for the police?"

I carefully watched both men as I broke the news. Its effect upon them was different in both cases. Mr. Raven started a little; exclaimed a little: he was more wonder-struck than horrified. But Mr. Cazalette's mask-like countenance remained immobile; only, a gleam of sudden, almost pleased interest showed itself in his black, shrewd eyes.

"Aye?" he exclaimed. "So you found your man dead and murdered, Middlebrook? Well, now, that's the very end I was thinking the fellow would come to! Not that I fancied it would be so soon, nor so close at hand. On one's own doorstep so to speak. Interesting! Very interesting!"

I was too much taken aback by his callousness to make any observation on these sentiments; instead, I looked at Mr. Raven. He was evidently too much surprised just then to pay any attention to his elder guest, he motioned me to follow him.

"Come with me to the telephone," he said. "Dear, dear, what a very sad thing. Of course, the poor fellow has been murdered for his money? You said he'd a lot of gold on him."

"It's not been for robbery," I answered. "His money and his watch are untouched. There's more in it than that."

He stared at me as if failing to comprehend.

"Some mystery?" he suggested.

"A very deep and lurid one, I think," I said. "Get the police out as quickly as possible, and bid them bring a doctor."

"They'll bring their own police surgeon," he remarked, "but we have a medical man closer at hand. I'll ring him up, too. Yet...what can they do?"

"Nothing for him," I replied. "But they may be able to tell us at what hour the thing took place. And that's important."

When we left the telephone we went to the morning-room, to get a mouthful of food before going down to the beach. Miss Raven was there...so was Cazalette. I saw at once he had told her the news. She was sitting behind her tea and coffee things, staring at him, a cup of tea in one hand, a dry biscuit in the other, was marching up and down the room sipping and munching, and holding forth, in didactic fashion, on crime and detection. Miss Raven gave me a glance as I slipped into a place at her side.

"You found this poor man?" Marcia whispered. "How dreadful for you!"

"For him, too and far more so," I said. "I didn't want you to know until later. Mr. Cazalette oughtn't to have told you."

Marcia arched her eyebrows in the direction of the odd, still orating figure.

"Oh!" Marcia murmured. "He's no reverence for anything...life or death. I believe he's positively enjoying this. He's been talking like that ever since he came in and told me of it."

Mr. Raven and I made a very hurried breakfast and prepared to join Tarver. The news of the murder had spread through the household. We found two or three of the men-servants ready to accompany us. And Mr. Cazalette was ready, too, and, I thought, more eager than any of the rest. Indeed, when we set out from the house he led the way, across the gardens and pleasure-grounds, along the yew-hedge at which he never so much as gave a glance and through the belt of pine wood. At its further extremity he glanced at Mr. Raven.

"From what Middlebrook says, this man must be lying in Kernwick Cove," he said. "Now, there's a footpath across the headlands and the field above from Long Houghton village to that spot. Quick must have followed it last night. But how came he to meet his murderer or did his murderer follow him? And what was Quick doing down here? Was he directed here or led here?"

Mr. Raven seemed to think these questions impossible of immediate answer. His one anxiety at that moment appeared to be to set the machinery of justice in motion. He was manifestly relieved when, as we came to the open country behind the pines and firs, where a narrow lane ran down to the sea, we heard the rattle of a light dog-cart and turned to see the inspector of police and a couple of his men, who had evidently hurried off at once on receiving the telephone message. With them, seated by the inspector on the front seat of the trap, was a professional looking man who proved to be the police surgeon. We all trooped down to the beach, where Tarver was keeping his unpleasant vigil. He had been taking a look round the immediate scene of the murder, he said, during my absence, thinking he might find something in the way of a clue. But he had found nothing.

There were no signs of any struggle anywhere near. It seemed clear the two men had crossed the land, descended the low cliffs, and one had fallen on the other as soon as the sands were reached...the footmarks indicated as much. I pointed them out to the police, who examined them carefully, and agreed with me one set was undoubtedly made by the boots of the dead man while the other was caused by the pressure of some light-footed, lightly-shoe person.

And there being nothing else to be seen or done at that place, Salter Quick was lifted on to an improvised stretcher which the servants had brought down from the Court and carried by the way we had come to an outhouse in the gardens, where the police surgeon proceeded to make a more careful examination of his body. He was presently joined in this by the medical man of whom Mr. Raven had spoken...a Dr. Lorrimore, who came hurrying up in his motor-car, and at once took a hand in his fellow-practitioner's investigations. But there was little to investigate...just as I had thought from the first. Quick had been murdered by a knife-thrust from behind...dealt with evident knowledge of the right place to strike, said the two doctors, for his heart had been transfixed, and death must have been instantaneous. Mr. Raven shrank away from these gruesome details, but Mr. Cazalette showed the keenest interest in them, and would not be kept from the doctor's elbows. He was pertinacious in questioning them.

"And what sort of a weapon was it, do you suppose the assassin used?" he asked. "That'll be an important thing to know, I'm thinking."

"It might have been a seaman's knife," said the police surgeon. "One of those with a long, sharp blade."

"Or," said Dr. Lorrimore, "a stiletto such as foreigners carry."

"Aye," remarked Mr. Cazalette, "or with an operating knife...such as you medicos use. Any one of those fearsome things would serve, no doubt. But we'll be doing more good, Middlebrook, just to know what the police are finding in the man's pockets."

The police inspector had gotten all Quick's belongings in a little heap. They were considerable. Over thirty pounds in gold and silver. Twenty pounds in notes in an old pocket-book. His watch...certainly a valuable one. A pipe, a silver match-box, a tobacco-box of some metal, quaintly chased and ornamented. Various other small matters...but, with one exception, no papers or letters. The one exception was a slightly torn, dirty envelope addressed in an ill-formed handwriting to Mr. Salter Quick, care of Mr. Noah Quick, The Admiral Parker, Haulaway Street, Devonport.

There was no letter inside it, nor was there another scrap of writing anywhere about the dead man's pockets. The police allowed Mr. Cazalette to inspect these things according to his fancy. It was very clear to me by that time the old gentleman had some taste for detective work, and I watched him with curiosity while he carefully examined Quick's money, his watch...which he took particular notice, even going so far as to jot down its number and the name of its maker on his shirt cuff, and the rest of his belongings. But nothing seemed to excite his interest very deeply until he began to finger the tobacco-box; then, indeed, his eyes suddenly coruscated, and he turned to me almost excitedly.

"Middlebrook!" he whispered, edging me away from the others. "Do you look here, my lad! Do you see the inside of the lid of this box? There's been something...a design, a plan, something of that sort, anyway scratched into it with the point of a nail, or a knife. Look at the lines and see, there's marks and there's figures! Now I'd like to know what all that signifies? What are you going to do with all these things?" he asked, turning suddenly on the inspector. "Take them away?"

"They'll all be carefully sealed up and locked up till the inquest, sir," replied the inspector. "No doubt the dead man's relatives will claim them."

Mr. Cazalette laid down the tobacco-box, left the place, and hurried away in the direction of the house. Within a few minutes he came hurrying back, carrying a camera. He went up to the inspector with an almost wheedling air.

"You'll just indulge an old man's fancy?" he said. "There's some queer marking inside the lid of that bit of a box the poor man kept his tobacco in. I'd like to take a photograph of them. Man! you don't know that an examination of them mightn't be useful."

Chapter 5

The police inspector, a somewhat silent, stolid sort of man, looked down from his superior height on Mr. Cazalette's eager face with a half-bored, half-tolerant expression; he had already seen a good deal of the old gentleman's fussiness.

"What is it about the box?" he demanded.

"Certain marks on it...inside the lid that I'd like to photograph," answered Mr. Cazalette. "They're small and faint, but if I get a good negative of them I can enlarge it. And I say again, you don't know what one mightn't find out and any little detail is of value in a case of this sort."

The inspector picked up the metal tobacco-box from where it lay a midst Quick's belongings and looked inside the lid. It was very plain that he saw nothing there but some...to him meaningless scratches and he put the thing into Mr. Cazalette's hands with an air of indifference.

"I see no objection," he said. "Let's have it back when you've done with it. We shall have to exhibit these personal properties before the coroner."

Mr. Cazalette carried his camera and the tobacco box outside the shed in which the dead man's body lay and began to be busy. A gardener's potting-table stood against the wall; on this, backed by a black cloth which he had brought from the house, he set up the box and prepared to photograph it. It was evident that he attached great importance to what he was doing.

"I shall take two or three negatives of this, Middlebrook," he observed, consequentially. "I'm an expert in photography, and I've got an enlarging apparatus in my room. Before the day's out, I shall show you something."

Personally, I had seen no more in the inner lid of the tobacco box than the inspector seemed to have seen...a few lines and scratches, probably caused by thumb or fingernail and I left Mr. Cazalette to his self-imposed labors and rejoined the doctors and the police who were discussing the next thing to be done. That Quick had been murdered there was no doubt; there would have to be an inquest, of course, and for that purpose his body would have to be removed to the nearest inn, a house on the cross-roads just beyond Ravensdene Court; search would have to be set up at once for suspicious characters, and Noah Quick, of Devonport, would have to be communicated with.

All this the police took in hand, and I saw Mr. Raven was heartily relieved when he heard the dead man would be removed from his premises and the inquest would not be held there. Ever since I had first broken the news to him, he had been upset and nervous: I could see he was one of those men who dislike fuss and publicity. He looked at me with a sort of commiseration when the police questioned me closely about my knowledge of Salter Quick's movements on the previous day, and especially about his visit to the Mariner's Joy.

"Yet," I said, finishing my account of that episode, "it is very evident the man was not murdered for the sake of robbery, seeing that his money and his watch were found on him untouched."

The inspector shook his head.

"I'm not so sure," he remarked. "There's one thing that's certain...the man's clothes had been searched. Look here!"

He turned to Quick's garments, which had been removed, preparatory to laying out the body in decent array for interment, and picked up the waistcoat. Within the right side, made in the lining, there was a pocket, secured by a stout button. That pocket had been turned inside out; so, too, had a pocket in the left hip of the trousers, corresponding to that on the right in which Quick had carried the revolver he had shown to us at the inn. The waistcoat was a thick, quilted affair...its lining, here and there, had been ripped open by a knife. And the lining of the man's hat had been torn out, too, and thrust roughly into place again: clearly, whoever killed him had searched for something.

"It wasn't money they were after," observed the inspector, "but there was an object he had on him that his murderer was anxious to get. And the fact the murderer left all this gold untouched is the worst feature of the affair from our point of view."

"Why, now?" inquired Mr. Raven.

"Because, sir, it shows the murderer, whoever he was, had plenty of money on him," replied the inspector grimly. "And as he had have little difficulty in getting away. Probably he got an early morning train, north or south, and is hundreds of miles off by this time. But we must do our best and we'll get to work now."

Leaving everything to the police obviously with relief and thankfulness Mr. Raven retired from the scene, inviting the two medical men and the inspector into the house with him, to take, as he phrased, a little needful refreshment. He sent out a servant to minister to the constables in the same fashion. Leaving him and his guests in the morning-room and refusing Mr. Cazalette's invitation to join him in his photographic enterprise, I turned into the big hall and there found Miss Raven. I was glad to find her alone; the mere sight of her, in her morning freshness, was welcome after the gruesome business in which I had just been engaged. I think she saw something of my thoughts in my face, for she turned to me sympathetically.

"What a very unfortunate thing this should have happened at the very beginning of your visit!" she exclaimed. "Didn't it give you an awful shock, to find that poor fellow so unexpectedly!"

"It was certainly not a pleasant experience," I answered. "But I was not quite as surprised as you might think."

"Why not?" she asked.

"Because I can't explain it, quite...I felt, yesterday, the man was running risks by showing his money as foolishly as he did," I replied. "And, of course, when I found him, I thought he'd been murdered for his money."

"And yet he wasn't!" she said. "For you say it was all found on him. What an extraordinary mystery! Is there no clue? I suppose he must really have been killed by that man who was spoken of at the inn? You think they met?"

"To tell you the truth," I answered, "at present I don't know what to think...except this is merely a chapter in some mystery...an extraordinary one, as you remark. We shall hear more. And, in the meantime a much pleasanter thing...won't you show me round the house? Mr. Raven is busy with the police inspector and the doctors, and I'm anxious to know what the extent of my labors may be."

She at once acquiesced in this proposition, and we began to inspect the accumulations of the dead and gone master of Ravensdene Court. As his successor had remarked in his first letter to me, Mr. John Christopher Raven, though obviously a great collector, had certainly not been a great exponent of system and order...except in the library itself, where all his most precious treasures were stored in tall, locked book-presses, his gatherings were lumped together anyhow and anywhere, all over the big house.

The north wing was indeed a lumber-house. He appeared to have bought books, pamphlets, and manuscripts by the cart-load, and it was very plain to me, as an expert, the greater part of his possessions of these sorts had never even been examined before. Miss Raven and I had spent an hour in going from one room to another I had arrived at two definite conclusions...one, the dead man's collection of books and papers was about the most heterogeneous I had ever set eyes on, containing much of great value and much of none whatever; the other, it would take me a long time to make a really careful and proper examination of it, and longer still to arrange it in proper order.

Clearly, I should have to engage Mr. Raven in a strictly business talk, and find out what his ideas were in regard to putting his big library on a proper footing. Mr. Raven at last joined us, in one of the much-encumbered rooms. With him was the doctor, Lorrimore, whom he had mentioned to me as living near Ravensdene Court. He introduced him to his niece, with, I thought, some signs of pleasure; then to me, remarking that we had already seen each other in different surroundings...now we could foregather in pleasanter ones.

"Dr. Lorrimore," he continued, glancing from me to Miss Raven and then to the doctor with a smile that was evidently designed to put us all on a friendly footing, "Dr. Lorrimore and I have been having quite a good talk. It turns out he has spent a long time in India. So we have a lot in common."

"How very nice for you, Uncle Francis!" said Marcia. "I know you've been bored to death with having no one you could talk to about curries and brandy-pawnees and things...now Dr. Lorrimore will come and chat with you. Were you long in India, Dr. Lorrimore?"

"Twelve years," answered the doctor. "I came home just a year ago."

"To bury yourself in these wilds!" remarked Marcia. "Doesn't it seem quite out of the world here...after that?"

Dr. Lorrimore glanced at Mr. Raven and showed a set of very white teeth in a meaning smile. He was a tall, good-looking man, dark of eye and hair; mustache and bearded; apparently under forty years of age...yet, at each temple, there was the faintest trace of silvery gray. A rather notable man, too, I thought, and one who was evidently scrupulous about his appearance...yet his faultlessly cut frock suit of raven black, his glossy linen, and smart boots looked more fitted to a Harley Street consulting-room than to the Northumbrian cottages and farmsteads among which his lot must necessarily be cast. He transferred his somewhat gleaming, rather mechanical smile to Miss Raven.

"On the contrary," he said in a quiet almost bantering tone, "this seems quite gay. I was in a part of India where one had to travel long distances to see a white patient and one doesn't count the rest. And I bought this practice, knowing it to be one that would not make great demands on my time, so I could devote myself a good deal to certain scientific pursuits in which I am deeply interested. No! I don't feel out of the world, Miss Raven, I assure you."

"He has promised to put in some of his spare time with me, when he wants company," said Mr. Raven. "We shall have much in common."

"Dark secrets of a dark country!" remarked Dr. Lorrimore, with a sly glance at Miss Raven. "Over our cheroots!"

Then, excusing himself from Mr. Raven's pressing invitation to stay to lunch, he took himself off, and my host, his niece, and myself continued our investigations. These lasted until the lunch hour They afforded us abundant scope for conversation, too, and kept us from any reference to the grim tragedy of the early morning. Mr. Cazalette made no appearance at lunch. I heard a footman inform Miss Raven, in answer to her inquiry, he had just taken Mr. Cazalette's beef-tea to his room and he required nothing else. And I did not see him again until late that afternoon, when, as the rest of us were gathered about the tea-table in the hall, before a cheery fire, he suddenly appeared, a smile of grim satisfaction on his queer old face. He took his usual cup of tea and dry biscuit and sat down in silence. But by that time I was getting inquisitive.

"Well, Mr. Cazalette," I said, "have you brought your photographic investigations to any successful conclusion?"

"Yes, Mr. Cazalette," chimed in Marcia, whom I had told of the old man's odd fancy about the scratches on the lid of the tobacco box. "We're dying to know if you've found out anything. Have you and what is it?"

He gave us a knowing glance over the rim of his tea-cup.

"Aye!" he said. "Young folks are full of curiosity. But I'm not going to say what I've discovered, nor how far my investigations have gone. You must just die a bit more, Miss Raven, and maybe when you're on the point of demise I'll resuscitate you with the startling news of my great achievements."

I knew by that time when Mr. Cazalette relapsed into his native Scotch he was most serious, and his bantering tone was assumed as a cloak. It was clear we were not going to get anything out of him just then. But Mr. Raven tried another tack, fishing for information.

"You really think those marks were made of a purpose, Cazalette?" he suggested. "You think they were intentional?"

"I'll not say anything at present," answered Mr. Cazalette. "The experiment is in course of process. But I'll say this, as a student of this sort of thing the murderer was far from the ordinary."

Miss Raven shuddered a little.

"I hope the man who did it is not hanging about!" Marcia said.

Mr. Cazalette shook his head with a knowing gesture.

"You need have no fear of that, lassie!" he remarked. "The man that did it had put a good many miles between himself and his victim long before Middlebrook there made his remarkable discovery."

"Now, how do you know that, Mr. Cazalette?" I asked, feeling a bit restive under the old fellow's cock-sureness. "Isn't that guess work?"

"No!" Mr. Cazalette said. "It's deduction and common sense. Mine's a nature that's full of both those highly admirable qualities, Middlebrook."

He went away then, as silently as he had come. And when, a few minutes later, I, too, went off to some preliminary work that I had begun in the library. I began to think over the first events of the morning, and to wonder if I ought not to ask Mr. Cazalette for some explanation of the incident of the yew-hedge. He had certainly secreted a piece of blood-stained, mud-discolored linen in that hedge for an hour or so.

Why? Had it anything to do with the crime? Had he picked it up on the beach when he went for his dip? Why was he so secretive about it? And why, if it was something of moment, had he not carried it straight to his own room in the house, instead of hiding it in the hedge while he evidently went back to the house and made his toilet? The circumstance was extraordinary, to say the least of it.

But on reflection I determined to hold my tongue and abide my time. For anything I knew, Mr. Cazalette might have cut one of his feet on the sharp stones on the beach, used his handkerchief to staunch the wound, thrown it away into the hedge, and then, with a touch of native parsimony, have returned to recover the discarded article. Again, he might be in possession of some clue, to which his tobacco box investigations were ancillary altogether, it was best to leave him alone. He was clearly deeply interested in the murder of Salter Quick, and I had gathered from his behavior and remarks this sort of thing...investigation of crime had a curious fascination for him.

Let him, then, go his way; something, perhaps, might come of it. One thing was very sure, and the old man had grasped it readily...this crime was no ordinary one. As the twilight approached, making my work in the library impossible, and having no wish to go on with it by artificial light, I went out for a walk. The fascination which is invariably exercised on any of us by such affairs led me, half-unconsciously, to the scene of the murder. The tide, which had been up in the morning, was now out, though just beginning to turn again, and the beach, with its masses of bare rock and wide-spreading deposits of sea-weed, looked bleak and desolate in the uncertain grey light. But it was not without life...two men were standing near the place where I had come upon Salter Quick's dead body. Going nearer to them, I recognized one as Claigue, the landlord of the Mariner's Joy.

He recognized me at the same time, and touched his cap with a look that was alike knowing and confidential.

"So it came about as I'd warned him, sir!" he said, without preface. "I told him how it would be. You heard me! A man carrying gold about him like that and showing it to all and sundry. Why, he was asking for trouble!"

"The gold was found on him," I answered. "And his watch and other things. He wasn't murdered for his property."

Claigue uttered a sharp exclamation. He was evidently taken aback.

"You hadn't heard that, then?" I suggested.

"No," he replied. "I hadn't heard that, sir. Bless me! his money and valuables found on him. No! we've heard nothing except he was found murdered, here, early this morning. Of course, I concluded it had been for the sake of his money he'd been pulling it out in some public-house or other, and had been followed. Dear me! that puts a different complexion on things. Now, what's the meaning of it, in your opinion, sir?"

"I have none," I answered. "The whole thing's a mystery so far. But, as you live hereabouts, perhaps you can suggest something. The doctors are of the opinion he was murdered... here...yesterday evening: that his body had been lying here, just above high-water mark, since, probably, eight or nine o'clock last night. Now, what could he be doing down at this lonely spot? He went inland when he left your house."

The man who was with Claigue offered an explanation. There was, he said, a coast village or two further along the headlands; it would be a short cut to them to follow the beach.

"Yes," I said, "but that would argue he knew the lie of the land. And, according to his own account, he was a complete stranger."

"Aye!" broke in Claigue. "But he wasn't alone, sir, when he came here! He'd fallen in with somebody, somewhere, that brought him down here and left him, dead. And...who was it?"

There was no answering that question, and presently we parted, Claigue and his companion going back towards his inn, and I to Ravensdene Court. The dusk had fallen by that time, and the house was lighted when I came back. Entering by the big hall, I saw Mr. Raven, Mr. Cazalette, and the police inspector standing in close conversation by the hearth. Mr. Raven beckoned me to approach.

"Here's some most extraordinary news from Devonport...where Quick came from," he said. "The inspector wired to the police there this morning, telling them to communicate with his brother, whose name, you know, was found on him. He's had a wire from them this afternoon...read it!"

He turned to the inspector, who placed a telegram in my hand. It ran thus: *"Noah Quick was found murdered at lonely spot on riverside near Saltash at an early hour this morning. So far no clue whatever to murderer."*

Chapter 6

I handed the telegram back to the police inspector with a glance that took in the faces of all three men. It was evident that they were thinking the same thought that had flashed into my own mind. The inspector put it into words.

"This," he said in a low voice, tapping the bit of flimsy paper with his finger, "this throws a light on the affair of this morning. No ordinary crime, that, gentlemen! When two brothers are murdered on the same night, at places hundreds of miles apart, it signifies something out of the common. Somebody has had an interest in getting rid of both men!"

"Wasn't this Noah Quick mentioned in some paper you found on Salter Quick?" I asked.

"An envelope," replied the inspector. "We have it, of course. Landlord...so I took it to mean...of the Admiral Parker, Haulaway Street, Devonport. I wired to the police authorities there, telling them of Salter Quick's death and asking them to communicate at once with Noah. Their answer is...this!"

"It'll be at Devonport that the secret lies," observed Mr. Cazalette suddenly. "Aye...that's where you'll be seeking for news!"

"We've got none here...about our affair," remarked the inspector. "I set all my available staff to work as soon as I got back to headquarters this forenoon, and up to the time I set off to show you this, Mr. Raven, we'd learned nothing. It's a queer thing, but we haven't come across anybody who saw this man after he left you, Mr. Middlebrook, yesterday afternoon. You say he turned inland, towards Denwick, when he left you after coming out of Claigue's place...well, my men have inquired in every village and at every farmstead and wayside cottage within an area of ten or twelve miles, and we haven't heard a word of him. Where did he go? Whom did he come across?"

"I should say that's obvious," I said. "He came across the man of whom he heard at the Mariner's Joy...the man who, like himself, was asking for information about an old churchyard in which people called Netherfield are buried."

"We've heard all about that from the man who told him...Jim Gelthwaite, the drover," replied the inspector. "He's told us of his meeting with such a man, a night or two ago. But we can't get any information on that point, either. Nobody else seems to have seen that man, any more than they've seen Salter Quick!"

"I suppose there are places along this coast where a man might hide?" I suggested.

"Caves, now?" put in Mr. Cazalette.

"There may be," admitted the inspector. "Of course I shall have the coast searched."

"Aye, but you'll not find anything...now!" affirmed Mr. Cazalette. "The man, Jim the drover told of, he might be hiding here or there in a cave, or some out of the way place, of which there's plenty in this part, till he did the deed, but when it was once done, he'd be away! The railway's not that far, and there's early morning trains going north and south."

"We've been at the railway folk, at all the near stations," remarked the inspector. "They could tell nothing. It seems to me," he continued, turning to Mr. Raven, and nodding sidewise at Mr. Cazalette, "this gentleman hits the nail on the head when he says it's to Devonport that we'll be turning for explanations. I'm coming to the conclusion the whole affair has been engineered from that quarter."

"Aye!" said Mr. Cazalette, laconically confident. "You'll learn more about Salter when you hear more about Noah. And it's a very bonny mystery and with an uncommonly deep bottom to it!"

"I've wired to Devonport for full particulars about the affair there," said the inspector. "No doubt I shall have them by the time our inquest opens tomorrow."

I forget whether these particulars had reached him, when, next morning, Mr. Raven, Mr. Cazalette, the gamekeeper Tarver, and myself walked across the park to the wayside inn to which Salter Quick's body had been removed, and where the coroner was to hold his inquiry. I remember, however, that nothing was done that morning beyond a merely formal opening of the proceedings, and a telegram was received from the police at Devonport in which it was stated they were unable to find out if the two brothers had any near relations...no one there knew of any. Altogether, I think, nothing was revealed that day beyond what we knew already, and so far as I remember matters, no light was thrown on either murder for some time. But I was so much interested in the mystery surrounding them that I carefully collected all the newspaper accounts concerning the murder at Saltash and at Ravensdene Court, and pasted the clippings into a book, and from these I can now give something like a detailed account of all that was known of Salter and Noah Quick previous to the tragedies of that spring.

Somewhere about the end of the year 1910, Noah Quick, hailing, evidently, from nowhere in particular, but, equally evidently, being in possession of plenty of cash, became licensee of a small tavern called the Admiral Parker, in a back street in Devonport. It was a fully-licensed house, and much frequented by seamen. Noah was a thick-set, sturdy, middle-aged man, reserved, taciturn, very strict in his attention to business; a steady, sober man, keen on money matters.

He was a bachelor, keeping an elderly woman as housekeeper, a couple of stout women servants, a barmaid, and a pot-man. His house was particularly well-conducted; it was mentioned at the inquest on him the police had never once had any complaint in reference to it, and Noah, who had to deal with a rather rough class of customers, was peculiarly adept in keeping order...one witness, indeed, said that having had opportunities of watching him, he had formed the opinion that Noah, before going into the public-house business, had held some position of authority and was accustomed to obedience.

Everything seemed to be going very well with him and the Admiral Parker, when, in February, 1912, his brother, Salter, made his appearance in Devonport. Nobody knew anything about Salter, except that he was believed to have come to Devonport from Wapping or Rotherhithe, or somewhere about those Thames-side quarters. He was very like his brother in appearance, and in character, except he was more sociable, and more talkative. He took up his residence at the Admiral Parker, and he and Noah evidently got on together very well: they were even affectionate in manner toward each other. They were often seen in Devonport and in Plymouth in company, but those who knew them best at this time noted they never paid visits to, nor received visits from, any one coming within the category of friends or relations. And one man, giving evidence at the inquest on Noah, said he had some recollection that Salter, in a moment of confidence, had once told him that he and Noah were orphans, and hadn't a blood-relation in the world. According to all that was brought out, matters went quite smoothly and pleasantly at the Admiral Parker until the 5th of March, 1912, three days, it will be observed, before I left London for Ravensdene Court.

On that date, Salter, who had a banking account at a Plymouth bank, to which he had been introduced by Noah, who also banked there, cashed a check for sixty pounds. That was in the morning...in the early afternoon, he went away, remarking to the barmaid at his brother's inn he was first going to London and then north. Noah accompanied him to the railway station. As far as anyone knew, Salter was not burdened by any luggage, even by a handbag.

After he had gone, things went on just as usual at the Admiral Parker. Neither the housekeeper, nor the barmaid, nor the pot-man, could remember the place was visited by any suspicious characters, nor that its landlord showed any signs of having any trouble or any extraordinary business matters. Everything was as it should be, when, on the evening of the 9th of March...the very day on which I met Salter on the Northumbrian coast, Noah told his housekeeper and barmaid he had to go over to Saltash, to see a man on business, and should be back about closing-time. He went away about seven o'clock, but he was not back at closing-time. The pot-man sat up for him until midnight: he was not back then. And none of his people at the Admiral Parker heard any more of him until just after breakfast next morning, when the police came and told them their employer's body had been found at a lonely spot on the bank of the river a little above Saltash, and he had certainly been murdered.

There were some points of similarity between the murders of Salter and Noah. The movements and doings of each man were traceable up to a certain point, after which nothing whatever could be discovered respecting them. As regards Noah he had crossed the river between Keyham and Saltash by the ferry-boat, landing just beneath the great bridge which links Devon with Cornwall. It was then nearly dark, but he was seen and spoken to by several men who knew him well. He was seen, too, to go up the steep street towards the head of the queer old village: there he went into one of the inns, had a glass of whiskey at the bar, exchanged a word or two with some men sitting in the parlor, and after a while, glancing at his watch, went out and was never seen again alive. His dead body was found next morning at a lonely spot on an adjacent creek, by a fisherman...like Salter, he had been stabbed, and in similar fashion. And as in Salter's case, robbery of money and valuables had not been the murderer's object.

Noah, when found, had money on him, gold, silver; he was also wearing a gold watch and chain and a diamond ring; all these things were untouched, as if the murderer had felt contemptuous of them. But here again was a point of similarity in the two crimes...Noah's pocket's had been turned out; the lining of his waistcoat had been slashed and slit; his thick reefer jacket had been torn off him and subjected to a similar search...its lining was cut to pieces, and it and his overcoat were found flung carelessly over the body. Close by lay his hard felt hat...the lining had been torn out.

This, according to the evidence given at the inquests and to the facts collected by the police at the places concerned, was all that came out. There was not the slightest clue in either case. No one could say what became of Salter after he left me outside the Mariner's Joy; no one knew where Noah went when he walked out of the Saltash inn into the darkness.

At each inquest a verdict of willful murder against some person or persons unknown was returned, and the respective coroners uttered some platitudes about coincidence and mystery and all the rest of it. But from all that had transpired it seemed to me there were certain things to be deduced, and I find that I tabulated them at the time, writing them down at the end of the newspaper clippings, as follows:

1. Salter and Noah Quick were in possession of some secret.

2. They were murdered by men who wished to get possession of it for themselves.

3. The actual murderers were probably two members of a gang.

4. Gang...if a gang and murderers were at large, and, if

51

they had secured possession of the secret would be sure to make use of it.

Out of this arose the question...what was the secret? Something, I had no doubt whatever, that related to money. But what, and how? I exercised my speculative faculties a good deal at the time over this matter, and I could not avoid wondering about Mr. Cazalette and the yew-hedge affair. He never mentioned it; I was afraid and nervous about telling him what I had seen. Nor for some time did he mention his tobacco box labors indeed, I don't remember that he mentioned them directly at all. But, about the time the inquests on the two murdered men came to an end, I observed Mr. Cazalette, most of whose time was devoted to his numismatic work, was spending his leisure in turning over whatever books he could come across at Ravensdene Court which related to local history and topography; he was also studying old maps, charts and the like. Also, he got from London the latest Ordnance Map. I saw him studying that with deep attention. Yet he said nothing until one day, coming across me in the library, alone, he suddenly plumped me with a question.

"Middlebrook!" he said, "the name which that poor man mentioned to you as you talked with him on the cliff was... Netherfield?"

"Netherfield," I said. "That was it...Netherfield."

"He said there were Netherfields buried hereabouts?" he asked.

"Just so...in some churchyard or other," I answered. "What of it, Mr. Cazalette?"

He helped himself to a pinch of snuff, as if to assist his thoughts.

"Well," he said presently, "and it's a queer thing that at the time of the inquest nobody ever thought of inquiring if there is such a churchyard and such graves."

"Why didn't you suggest it?" I asked.

"I'd rather find it out for myself," he said, with a knowing look. "And if you want to know, I've been trying to do so. But I've looked through every local history there is...and I think the late John Christopher Raven collected every scrap of printed stuff relating to this corner of the country that's ever left a press and I can't find any reference to such a name."

"Parish registers?" I suggested.

"Aye, I thought of that," he said. "Some of them have been printed, and I've consulted those that have, without result. And, Middlebrook, I'm more than ever convinced the dead man knew what he was talking about, and there's dead and gone Netherfields lying somewhere in this quarter, and the secret of his murder is, somehow, to be found in their ancient tombs! Aye!"

He took another big pinch of snuff, and looked at me as if to find out whether or not I agreed with him. Then I let out a question.

"Mr. Cazalette, have you found out anything from your photographic work on that tobacco box lid?" I asked. "You thought you might."

Much to my astonishment, he turned and shuffled away.

"I'm not through with that matter, yet," he answered. "It's...progressing."

I told Miss Raven of this little conversation. She and I were often together in the library; we often discussed the mystery of the murders.

"What was there, really, on the lid of the tobacco box?" Marcia asked. "Anything that could actually arouse curiosity?"

"I think Mr. Cazalette exaggerated their importance," I replied, "but there were certainly some marks, scratches, which seemed to have been made by design."

"And what," Marcia asked again, "did Mr. Cazalette think they might mean?"

"Heaven knows!" I answered. "Some deep and dark clue to Quick's murder, I suppose."

"I wish I had seen the tobacco box," she remarked. "Interesting, anyway."

"That's easy enough," I said. "The police have it and all the rest of Quick's belongings. If we walked over to the police station, the inspector would willingly show it to you."

I saw that this proposition attracted her...she was not beyond feeling something of the fascination which is exercised upon some people by the inspection of the relics of strange crimes.

"Let us go, then," Marcia said. "This afternoon?"

I had a mind, myself, to have another look at that tobacco box. Mr. Cazalette's hints about it, and his mysterious secrecy regarding his photographic experiments, made me inquisitive. So after lunch Miss Raven and I walked across country to the police station, where we were shown into the presence of the inspector, who, in the midst of his politeness, frankly showed his wonder at our pilgrimage.

"We have come with an object," I said, giving him an informing glance. "Miss Raven, like most ladies, is not devoid of curiosity. She wishes to see that metal tobacco box which was found on Salter."

The inspector laughed.

"Oh!" he exclaimed. "The thing the old gentleman... what's his name? Mr. Cazalette was so keen about photographing. Why, I don't know...I saw nothing but two or three surface scratches inside the lid. Has he discovered anything?"

"That," I answered, "is only known to Mr. Cazalette. He preserves a strict silence on that point. He is very mysterious about the matter. It is his secrecy, and his mystery, that makes Miss Raven inquisitive."

"Well," remarked the inspector, indulgently, "it's a curiosity that can very easily be satisfied. I've got all Quick's belongings here...just as they were put together after being exhibited before the coroner." He unlocked a cupboard and pointed to two bundles...one, a large one, was done up in linen; the other, a small one, in a wrapping of canvas. "That," he continued, pointing to the linen-covered package, "contains his clothing; this, his effects: his money, watch and chain, and so on. It's sealed, as you see, but we can put fresh seals on after breaking these."

"Very kind of you to take so much trouble," said Miss Raven. "All to satisfy a mere whim."

The inspector assured her that it was no trouble, and broke the seals of the small, carefully-wrapped package. There, neatly done up, were the dead man's effects, even down to his pipe and pouch. His money was there, notes, gold, silver, copper; there was a stump of lead-pencil and a bit of string; every single thing found upon him had been kept. But the tobacco box was not there.

"I...I don't see it!" exclaimed the inspector. "How's this?"

He turned the things over again, and yet again...there was no tobacco box. And at that, evidently vexed and perplexed, he rang a bell and asked for a particular constable, who presently entered. The inspector indicated the various properties.

"Didn't you put these things together when the inquest was over?" he demanded. "They were all lying on the table at the inquest...we showed them there. I told you to put them up and bring them here and seal them."

"I did, sir," answered the man. "I put together everything that was on the table, at once. The package was never out of my hands till I got it here, and sealed it. Sergeant Brown and myself counted the money, sir."

"The money is all right," observed the inspector. "But there's a metal box...a tobacco box missing. Do you remember it?"

"Can't say I do, sir," replied the constable. "I packed up everything that was there."

The inspector nodded a dismissal; when we were alone again, he turned to Miss Raven and me with a queer expression.

"That box has been taken at the inquest!" he said, "Now then...by whom and why?"

Chapter 7

It was very evident the inspector was considerably puzzled, not to say upset, by the disappearance of the tobacco box, and I fancied that I saw the real reason of his discomfiture. He had pooh-poohed Mr. Cazalette's almost senile eagerness about the thing, treating his request as of no importance; now he suddenly discovered somebody had conceived a remarkable interest in the tobacco box and had cleverly taken it under his very eyes and he was angry with himself for his lack of care and perception. I was not indisposed to banter him a little.

"The second of your questions might be easily answered," I said. "The thing has been appropriated because somebody believes, as Mr. Cazalette evidently does, or did, there may be a clue in those scratches, or marks, on the inside of the lid. But as to who it was that believed this, and managed to secrete the box...that's a far different matter!"

He was thinking, and presently he nodded his head.

"I can call to mind everybody who sat round that table, where these things were laid out," he remarked, confidently. "There were two or three officials, like myself. There was our surgeon and Dr. Lorrimore. Two or three of the country gentlemen...all magistrates; all well known to me. And at the foot of the table there were a couple of reporters: I know them, too, well enough. Now, who, out of that lot, would be likely to steal...for that's what it comes to...this tobacco box? A thing that had scarcely been mentioned...if at all during the proceedings!"

"Well, I don't know," I remarked. "But you're forgetting one thing, inspector. That's...curiosity!"

He looked at me blankly...clearly, he did not understand. Neither, I saw, did Miss Raven.

"There are some people," I continued, "who have an itching...perhaps a morbid desire to collect and possess relics, memento's of crime and criminals. I know a man who has a cabinet filled with such things...very proud of the fact he owns a flute which once belonged to Charles Pease; a purse that was found on Frank Muller; a reputed riding-whip of Dick Turpin's and the like. How do you know that one or other of the various men who sat round the table you're talking of hasn't some such mania and appropriated the tobacco box as a memento of the Ravensdene Court mania?"

"I don't know," he replied. "But I don't think it likely: I know the lot of them, more or less, and I think they've all too much sense."

"All the same, the thing's gone," I remarked. "And you'll excuse me for saying it...you're a bit concerned by its disappearance."

"I am!" he said, frankly. "And I'll tell you why. It's just because no particular attention was drawn to it at the inquest. So far as I remember it was barely mentioned...if it was, it was only as one item, an insignificant one, among more important things; the money, the watch and chain, and so on. But somebody...somebody there considered it of so much importance as to appropriate it. Therefore, it is...just what I thought it wasn't a matter of moment. I ought to have taken more care about it, from the time Mr. Cazalette first drew my attention to those marks inside the lid."

"You're sure it was on the table at the inquest?" I suggested.

"I'm sure of that," he replied with conviction, "for I distinctly remember laying out the various objects myself. When the inquest was over, I told the man you've just seen to put them all together and to seal the package when he brought it back here. No...that tobacco box was picked up...stolen off that table."

"Then there's more in the matter than lies on the surface," I said.

"Evidently," he said. He looked dubiously from Miss Raven to myself. "I suppose the old gentleman...Mr. Cazalette is to be...trusted? I mean you don't think he's found out anything with his photography, and is keeping it dark?"

"Miss Raven and myself," I replied, "know nothing whatever of Mr. Cazalette except that he is a famous authority on coins and medals, a very remarkable person for his age, and Mr. Raven's guest. As to his keeping the result of 'his investigations dark, I should say that no one could do that sort of thing better!"

"Aye, so I guessed," muttered the inspector. "I wish he'd tell us, though, if he has discovered anything. But I suppose he'll take his time?"

"Precisely," I said. "Men like Mr. Cazalette do. Time is regarded by men of his peculiar temperament in somewhat different fashion to the way in which we younger folk regard it...having come a long way along the road of life, they refuse to be hurried. Well I suppose you'll make some inquiries about that box? By the way, if it's not a professional secret, have you heard any more of the affair at Saltash?"

"They haven't found out another thing," he answered, with a shake of the head. "That's as big a mystery as this!"

"What do you think, from your standpoint, of the two affairs?" I asked, more for the delectation of Miss Raven than for my own satisfaction. I knew she was curious about the double mystery. "Have you formed any conclusion?"

"I've thought a great deal about it," he replied. "It seems to me the two brothers, Salter and Noah Quick, were men who had what's commonly called a past, and there was some strange secret in it...probably one of money. I think in their last days they were tracked, shadowed, whatever you like to call it, by some old associates of theirs, who murdered them in the expectation of getting hold of something...papers, or what not. And what I would like to know is why did Salter Quick come down here, to this particular bit of the North Country?"

"He said to look for the graves of his ancestors on the mother's side, the Netherfields," I answered.

"Aye, well!" remarked the inspector, almost triumphantly. "I know he did...but I've had the most careful inquires made. There isn't such a name in any churchyard of these parts. There isn't such a name in any parish register between Alnmouth Bay and Fenham Flats and that's a pretty good stretch of country! I set to work on those investigations as soon as you told me about your first meeting with Salter Quick, and every clergyman and parish clerk in the district and further afield has been at work. The name of Netherfield is absolutely unknown in the past or present."

"And yet," suddenly broke in Marcia, "it was not Salter Quick alone who was seeking the graves of the Netherfields! There was another man."

The inspector gave her an appreciative look.

"The most mysterious feature of the whole case!" he exclaimed. "You're right, Miss Raven! There was another man asking for the same information. Who was he! Where is he? If only I could clap a hand on him..."

"You think you'd be clapping a hand on Salter Quick's murderer?" I said sharply.

To my surprise he gave me an equally sharp look and shook his head.

"I'm not at all sure of that, Mr. Middlebrook," he answered quietly. "Not at all sure! But I think I could get some information out of him that I should be very glad to secure."

Miss Raven and I rose to leave; the inspector accompanied us to the door of the police station. And as we were thanking him for his polite attentions, a man came along the street, and paused close by us, looking inquiringly at the building from which we had just emerged and at our companion's smart semi-uniform. Finally, as we were about to turn away, he touched his cap.

"Begging your pardon," he said; "is this here the police office?"

There was a suggestion in the man's tone which made me think he had come there with a particular object, and I looked at him more attentively. He was a short, thick-set man, hound-faced, frank of eye and lip; no beauty, for he had a shock of sandy-red hair and three or four days stubble on his cheeks and chin; yet his apparent frankness and a certain steadiness of gaze set him up as an honest fellow. His clothing was rough; there were bits of straw, hay, wood about it, as if he were well acquainted with farming life; in his right hand he carried a stout ash-plant stick.

"You are right, my friend," answered the inspector. "It is! What are you wanting?"

The man looked up the steps at his informant with a glance in which there was a decided sense of humor. Something in the situation seemed to amuse him.

"You'll not know me," he replied. "My name's Beeman... James Beeman. I come from near York. I'm the chap that were mentioned by one of the witnesses at the inquest on that strange man that were murdered hereabouts. I should had called to see you about the matter before now, but I've not but just come back into this part of the country; I been away up in the Cheviot Hills there."

"Oh?" said the inspector. "And what mention was made of you?"

James showed a fine set of teeth in a grin that seemed to stretch completely across his homely face.

"I'm the chap that were spoken of as asking about the graves of the Netherfield family," he answered. "You know...on the roadside one night, off a fellow that I chanced to meet with outside Lesbury. That's who I am!"

The inspector turned to Miss Raven and myself with a look which meant more than he could express in words.

"Talk about coincidence!" he whispered. "This is the very man we'd just mentioned. Come back to my office and hear what he's got to tell. Follow me," he continued, beckoning the caller. "I'm much obliged to you for coming. Now," he continued, when all four of us were within his room. "What can you tell me about that? What do you know about the grave of the Netherfields?"

James laughed, shaking his round head. Now that his old hat was removed, the fiery hue of his poll was almost alarming in its crudeness of hue.

"Not," he said, "Not at all! I'll tell you all about it...that's what I've come here for, hearing as you were wondering who I was and what had come of me. I come up here...yes, it were on the sixth of March to see about some sheep stock for our master, Mr. Dimbleby, and I put up for the first night at a Temperance in Alnwick yonder. But of course, Temperance is all right for sleeping and breakfasting, but not for anything else, so when I'd tea there, I went down the street for a comfortable public, where I could smoke my pipe and have a glass or two. And while I was there, a man come in and from his description in the papers, would be this here fellow that were murdered. I didn't talk none to him, but, after a bit, I heard him talking to the landlord. And, after a deal of talk about fishing hereabouts, I heard him asking the landlord, as seemed to be a great fisherman and knew all the countryside, if he knew any places, churchyards, where there were Netherfields buried? He talked so much about them, that the name got right fixed on my mind. The next day I had business outside Alnwick, at one or two farms, and that night I made further north, to put up at Embleton. Now then, as I were walking that way, after dark I chanced in with a man near Lesbury, and walked with him a piece, and I asked him, finding he were a native, if he knew of the Netherfield graves. And that would be the man that told you that he'd met such a person. All right! I'm the person."

"Then you merely asked the question out of curiosity?" suggested the inspector.

"Aye...just because I'd heard the strange man inquire," assented James. "I just wondered if it were some family of what they call consequence."

"You never saw the man again whom you speak of as having seen at Alnwick?" the inspector asked. "And had no direct conversation with him yourself?"

"Never saw the fellow again, nor had a word with him," replied James. "He had his glass or two of rum, and went away. But I reckon he was the man who was murdered."

"And where have you been, yourself, since the time you tell us about?" asked the inspector.

"Right away across country," answered James readily. "I went across to Chillingham and Wooler, then forward to some farms in the Cheviots, and back by Alnham and Whittingham to Alnwick. And then I heard all about this affair, and so I thought good to come and tell you what bit I knew."

"I'm much obliged to you, Mr. Beeman," said the inspector. "You've cleared up something, at any rate. Are you going to stay longer in the neighborhood?"

"I shall be here...least-ways, at Alnwick yonder, at the Temperance...for two or three days yet, while I've collected some sheep together that I've bought for our master, on one farm and another," replied James. "Then I shall be away. But if you ever want me, at the Sizes, or what of that sort, my directions is James Beeman, foreman to Mr. Thomas Dimbleby, Cross-houses Manor, York."

When this candid and direct person had gone, the inspector looked at Miss Raven and me with glances that indicated a good deal. "That settles one point and seems to establish another," he remarked significantly. "Salter Quick was not murdered by somebody who had come into these parts on the same errand as himself. He was murdered by somebody who was...here already!"

"And who met him?" I suggested.

"And who met him," assented the inspector. "And now I'm more anxious than ever to know if there is anything in that tobacco box theory of Mr. Cazalette's. Couldn't you young people cajole Mr. Cazalette into telling you a little? Surely he would oblige you, Miss Raven?"

"There are moments when Mr. Cazalette is approachable," replied Marcia. "There are others at which I should as soon think of asking a question of the Sphinx."

"Wait!" I said. "Mr. Cazalette, I firmly believe, knows something. And now...you know more than you did. One mystery has gone by the board."

"It leaves the main one all the blacker," answered the inspector. "Who, of all the folk in these parts, is one to suspect? Yet...it would seem Salter Quick found somebody here to whom his presence was so decidedly unwelcome there was nothing for it but swift and certain death! Why? Well...death ensures silence."

Miss Raven and I took our leave for the second time. We walked some distance from the police station before exchanging a word: I do not know what she was thinking of; as for myself, I was speculating on the change in my opinion brought about by the rough and ready statement of the brusque Yorkshire-man. For until then I had firmly believed the man who had accosted our friend of the Mariner's Joy, Jim Gelthwaite, the drover, was the man who had murdered Salter Quick. My notion was this man, whoever he was, had fore-gathered somewhere with Quick, they were known to each other, and had a common object, and he had knifed Quick for purposes of his own. And now that idea was exploded, and so far as I could see, the search for the real assassin was yet to begin.

Suddenly Marcia spoke. "I suppose it's scarcely possible the murderer was present at that inquest?" Marcia asked, half-timidly, as if afraid of my ridiculing her suggestion.

"Quite possible," I said. "The place was packed to the doors with all sorts of people. But why?"

"I thought perhaps that he might have contrived to abstract that tobacco box, knowing that as long as it was in the hands of the police there might be some clue to his identity," Marcia suggested.

"Good notion!" I replied. "But there's just one thing against it. If the murderer had known that, if he felt that, he'd have secured the box when he searched Quick's clothing, as he undoubtedly did."

"Of course!" Marcia admitted. "I ought to have thought of that. But there are such a lot of things to think of in connection with this case...threads interwoven with each other."

"You've been thinking much about it?" I asked.

She made no reply for a moment, and I waited, wondering.

"I don't think it's a very comfortable thing to know that one's had a particularly brutal murder at one's very door and for all one knows, the murderer may still be close at hand," Marcia said at last. "There's such a disagreeable feeling of uneasiness about this affair. I know that Uncle Francis is most awfully upset by it."

I looked at her in some surprise. I had not seen any marked signs of concern in Mr. Raven.

"I hadn't observed that," he said.

"Perhaps not," Marcia answered. "But I know him better. He's an unusually nervous man. Do you know that since this happened he's taken to going round the house every night, examining doors and windows? And he's begun to carry a revolver."

The last statement made me think. Why should Mr. Raven expect or, if not expect, be afraid of, any attack on himself? But before I could make any comment on my companion's information, my attention to the subject was diverted. All that afternoon the weather had been threatening to break...there was thunder about. And now, with startling suddenness, a flash of lightning was followed by a sharp crack, and that on the instant by a heavy downpour of rain. I glanced at Miss Raven's light dress...early spring though it was, the weather had been warm for more than a week, and she had come out in things that would be soaked through in a moment. But just then we were close to an old red-brick house, which stood but a yard or two back from the road, and was divided from it by nothing but a strip of garden. It had a deep doorway, and without ceremony, I pushed open the little gate in front, and drew Miss Raven within its shelter. We had not stood there many seconds, our back to the door...which I never heard opened, when a soft mellifluous voice sounded close to my startled ear.

"Will you not step inside and shelter from the storm?"

Turning round sharply, I found myself staring at the slit-like eyes and old parchment-hued face of a smiling Chinaman.

Chapter 8

Had Miss Raven and I suddenly been caught up out of that little coast village and transported to the far East on a magic carpet, to be set down in the twinkling of an eye on some Oriental threshold, we could scarcely have been more surprised than we were at the sight of that bland, smiling countenance. For the moment I was at a loss to think who and what the man could be; he was in the dress of his own country, a neat, close-fitting, high-buttoned blue jacket; there was a little cap on his head, and a pigtail dependent from behind it.

I was not sufficiently acquainted with Chinese costumes to gather any idea of his rank or position from these things for anything I knew to the contrary, he might be a mandarin who, for some extraordinary reason, had found his way to this out-of-the-world spot. And my answer to his courteous invitation doubtless sounded confused and awkward.

"Oh, thank you," I said, "pray don't let us put you to any trouble. If we may just stand under your porch a moment..."

He stood a little aside, waving us politely into the hall behind him.

"Dr. Lorrimore would be very angry with me if I allowed a lady and gentleman to stand in his door and did not invite them into his house," he said, in the same even, mellifluous tones. "Please to enter."

"Oh, is this Dr. Lorrimore's?" I said. "Thank you...we'll come in. Is Dr. Lorrimore at home?"

"Presently," he answered. "He is in the village."

He closed the door as we entered, passed us with a bow, preceded us along the hall, and threw open the door of a room which looked out on a trim garden at the rear of the house. Still smiling and bland he invited us to be seated, and then, with another bow, left the room, apparently walking on velvet. Miss Raven and I glanced at each other.

"So Dr. Lorrimore has a Chinese man servant?" she said. "How...picturesque!"

"Um!" I muttered.

She gave me a questioning, half-amused glance, and dropped her voice.

"Don't you like...Easterners?" Marcia whispered.

"I like them in the East," I replied. "In Northumberland they don't...shall we say they don't fit in with the landscape."

"I think he fits in...here," Marcia retorted, looking round. "This is a bit Oriental."

She was right in that. The room into which we had been ushered was certainly suggestive of what one had heard of India. There were fine Indian rugs on the floor; ivories and brasses in the cabinets; the curtains were of fabric that could only have come out of some Eastern bazaar; there was a faint, curious scent of sandal-wood and of dried rose-leaves. And on the mantelpiece, where, in English households, a marble clock generally stands, reposed a peculiarly ugly Hindu god, cross-legged, hideous of form, whose baleful eyes seemed to follow all our movements.

"Yes," I admitted, reflectively. "I think he fits in...here. Dr. Lorrimore said he had been in India for some years, didn't he? He appears to have brought some of it home with him."

"I suppose this is his drawing-room," said Marcia. "Now, if only it looked out on palm-trees, and...and all other things that one associates with India."

"Just so," I said. "What it does look out on, however, is a typical English garden on which, at present, about a ton of rain is descending. And we are nearly three miles from Ravensdene Court!"

"Oh, but it won't keep on like that, for long," Marcia said. "And I suppose, if it does than we can get some sort of a conveyance...perhaps, Dr. Lorrimore has a brougham that he'd lend us."

"I don't think that's very likely," I said. "The country practitioner, I think, is more dependent on a bicycle than on a brougham. But here is Dr. Lorrimore."

I had just caught sight of him as he entered his garden by a door set in its ivy-covered wall. He ran hastily up the path to the house...within a minute or two, divested of his mackintosh, he opened the door of our room.

"So glad you were near enough to turn in here for shelter!" he exclaimed, shaking hands with us warmly. "I see that neither of you expected rain...now, I did, and I went out prepared."

"We made for the first door we saw," said Marcia. "But we'd no idea it was yours, Dr. Lorrimore. And do tell me...the Chinese," she continued, in a whisper. "Is he your man-servant?"

Lorrimore laughed, rubbing his hands together. That day he was not in the solemn, raven-hued finery in which he had visited Ravensdene Court; instead he wore a suit of grey tweed, in which, I thought, he looked rather younger and less impressive than in black. But he was certainly no ordinary man, and as he stood there smiling at Miss Raven's eager face, I felt conscious that he was the sort of somewhat mysterious, rather elusive figure in which women would naturally be interested.

"Man-servant!" he said, with another laugh. "He's all the servant I've got. Wing...he's too or three other monosyllabic patronymics, but Wing suffices...is an invaluable person. He's a model cook, valet, launderer, general factotum... there's nothing that he can't or won't do, from making the most perfect curries. I must have Mr. Raven to try them against the achievements of his man...to taking care about the halfpennies, when he goes his round of the tradesmen. Oh, he's a treasure I assure you, Miss Raven, you could go the round of this house, at any moment, without finding a thing out of place or a speck of dust in any corner. A model!"

"You brought him from India, I suppose?" I said.

"I brought him from India, yes," he answered. "He'd been with me for some time before I left. So, of course, we're thoroughly used to each other."

"And does he really like living...here?" asked Marcia. "In such absolutely different surroundings?"

"Oh, well, I think he's a pretty good old hand at making the best of the moment," laughed Lorrimore. "He's a philosopher. Deep inscrutable in short, he's Chinese. He has his own notions of happiness. At present he's supremely happy in getting you some tea...you mightn't think it, but that saffron-faced Eastern can make an English plum-cake that would put the swellest London pastry-cook to shame! You must try it!"

The China-man presently summoned us to tea, which he had laid out in another room...obviously Lorrimore's dining-room. There was nothing Oriental in that; rather, it was eminently Victorian, an affair of heavy furniture, steel engravings, and an array, on the sideboard, of what, I suppose, was old family plate. Wing ushered us and his master in with due ceremony and left us; when the door had closed on him, Lorrimore gave us an arch glance.

"You see how readily and skillfully that chap adapts himself to the needs of the moment," he said. "Now, you mightn't think it, but this is the very first time I have ever been honored with visitors to afternoon tea. Observe how Wing immediately falls in with English taste and custom! Without a word from me, out comes the silver tea-pot, the best china, the finest linen! He produces his choicest plum-cake; the bread-and-butter is cut with wafer-like thinness; and the tea...ah, well, no Englishwoman, Miss Raven, can make tea as a Chinese man-servant can!"

"It's quite plain that you've got a treasure in your house, Dr. Lorrimore," said Marcia. "But then, the Chinese are very clever, aren't they?"

"Very remarkable people, indeed," assented our host. "Shrewd, observant, penetrative. I have often wondered if this man of mine would find any great difficulty in seeing through a brick wall!"

"He would be a useful person, perhaps, in solving the present mystery," I said. "The police seem to have got no further."

"Ah, the Quick business?" remarked Lorrimore. "Um... well, as regards that, it seems to me that whatever light is thrown on it will have to be thrown from the other angle...from Devonport. From all that I heard and gathered, it's very evident what is really wanted is a strict examination into the immediate happenings at Noah Quick's inn, and also into the antecedents of Noah and Salter. But is there anything fresh?"

I told him, briefly, all that had happened that afternoon...of the information given by James Beeman and of the disappearance of the tobacco box.

"That's odd!" he remarked. "Let's see...it was the old gentleman I saw at Ravensdene Court who had some fancy about that box, wasn't it? Mr. Cazalette. What was his idea, now?"

"Mr. Cazalette," I replied, "saw, or fancied he saw,

certain marks or scratches within the lid of the box which he took to have some meaning: they were, he believed, made with design...with some purpose. He thought by photographing them, and then enlarging his photograph, he would bring out those marks more clearly, and possibly find out what they were really meant for."

"Yes?" said Lorrimore. "Well...what has he discovered?"

"Up to now nobody knows," said Marcia. "Mr. Cazalette won't tell us anything."

"That looks as if he had discovered something," observed Lorrimore. "But...old gentlemen are a little queer, and a little vain. Perhaps he's suddenly going to let loose a tremendous theory and wants to perfect it before he speaks. Oh, well!" he added, almost indifferently, "I've known a good many murder mysteries in my time...out in India and I always found the really good way of getting at the bottom of them was to go right back...as far back as possible. If I were the police in charge of these cases, I should put one question down before me and do nothing until I'd exhausted every effort to solve it."

"And that would be...what?" I asked.

"This," he said. "What were the antecedents of Noah and Salter Quick?"

"You think they had a past?" suggested Marcia.

"Everybody has a past," answered Lorrimore. "It may be this; it may be that. But nearly all the problems of the present have their origin and solution in the past. Find out what and where those two middle-aged men had been, in their time and then there'll be a chance to work forward."

The rain cleared off soon after we had finished tea, and presently Miss Raven and I took our leave. Lorrimore informed us Mr. Raven had asked him to dinner on the following evening; he would accordingly see us again very soon.

"It will be quite an event for me!" he said, gaily, as he opened his garden gate. "I live like an anchorite in this place. A little...a very little practice the folk are scandalously healthy and a great deal of scientific investigation...that's my lot."

"But you have a treasure of a servant," observed Marcia. "Please tell him that his plum-cake was perfection."

The Chinaman was just then standing at the open door, in waiting on his master. Miss Raven threw him a laughing nod to which he responded with a deep bow. We left them with that curious picture in our minds: Lorrimore, essentially English in spite of his long residence in the East; the Chinaman, bland, suave, smiling.

"A curious pair and a strange combination!" I remarked as we walked away. "That house, at any rate, has a plenitude of brain-power in it. What amazes me is that a clever chap like Master Wing should be content to bury his talents in a foreign place, out of the world...to make curries and plum-cake!"

"Perhaps he has a faithful devotion to his master," said Marcia. "Anyway, it's very romantic, and picturesque, and that sort of thing, to find a real live China-man in an English village. I wonder if the poor man gets teased about his queer clothes and his pigtail?"

"Didn't Lorrimore say he was a philosopher?" I said. "Therefore he'll be indifferent to criticism. I dare say he doesn't go about much."

That the China-man was not quite a recluse, however, I discovered a day or two later, when, going along the headlands for a solitary stroll after a stiff day's work in the library, I turned into the Mariner's Joy for a glass of Claigue's undeniably good ale. Wing was just coming out of the house as I entered it. He was as neat, as bland, and as smiling as when I saw him before; he was still in his blue jacket, his little cap. But he was now armed with a very large umbrella, and on one arm he carried a basket, filled with small parcels; evidently he had been on a shopping expedition. He greeted me with a deep obeisance and respectful smile and went on his way. I entered the inn and found its landlord alone in his bar-parlor.

"You get some queer customers in here, Mr. Claigue," I observed as he attended to my modest wants. "Yet it's not often, I should think, that a real live China-man walks in on you."

"He's been in two or three times, that one," replied Claigue. "China-man he is, no doubt, sir, but it strikes me he must know as much of this country as he knows of his own, for he speaks our tongue like a native...a bit soft and mincing-like, but never at a loss for a word. Dr. Lorrimore's servant, I understand."

"He has been in Dr. Lorrimore's service for some years," I answered. "No doubt he's had abundant opportunities of picking up the language. Still...it's an odd sight to see a China-man, pigtail and all, in these parts, isn't it?"

"Well, I've had all sorts in here, time and again," replied Claigue reflectively. "Sailor men, mostly. But," he added, with a meaning look, "of all the lot, that poor chap as got knifed the other week was the most mysterious! What do you make of it, sir?"

"I don't know what to make of it," I said. "I don't think anybody knows what to make of it. The police don't, anyhow!"

"The police!" he exclaimed, with a note of derision. "Yeah! They're worse than a parcel of old women! Have they ever tried? Just a bit of surface inquiry and the thing slips past. Of course, the man was a stranger. Nobody cares; that's about it. My notion is that the police don't care the value of that match whether the thing's ever cleared up or not. Nine days wonder, you know, Mr. Middlebrook. Still...there's a deal of talk about."

"I suppose you hear a good deal in this parlor of yours?" I suggested.

"Nights...yes," he said. "A murder's always a good subject of conversation. At first, those who come in here of an evening...regular set there, in from the village at the back of the cliffs. They could talk of nothing else, starting first this and that theory. It's died down a good deal, to be sure...there's been nothing new to start it afresh, on another tack...but there is some talk, even now."

"And what's the general opinion?" I inquired. "I suppose there is one?"

"Aye, well, I couldn't say that there's a general opinion," he answered. "There's a many opinions. And some queer notions, too!"

"Such as what?" I asked.

"Well," he said, with a laugh, as if he thought the suggestion ridiculous, "there's one that comes nearer being what you might call general than any of the others. There's a party of the older men that come here who're dead certain that Quick was murdered by a woman"

"A woman!" I exclaimed. "Whatever makes them think that?"

"Those foot-marks," answered Claigue. "You'll remember, Mr. Middlebrook, there were two sets of prints in the sand thereabouts. One was certainly Quick's...they fitted his boots. The other was very light...delicate, you might call them...made, without doubt, by some light-footed person. Well, some of the folk hereabouts went along to Kernwick Cove the day of the murder, and looked at those prints. They say the lighter ones were made by a woman."

I let my recollections go back to the morning on which I had found Quick lying dead on the patch of yellow sand.

"Of course," I said, reflectively, "those marks are gone, now."

"Gone? Aye!" exclaimed Claigue. "Long since. There's been a good many tides washed over that spot since this, Mr. Middlebrook. But they haven't washed out the fact that a man's life was let out there! And whether it was man or woman that stuck that knife into the poor fellow's shoulders, it'll come out, some day."

"I'm not so sure of that," I said. "There's a goodly percentage of unsolved mysteries of that kind."

"Well, I believe in the old saying," he declared. "Murder will out! What I don't like is the notion the murderer may be walking about this quarter, free, unsuspected. Why, I may have served him with a glass of beer! What's to prevent it? Murderers don't carry a label on their foreheads!"

"What do you think the police ought to do or ought to have done?" I asked.

"I think they should have started working backward," he replied, with decision. "I read all I could lay hands on in the newspapers, and I came to the conclusion there was a secret behind those two men. Come! two brothers murdered on the same night...hundreds of miles apart! That's no common crime, Mr. Middlebrook. Who were these two men...Noah and Salter Quick? What was their past history? That's what the police ought to have busied themselves with. If they lost or couldn't pick up the scent here, they should have tried far back. Go backward they should...if they want to go forward."

That was the second time I had heard that advice, and I returned to Ravensdene Court reflecting on it. Certainly it was sensible. Who, after all, were Noah and Salter Quick...what was their life-story.

I was wondering how that could be brought to light, when, having dressed for dinner, and I was going downstairs,

Mr. Cazalette's door opened and he quietly drew me inside his room.

"Middlebrook!" he whispered...though he had carefully shut the door, "you're a sensible lad, and I'll acquaint you with a matter. This very morning, as I was taking my bit of a dip, my pocket-book was stolen out of the jacket that I'd left on the shore. Stolen, Middlebrook!"

"Was there anything of great value in it?" I asked.

"Aye, there was!" answered Mr. Cazalette. "There was that in it which, in my opinion, might be some sort of a clue to the real truth about the man's murder!"

Chapter 9

I was dimly conscious, in a vague, uncertain fashion, Mr. Cazalette was going to tell me secrets and I was about to hear something which would explain his own somewhat mysterious doings on the morning of the murder; a half-excited, anticipating curiosity rose in me. I think he saw it, for he signed to me to sit down in an easy chair close by his bed; he was a queer, odd figure in his quaint, old-fashioned clothes, perched himself on the edge of the bed.

"Sit you down, Middlebrook," he said. "We've sometime yet before dinner, and I'm wanting to talk to you...in private, you'll bear in mind. There's things I know that I'm not willing... as yet...to tell to everybody. But I'll tell them to you, Middlebrook...for you're a sensible young fellow, and we'll take a bit of counsel together. Aye...there was that in my pocket-book that might be...I'll not say positively that it was, but that it might be a clue to the identity of the man that murdered Salter Quick, and I'm sorry now that I've lost it and didn't take more care of it. But man! Who'd thought that I'd have my pocket-book stolen from under my very nose! And that's a convincing proof there's uncommonly sharp and clever criminals around us in these parts, Middlebrook."

"You lost your pocket-book while you were bathing, Mr. Cazalette?" I asked, wishful to know all his details. He turned on his bed, pointing to a venerable Norfork jacket which hung on a peg in a recess by the washstand. I knew it well enough: I had often seen him in it, first thing of a morning.

"It's my custom," he said, "to array myself in that old coat when I go for my bit dip, you see...it's thick and it's warm, and I've had it twenty years or more...good tweed it is, and homespun. And whenever I've gone out here of a morning, I've put my pocket-book in the inside pocket, and laid the coat itself and the rest of my scanty attire on the bank there down at Kernwick Cove while I went in the water. And I did that very same thing this morning and when I came to my clothes again, the pocket-book was gone!"

"You saw nobody about?" I suggested.

"Nobody," he said. "But Lord, man, I know how easy it was to do the thing! You'll bear in mind that on the right hand side of that cove the plantation comes right down to the edge of the bit of cliff...well, a man lurking among the shrubs and undergrowth would have nothing to do but reach his arm to the bank, draw my coat to his nefarious self, and abstract my property. And by the time I was on dry land again, and wanting my garments, he'd be a quarter of a mile away!"

"And the clue?" I asked.

He edged a little nearer to me, and dropped his voice still lower.

"I'm telling you," he said. "Now you'll let your mind go back to the morning where you found the man Quick lying dead and murdered on the sand? And you'll remember that before ever you were down at the place, I'd been there before you. You'll wonder how it comes about that I didn't find what you found, but then, there's a many big rocks and boulders standing well up on that beach, and its very evident the corpse was obscured from my view by one or other and maybe more of them. Anyway, I didn't find Salter Quick...but I did find something that maybe...mind, I'm saying maybe, Middlebrook...had to do with his murder."

"What, Mr. Cazalette?" I asked, though I knew well enough what it was. I wanted him to say, and have done with it; his circumlocution was getting wearisome. But he was one of those old men who won't allow their cattle to be hurried, and he went on in his long-winded way.

"You'll be aware," he continued, "there's a deal of gorse and bramble growing right down to the very edge of the coast thereabouts, Middlebrook. Scrub...that sort of thing. The stuff that if it catches anything loose, anything protruding from say, the pocket of a garment, I'll lay hold and stick to it. Aye, well, on one of those bushes, gorse or bramble I cannot rightly say which, just within the entrance to the plantation. I saw, fluttering in the morning breeze that came sharp and refreshing off the face of the water, a handkerchief. And there was two sorts of stains on it...caused in the one case by mud... the soft mud of the adjacent beach and in the other by blood. A smear of blood as if somebody had wiped blood off his fingers, you'll understand. But it was not that, not the blood, made me give my particular attention to the thing, which I'd picked off with my thumb and finger. It was that I saw at once this was no common man's property, for there was a crest woven into one corner, and a monogram of initials underneath it, and the stuff itself was a sort that I'm unfamiliar with...it wasn't linen, though it looked like it, and it wasn't silk, for I'm well acquainted with that fabric...maybe it was a mixture of the two, but it had not been woven or made in any British factory: the thing, Middlebrook, was of foreign origin."

"What were the markings you speak of?" I asked.

"Well, I tell you there was a crest; anyhow it was a coronet, or that make of a thing," he answered. "Woven in one corner...I mean worked in by hand. And the letters beneath it were a V and a de...small, that last and a C. Man! that handkerchief was the property of some man of quality! And the stains being wet...the mud-stains, at any rate, though the smear of blood was dry. I gathered that it had been but recently deposited, by accident, where I found it. I reckoned it up this way, do you see, Middlebrook...the man who'd left it there had used it on the beach...maybe he'd cut his toe, bathing, or something of that sort, or likely a cut finger, gathering a shell or a fossil and had thrust it carelessly into a side-pocket, for a thorn to catch hold of as he passed. But there it was, and there I found it."

"And what did you do with it, Mr. Cazalette?" I inquired with seeming innocence.

"I'm telling you," he replied. "I had no knowledge, you're aware, of what lay behind me on the sands: I just thought it a queer thing that a man of quality's handkerchief should be there. And I slipped it among my towels, to bring along with me to the house here. But I'm whiles given to absent-mindedness, and not liking that I should put the blood-stained thing down on my dressing-table there and cause the maids to wonder, I thrust it into a hedge as I was passing along, till I could go back and examine it at my leisure. And when I'd got myself dressed, I went back and took it, and put it in a stout envelope into my pocket and then you came along, Middlebrook, with your story of the murder, and I saw then before saying a word to anybody, I'd keep my own counsel and examine that thing more carefully. And man alive! I've no doubt whatever the man who left the handkerchief behind him was the man who knifed Salter Quick."

"I gather, from all you've said, the handkerchief was in the pocket-book you had stolen this morning?" I suggested.

"You're right in that," he said. "Oh, it was! Wrapped up in a bit of oiled paper, and in an envelope, sealed down and attested in my handwriting, Middlebrook...date and particulars of my discovery of it, all in order. Aye, and there was more. Letters and papers of my own, to be sure, and a trifle money... bank-notes. But there was yet another thing that, in view of all we know, may be a serious thing to have fall into the hands of ill-doers. A print, Middlebrook, of the enlarged photograph I got of the inside of the lid of the dead man's tobacco box!"

He regarded me with intense seriousness as he made this announcement, and not knowing exactly what to say, I remained silent.

"And," he continued, "it's my distinct and solemn belief that it's what the thief was after! You see, Middlebrook, it's been spoken of...not widely noised abroad, as you might say, but still spoken of, and things spread, that I was keenly interested in those marks, scratches, whatever they were, on the inside of that lid, and got the police to let me make a photograph, and it's my impression there's somebody about who's been keenly anxious to know what results I obtained."

"You really think so?" I said. "Why...who could there be?"

"Aye, man, and who could there be, with a crest and monogram on his kerchief, that would murder the man the secret way he has?" he retorted, answering my incredulous look with one of triumph. "Tell me that, my laddie! I'm telling you, Middlebrook, this was no common murder any more than the murder of the man's own brother down yonder at Saltash, which is a Cornish riverside place, and a good four or five hundred miles away, was a common, ordinary crime! Man! We're living in the very midst of a mystery and that there's bloody minded, aye, and bloody handed men, maybe within our gates, but surely close by us, is as certain to me as that I'm looking at you!"

"I thought you believed that Salter Quick's murderer was miles away before ever he was cold?" I observed.

"I did and I've changed my mind," he answered. "I'm

not thinking it anymore, and all the less since I was robbed of my venerable pocket-book, with those two exhibits of the crime in its name. The murderer is about! and though he mayn't have thought to get his handkerchief, he may have hoped that he'd secure some result of my labors in the photographic line."

"Mr. Cazalette!" I said, "what were the results of your labors? I don't suppose the print which was in your pocket-book was the only one you possess?"

"You're right there," he replied. "It wasn't. If the thief thought he was securing something unique, he was mistaken. But...I didn't want him, or anybody, to get hold of even one print, for as sure as we're living men, Middlebrook, what was on the inside of that lid was...a key to something!"

"You forget the tobacco box has been stolen from the police's keeping," I reminded him.

"And I don't forget anything of the sort," he retorted. "And the fact you've mentioned makes me all the more assured, my man, that what I say is correct! There's him, or there's them...in all likelihood it's the plural that's uncommonly anxious, feverishly anxious, to get hold of that key that I suspicion. What were Salter Quick's pockets turned out for? What were the man's clothes slashed and hacked for? Why did whoever slew Noah Quick at Saltash treat the man in similar fashion? It wasn't money the two men were murdered for...no, it was for information, a secret! Or, as I put it before, the key to something."

"And you believe, really and truly, this key is in the marks or scratches or whatever they are on the lid of the tobacco box?" I asked.

"Aye, I do!" he exclaimed. "And what's more, Middlebrook, I believe I'm an old fool! If I'd contrived to get a good, careful, penetrating look at that box, without saying anything to the police, I should have shown some common-sense. But like the blithering old idiot that I am, I spoke my thoughts aloud before a company, and I made a present of an idea to these miscreants. Until I said what I did, the murderous gang that knifed the two men hadn't a notion that Salter Quick carried a key in his tobacco box! Now they know."

"You don't mean to suggest any of the murderers were present when you asked permission to photograph the box!" I exclaimed. "Impossible!"

"There's very few impossibilities in this world, Middlebrook," he answered. "I'm not saying that any of the gang were present in Raven's outhouse, where they carried the poor fellow's body, but there were a dozen or more men heard what I said to the police inspector, like the old fool I was, and saw me taking my photograph. And men talk...no matter of what degree they are."

"Mr. Cazalette," I said, "I'd just like to see your results."

He got off his bed at that, and going over to a chest of drawers, unlocked one, and took out a writing-case, from which he presently extracted a sheet of cardboard, where he had mounted a photograph, beneath which, on the cardboard, were some lines of explanatory writing in its fine, angular style of calligraphy. This he placed in my hand without a word, watching me silently as I looked at it.

I could make nothing of the thing. It looked to me like a series...a very small one...of meaningless scratches, evidently made with the point of a knife, or even by a strong pin on the surface of the metal. Certainly, the marks were there, and, equally certainly, they looked to have been made with some intent...but what did they mean?

"What do you make of it, lad?" he inquired after a while. "Anything?"

"Nothing, Mr. Cazalette!" I replied. "Nothing whatever."

"Aye, well, and to be candid, neither do I," he confessed. "And yet, I'm certain there's something in it. Take another look and consider it carefully."

I looked again...this is what there was to look at: mere lines, and at the foot of the photograph, Mr. Cazalette's explanatory notes and suggestions: I sat studying this for a few moments. "I make nothing of it. It seems to be a plan. But of what?"

"It is a plan, Middlebrook," he answered. "A plan of some place. But there I'm done! What place? Somebody that's in the secret, to a certain point, might know...but who else could? I've speculated a deal on the meaning and significance of those lines and marks, but without success. Yet...they're the key to something."

"Probably to some place that Salter Quick knew of," I suggested.

"Aye, and that somebody else wants to know of!" he

exclaimed. "But what place, and where?"

"He was asking after a churchyard," I said, suddenly remembering Quick's questions to me and his evident eagerness to acquire knowledge. "This may be a rude drawing of a corner of it."

"Aye, and he wanted the graves of the Netherfields," remarked Mr. Cazalette, dryly. "And I've made myself assured of the fact there isn't a Netherfield buried anywhere about this region! No, it's my belief this is a key to some spot in foreign parts, and there are those who are anxious to get hold of it they'll not stop and haven't stopped at murder. And now they've got it!"

"They've got or somebody's got your pocket-book," I answered. "But really, you know, Mr. Cazalette, this, and the handkerchief, mayn't have been the thief's object. You see, it must be pretty well known that you go down there to bathe every morning, and are in the habit of leaving your clothes about and, well there may be those who're not particularly honest even in these Arcadian solitudes."

"No...I'm not with you, Middlebrook!" he said. "Somewhere around us there's what I say...crafty and bloody murderers! But you'll keep all this to yourself for a while, and..."

Just then the dinner-bell rang, and he put the photographic print away, and we went downstairs together. That was the evening on which Dr. Lorrimore was to dine with us. We found him in the hall, talking to Mr. Raven and his niece. Joining them, we found their subject of conversation was the same that had just engaged Mr. Cazalette and myself... the tobacco box. It turned out the police inspector had been round to Lorrimore's house, inquiring if Lorrimore, who, with the police surgeon, had occupied a seat at the table where the Quick relics were laid out at the inquest, had noticed the now missing and consequently all important object.

"Of course I saw it!" remarked Lorrimore, narrating this. "I told him I not only saw it, but handled it...so, too, did several other people. Mr. Cazalette there had drawn attention to the thing when we were examining the dead man, and there was some curiosity about it." Mr. Cazalette, standing close by me, nudged my elbow, to remind me of what he had just said upstairs. "And I told the inspector something else, or, rather, put him in mind of something he'd evidently forgotten," continued Lorrimore. "That inquest, or, to be precise, the adjourned inquest, was attended by a good many strangers, who had evidently been attracted by mere curiosity. There were a lot of people there who certainly did not belong to this neighborhood. And when the proceedings were over, they came crowding round that table, morbidly inquisitive about the dead man's belongings. What easier, as I said to the inspector, than for some one of them...perhaps a curio-hunter to quietly pick up that box and make off with it? There are people who'd give a good deal to lay hold of a souvenir of that sort."

Mr. Raven muttered something about no accounting for tastes, and we went in to dinner, and began to talk of less gruesome things. Lorrimore was a brilliant and accomplished conversationalist, and the time passed pleasantly until, as we men were lingering a little over our wine, and Miss Raven was softly playing the piano in the adjoining drawing-room, the butler came in and whispered to his master. Raven turned an astonished face to the rest of us.

"There's the police inspector here now," he said, "and with him a detective from Devonport. They are anxious to see me and you, Middlebrook. The detective has something to tell."

Chapter 10

I am not sure which, or how many, of us sitting at that table had ever come into personal contact with a detective. I had never met one in my life...but I am sure Mr. Raven's announcement there was a real live one close at hand immediately excited much curiosity. Miss Raven, in the adjoining room, the door of which was open, caught her uncle's last words, and came in, expectantly. I think she, like most of us, wondered what sort of being we were about to see.

And possibly there was a shade of disappointment on her face when the police inspector walked in followed, not by the secret, subtle, sleuth-hound-like person she had perhaps expected, but by a little, rotund, rather merry-faced man who looked more like a prosperous cheese-monger or successful draper than an emissary of justice: he was just the sort of person you would naturally expect to see with an apron round his comfortable waist-line or a pencil stuck in his ear and who was given to rubbing his fat, white hands...he rubbed them now and smiled, as his companion led him forward.

"Sorry to disturb you, Mr. Raven," said the inspector with an apologetic bow, "but we are anxious to have a little talk with you and Mr. Middlebrook. This is Mr. Scarterfield...from the police at Devonport. Mr. Scarterfield has been in charge of the investigations about the affair, Noah Quick, you know... down there, and he has come here to make some further inquiries."

Mr. Raven murmured some commonplace about being glad to see his visitors, and, with his usual hospitality, offered them refreshment. We made room for them at the table at which we were sitting, and some of us, I think, were impatient to hear what Mr. Scarterfield had to tell. But the detective was evidently one of those men who readily adapt themselves to whatever company they are thrown into, and he betrayed no eagerness to get to business until he had lighted one of Mr. Raven's cigars and pledged Mr. Raven in a whiskey and soda.

Then, equipped and at his ease, he turned a friendly, all-embracing smile on the rest of us.

"Which," he asked, looking from one to the other, "which of these gentlemen is Mr. Middlebrook?"

The general turning of several pairs of eyes in my direction gave him the information he wanted...we exchanged nods.

"It was you who found Salter Quick?" he suggested. "And who met him, the previous day, on the cliffs hereabouts, and went with him into the Mariner's Joy?"

"Quite correct," I said.

"I have read up everything that appeared in print in connection with the Salter Quick affair," he remarked. "It has, of course, a bearing on the Noah Quick business. Whatever is of interest in the one is of interest in the other."

"You think the two affairs one really...eh?" inquired Mr. Raven.

"One!" declared Scarterfield. "The object of the man who murdered Noah was the same object as the man who murdered Salter. The two murderers are, without doubt, members of a gang. But what gang, and what object...ah! That's just what I don't know yet!"

What we were all curious about, of course, was...what did he know that we did not already know? And I think he saw in what direction our thoughts were turning, for he presently leaned forward on the table and looked around the expectant faces as if to command our attention.

"I had better tell you how far my investigations have gone," he said quietly. "Then we shall know precisely where we are, and from what point we can, perhaps, make a new departure, now that I have come here. I was put in charge of this case...at least of the Saltash murder from the first. There's no need for me to go into the details of that now, because I take it that you have all read them, or quite sufficient of them. Now, when the news about Salter Quick came through, it seemed to me that the first thing to do was to find out a very pertinent thing...who were the brothers Quick? What were their antecedents? What was in their past, the immediate or distant past, likely to lead up to these crimes? A pretty stiff proposition, as you may readily guess! For, you must remember, each was a man of mystery. No one in our quarter knew anything more of Noah Quick than that he had come to Devonport some little time previous, taken over the license of the Admiral Parker, conducted his house very well, and had the reputation of being a quiet, close, reserved sort of man who was making money. As to Salter, nobody knew anything except that he had been visiting Noah for some time. Family ties, the two men evidently have none...not a soul has come forward to claim relationship. And there has been wide publicity."

"Do you think Quick was the real name?" asked Mr. Cazalette, who from the first had been listening with rapt attention. "Mayn't it have been an assumed name?"

"Well, sir," replied Scarterfield, "I thought of that. But you must remember that full descriptions of the two brothers appeared in the press, and portraits of both were printed alongside. Nobody came forward, recognizing them. And there has been a powerful, a most powerful, inducement for their relations to appear, never mind whether they were Quick, or Brown, or Smith, or Robinson, the most powerful inducement we could think of!"

"Aye!" said Mr. Cazalette. "And that was..."

"Money!" answered the detective. "Money! If these men left any relations...sisters, brothers, nephews, nieces...it's in the interest of these relations to come into the light, for there's money awaiting them. That's well known...I had it noised abroad in the papers, and let it be freely talked of in town. But, as I say, nobody's come along. I firmly believe, now, these two hadn't a blood relation in the world...a queer thing, but it seems to be so."

"And this money?" I asked. "Is it much?"

"That was one of the first things I went for," answered Scarterfield. "Naturally, when a man comes to the end which Noah met with, inquiries are made of his solicitors and his bankers. Noah had both in our parts. The solicitors knew nothing about him except that he had employed them now and then in trifling matters, and that of late he had made a will in which, in brief fashion, he left everything of which he died possessed to his brother Salter, whose address he gave as being the same as his own; about the same time they had made a will for Salter, in which he bequeathed everything he had to Noah. But as to the antecedents of Noah and Salter...nothing! Then I approached the bankers. There I got more information. When

Noah first went to Devonport he deposited a considerable sum of money with one of the leading banks at Plymouth, and at the time of his death he had several thousand pounds lying there to his credit: his bankers also had charge of valuable securities of his. On Salter's coming to the Admiral Parker, Noah introduced him to this bank: Salter deposited there a sum of about two thousand pounds, and of that he had only withdrawn about a hundred.

So he, too, at the time of his death, had a large balance; also, he left with the bankers, for safe keeping, some valuable scrip and securities, chiefly of Indian railways. Altogether, those bankers hold a lot of money that belongs to the two brothers, and there are certain indications they made their money...previous to coming to Devonport in the far East. But the bankers know no more of their antecedents than the solicitors do. In both instances...banking matters and legal matters the two men seem to have confined their words to strict business, and no more; the only man I have come across who can give me the faintest idea of anything respecting their past is a regular frequenter of the Admiral Parker who says that he once gathered from Salter that he and Noah were natives of Rotherhithe, or somewhere in that part, and they were orphans and the last of their lot."

"Of course, you have been to Rotherhithe...making inquiries?" suggested Mr. Raven.

"I have, sir," replied Scarterfield. "And I searched various parish registers there, and found nothing that helped me. If the two brothers did live at Rotherhithe, they must have been taken there as children and born elsewhere...they weren't born in Rotherhithe parish. Nor could I come across anybody at all who knew anything of them in seafaring circles thereabouts. I came to the conclusion that whoever those two men were, and whatever they had been, most of their lives had been spent away from this country."

"Probably in the far East, as you previously suggested," muttered Mr. Cazalette.

"Likely!" agreed Scarterfield. "Their money would seem to have been made there, judging by, at any rate, some of their securities. Well, there's more ways than one of finding things out, and after I'd knocked round a good deal of Thames side, and been in some queer places, I turned my attention to

Lloyds. Now, connected with Lloyds, are various publications having to do with shipping matters...the 'Weekly Shipping Index,' the 'Confidential Index,' for instance; moreover, with time and patience, you can find out a great deal at Lloyds not only about ships, but about men in them. And to cut a long story short, gentlemen, last week I did at last get a clue about Noah and Salter Quick which I now mean to follow up for all it's worth."

Here the detective, suddenly assuming a more business-like air than he had previously shown, paused, to produce from his breast-pocket a small bundle of papers, which he laid before him on the table. I suppose we all gazed at them as if they suggested deep and dark mystery...but for the time being Scarterfield let them lie idle where he had placed them.

"I'll have to tell the story in a sort of sequence," he continued. "This is what I have pieced together from the information I collected at Lloyds. In October, 1907, now nearly five years ago, a certain steam ship, the *Elizabeth Robinson*, left Hong-Kong, in Southern China, for Chemulpo, one of the principal ports in Korea. She was spoken in the Yellow Sea several days later. After that she was never heard of again, and according to the information available at Lloyds she probably went down in a typhoon in the Yellow Sea and was totally lost, with all hands on board. No great matter, perhaps...from all that I could gather she was nothing but a tramp steamer that did, so to speak, odd jobs anywhere between India and China; she had gone to Hong-Kong from Singapore: her owners were small folk in Singapore, and I imagine that she had seen a good deal of active service. All the same, she's of considerable interest to me, for I have managed to secure a list of the names of the men who were on her when she left Hong-Kong for Chemulpo and among those names are those of the two men we're concerned about: Noah and Salter Quick."

Scarterfield slipped off the India-rubber band which confined his papers, and selecting one, slowly unfolded it. Mr. Raven spoke.

"I understood this ship, the *Elizabeth Robinson*, was lost with all hands?" he said.

"So she is set down at Lloyds," replied Scarterfield. "Never heard of again...after being spoken in the Yellow Sea about three days from Chemulpo."

"Yet...Noah and Salter Quick were on her and were living five years later?" suggested Mr. Raven.

"Just so, sir!" agreed Scarterfield, dryly. "Therefore, if Noah and Salter Quick were on her, and as they were alive until recently, either the *Elizabeth Robinson* did not go down in a typhoon, or from any other reason, or the brothers Quick escaped. But here is a list of the men who were aboard when she sailed from Hong-Kong. She was, I have already told you, a low-down tramp steamer, evidently picking up a precarious living between one far Eastern port and another...a small vessel. Her list includes a master, or captain, and a crew of eighteen...I needn't trouble you with their names, except in two instances, which I'll refer to presently. But here are the names of Noah Quick, Salter Quick...set down as passengers. Passengers...not members of the crew. Nothing in the list of the crew strikes me but the two names I spoke of, and that I'll now refer to. The first name will have an interest for Mr. Middlebrook. It's Netherfield."

"Netherfield!" I exclaimed. "The name..."

"That Salter asked you particular questions about when he met you on the headlands, Mr. Middlebrook," answered Scarterfield, with a knowing look, "and that he was very anxious to get some news of William Netherfield, deck-hand, of Blyth, Northumberland...that's the name on the list of those who were aboard the *Elizabeth Robinson* when she went out of Hong-Kong and disappeared forever!"

"Of Blyth?" remarked Mr. Cazalette. "Um...Blyth lies some miles to the southward."

"I'm aware of it, sir," said Scarterfield, "and I propose to visit the place when I have made certain inquiries about this region. But I hope you appreciate the extraordinary coincidence, gentlemen? In October, 1907, Salter Quick is on a tramp steamer in the Yellow Sea in company, more or less intimate, with a sailor-man from Blyth, in Northumberland, whose name is Netherfield: in March, 1912, he is on the sea-coast near Alnmouth, asking anxiously if anybody knows of a churchyard or churchyards in these parts where people of the name of Netherfield are buried? Why? What had the man Netherfield who was with Salter Quick in Chinese waters in 1907 got to do with Salter Quick's presence here five years later?"

Nobody attempted to answer these questions, and presently I put one for myself.

"You spoke of two names on the list as striking you with some significance," I said. "Netherfield is one. What is the other?"

"That of a China-man," he replied promptly, referring to his documents. "Set down as cook...I'm told most of those coasting steamers in that part of the world carry China-men as cooks. Chuh Fen...that's the name. And why it's significant to me, when all the rest aren't, is this...during the course of my inquiries at Lloyds, I learned that about three years ago a certain Chinaman, calling himself Chuh Fen, dropped in at Lloyds and was very anxious to know if the steamer *Elizabeth Robinson*, which sailed from Hong-Kong for Chemulpo in October, 1907, ever arrived at its destination? He was given the same information that was afforded me, and on getting it went away, silent. Now then...was this man, this China-man, the Chuh Fen who turned up in London, the same Chuh Fen who was on the *Elizabeth Robinson*? If so, how did he escape a shipwreck which evidently happened? And why...if there was no shipwreck, and something else took place of which we have no knowledge...did he want to know, after two years lapse of time, if the ship did really get to Chemulpo?"

There was a slight pause then, suddenly broken by Dr. Lorrimore, who then spoke for the first time.

"Do you know what all this is suggesting to me?" he exclaimed, nodding at Scarterfield. "Something happened on that ship! It may be there was no shipwreck, as you said just now...something may have taken place of which we have no knowledge. But one fact comes out clearly...whether the *Elizabeth Robinson* ever reached any port or not, it's very evident...certain Noah and Salter Quick did. And considering the inquiry he made at Lloyds...so did the Chinaman, Chuh Fen. Now what could those three have told about the *Elizabeth Robinson*?"

No one made any remark on that, until Scarterfield remarked softly:

"I wish I had chanced to be at Lloyds when Chuh Fen called there! But...that's three years ago, and Chuh Fen may be...where?"

Something impelled Miss Raven and myself to glance at

Dr. Lorrimore. He nodded...he knew what we were thinking of. And he turned to Scarterfield.

"I happen," he said, "to have a China-man in my employ at present...one Wing, a very clever man. He has been with me for some years. I brought him from India, when I came home recently. An astute chap, like..."

He paused suddenly; the detective had turned a suddenly interested glance on him.

"You live hereabouts, sir?" he asked. "I...I don't think I've caught your name?"

"Dr. Lorrimore...our neighbor," said Mr. Raven hurriedly. "Close by."

I think Lorrimore saw what had suddenly come into Scarterfield's mind. He laughed, a little cynically.

"Don't get the idea, or suspicion, formed or half-fledged, that my man Wing had anything to do with the murder of Salter Quick!" he said. "I can vouch for him and his movements. I know where he was on the night of the murder. What I was thinking of was this...Wing is a man of infinite resource and of superior brains. He might be of use to you in tracing this Chuh Fen, if Chuh Fen is in England. When Wing and I were in London...we were there for some time after I returned from India, previous to my coming down here. Wing paid a good many visits to his fellow China-men in the East End, Limehouse way; he also had a holiday in Liverpool and another at Swansea and Cardiff, where, I am told, there are Chinese settlements. And I happen to know that he carries on an extensive correspondence with his compatriots. If you think he could give you any information, Mr. Scarterfield..."

"I'd like to have a talk with him, certainly," responded the detective, with some eagerness. "I know a bit about these chaps...some of them can see through a brick wall!"

Lorrimore turned to Mr. Raven.

"If your coachman could run across with the dog-cart, or anything handy," he said, "and would tell Wing that I want him, here, he'd be with me at once. And he may be able to suggest something. I know that before he came to me...I picked him up in Bombay, he had knocked about the ports of Southern China a great deal."

"Come with me and give my coachman instructions," said Mr. Raven. "He'll run over to your place in ten minutes;

and while we are discussing this affair we may as well have as much light as we can get on it."

He and Lorrimore left the room together; when they returned, the conversation reverted to a discussion of possible ways and means of finding out more about the antecedents of the Quicks. Half an hour passed in this...fruitlessly; then the door was quietly opened and behind the somewhat pompous figure of the butler I saw the bland, obsequious smile of the China-man.

Chapter 11

We sat round that table during the next hour or so must have made a strange group. Mr. Raven, always a little nervous and flustered in manner; his niece, fresh and eager, in her pretty dinner dress, a curious contrast to the antiquated garb and parchment face of old Cazalette, who sat by her, watchful and doubting; the officialdom-suggesting figure of the police-inspector, erect and rigid in his close-fitting uniform; the detective, rubicund and confident, though of what one scarcely knew; Lorrimore and myself, keen listeners and watchers, and last, but not by any means the least notable, the bland, suave China-man in his neat native dress, sitting modestly in the background, inscrutable as an image carved out of ivory.

I do not know what the rest thought, but it lay in my own mind that if there was one man in that room who might be trusted to find his way out of the maze in which we were wandering, that man was Dr. Lorrimore's servant. It was Lorrimore who, at the detective's request, explained to Wing why we had sent for him. The China-man nodded a grave assent when reminded of the Salter Quick affair...evidently he knew all about it. And if one really could detect anything at all in so carefully-veiled a countenance I thought detected an increased watchfulness in his eyes when Scarterfield began to ask him questions arising out of what Lorrimore had said.

"There is evidence," began the detective, "this man Salter and his brother Noah Quick, were mixed up in some affair that had connection with a trading steamer, the *Elizabeth Robinson*, believed to have been lost in the Yellow Sea, between Hong-Kong and Chemulpo, in October 1907. On board that steamer was a certain China-man, who, two years later, turned up in London. Now, Dr. Lorrimore tells me that when you and he were in London, some little time ago, you spent a good deal of time among your own people in the East End, and you also visited some of them in Liverpool, Cardiff, and Swansea. So I want to ask you...did you ever hear, in any of

91

these quarters, of a man named Chuh Fen? Here in London two years after the *Elizabeth Robinson* affair...that's three years back from now."

The China-man moved his head very slightly.

"No," he answered. "Not in London nor in England. But I knew a man named Chuh Fen ten, eleven, years ago, before I went to Bombay and entered my present service."

"Where did you know him?" asked Scarterfield.

"Two...perhaps three places," said Wing. "Singapore, Penang, perhaps Rangoon, too. I remember him."

"What was he?"

"A cook...very good cook."

"Would you be surprised to hear of his being in England three years ago?"

"Not at all. Many China-men come here. I myself...why not others? If Chuh Fen came here, three years ago, perhaps he came as cook on some ship trading from China or Burma. Then go back again."

"I wonder if he did!" muttered the detective. "Still," he continued, turning to Wing, "a lot of your people when they come here, stop, don't they?"

"Many stop in this country," said Wing.

"Laundry business, eating-houses, groceries, and so on?" suggested Scarterfield. "And chiefly in the places I've mentioned, eh? the East End of London, Liverpool, and the two big Welsh towns? Now, I want to ask you a question. This man I'm talking of, Chuh Fen, was certainly in London three years ago. Are there places and people in London where one could get to hear of him?"

"Where I could get to hear of him...yes," answered Wing.

"You say...where you could get to hear of him," remarked Scarterfield. "Does that mean you would get information which I shouldn't get?"

The very faintest ghost of a smile showed itself in the wrinkles about the Chinaman's eyes. He inclined his head a little, politely, and Lorrimore stepped into the arena.

"What Wing means is that being a China-man, naturally he could get news of a fellow-China-man from fellow-China-men where you, an Englishman, wouldn't get any at all!" he said with a laugh. "I dare say if you, Mr. Scarterfield, went down Limehouse way seeking particulars about Chuh Fen, you'd be met with blank faces and closed ears."

"That's just what I'm suggesting, doctor," answered the detective, good-humoredly. "I'll put the thing in a nutshell...my profound belief is that if we want to get at the bottom of these two murders we've got to go back a long way, to the *Elizabeth Robinson* time, and Chuh Fen is the only person I've heard of, up to now, who can throw a light on that episode. And it seems to me, to be plain about it, Mr. Wing there could be extremely useful."

"How?" asked Lorrimore. "He's at your service, I'm sure."

"Well, by finding out if this Chuh Fen, when he was here, three years since, made any revelations to his Chinese brethren in Limehouse or elsewhere," replied Scarterfield. "He may have known something about the brothers Quick and concerning that *Elizabeth Robinson* affair that would help immensely. Any little thing...a mere scrap of information, just a bit of chance gossip...a hint. You don't know how valuable these things are. The mere germ of a clue you know!"

"I know," said Lorrimore. He turned to his servant and addressed him in some strange tongue in which Wing at once responded: for some minutes they talked together, volubly: then Lorrimore looked round at Scarterfield.

"Wing says that if Chuh Fen was in London three years ago he can engage to find out how long he was here, when he came and why, and where he went," he said. "I gather there's a sort of freemasonry among these men...naturally, they seek each other out in strange lands, and there are places in London and the other parts to which a China-man resorts if he happens to land in England. This he can do for you...he's no doubt of it."

"There's another thing," said Scarterfield. "If Chuh Fen is still in England...as he may be...can he find him?"

Wing's smooth countenance, on hearing this, showed some sign of animation. Instead of replying to the detective, he again addressed his master in the foreign tongue. Lorrimore nodded and turned to Scarterfield with a slightly cynical smile.

"He says if Chuh Fen is anywhere in England he can lay hands on him, quickly," said Lorrimore. "But...he adds that it might not be at all convenient to Chuh Fen to come into the full light of day. Chuh Fen may have reasons of his own for

93

desiring strict privacy."

"I take you!" said Scarterfield, with a wink. "All right, doctor! If Mr. Wing can unearth Mr. Chuh Fen and that mysterious gentleman can give me a tip, I'll respect his privacy! So now...do we get at something? Do I understand that your man will help us by trying to find out some particulars of Chuh Fen, or laying hands on Chuh Fen himself? All expenses defrayed, you know," he went on, turning to Wing, "and a handsome remuneration if it leads to results. And follow your own plans! I know you China-men are smart and deep at this sort of thing!"

"Leave it to him," said Lorrimore. "To him and to me. If there's news to be had of this man Chuh Fen, he'll get it."

"Then that is something done!" exclaimed Scarterfield, rubbing his hands. "Good! I like to see even a bit of progress. But now, while I'm here, and while we're at business and I hope this young lady doesn't find it dull business...there's another matter. The inspector tells me there have been alarums and excursions about a certain tobacco-box which was found on Salter Quick, that Mr. Cazalette...you, sir, I think had various experiments in connection with it, and the thing has been stolen. Now, I want to know all about that...who can tell me most?"

Mr. Cazalette was sitting between Miss Raven and myself; I leaned close to him and whispered, feeling that now was the time to bring every known fact to light. "Tell all...all you told me just before dinner!" I urged upon him. "Table the whole pack of cards: let us get at something...now!"

He hesitated, looking half-suspiciously from one to the other of those opposite. "Do you think I'd be well advised, Middlebrook?" he whispered. "Is it wise policy to show all the cards you're holding?"

"In this case, yes!" I said. "Tell everything!"

"Well," he said. "Maybe. But it's on your advice, you'll remember, and I'm not sure this is the time, nor just the company. However..."

So, for the second time that day, Mr. Cazalette told the story of the tobacco box and of his pocket-book, and produced his photograph. It came as a surprise to all there but myself, and I saw Mr. Raven in particular was much perturbed by the story of the theft that morning. I knew what he was thinking...

the criminal or criminals were much too close at hand. He cut in now and then with a question, but the detective listened in grim, absorbed silence.

"Now, you know, this is really about the most serious and important thing I've heard, so far," he said, when Mr. Cazalette had finished. "Just let's sum it up. Salter Quick is murdered in a strange and lonely place. Not for his goods, for all his money and his valuables...not inconsiderable are found on him. But the murderer was in search of something that he believed to be on Salter Quick, for he thoroughly searched his clothing, slashed its linings, turned his pockets out and probably, no, we may safely say certainly, failed in his search. He did not get what he was after any more than his fellow-murderer who slew Noah Quick, some hundreds of miles away from here, about the very same time, got what he was after.

But now comes in Mr. Cazalette. Mr. Cazalette, inadvertently, never thinking what he was doing, draws public attention to certain marks and scratches, evidently made on purpose, in Salter's tobacco box. Do you see my point, gentlemen? The murderer hears of this and says to himself, 'That box is the thing I want!' So he appropriates it, at the inquest! But even then, so faint and almost illegible are the marks within the lid, he doesn't find exactly what he wants. But he knows that Mr. Cazalette was going to submit his photograph to an enlarging process, which would make the marks clearer; he also knows Mr. Cazalette's habits...a highly significant fact, so he sets himself to steal Mr. Cazalette's pocket-book, theorizing that Mr. Cazalette probably has a copy of the enlarged photograph within it. And, this morning, while Mr. Cazalette is bathing, he gets it! Gentlemen! What does this show? One thing as a certainty...the murderer is close at hand!"

There was a dead silence...broken at last by a querulous murmur from Mr. Cazalette.

"You may be as sure of that, my man, as that Arthur's Seat overlooks Edinburgh!" he said. "I wish I was as sure of his identity!"

"Well, we know something that's gradually bringing us toward establishing that," remarked Scarterfield. "Let me see that photograph again, if you please."

The rest of us watched Scarterfield as he studied the

thing over which Mr. Cazalette and I had exercised our brains in the half-hour before dinner. He seemed to get no more information from a long perusal of it than we had got, and he finally threw it away from him across the table, with a muttered exclamation which confessed discomfiture. Miss Raven picked up the photograph.

"Aye!" mumbled Mr. Cazalette. "Let the lassie look at it! Maybe a woman's brains is more use than a man's whiles."

"Often!" said the detective. "And if Miss Raven can make anything of that..."

I saw Miss Raven was already wishful to speak, and I hastened to encourage her by throwing a word to Scarterfield.

"You'd be infinitely obliged to her, I'm sure," I put in. "It would be a help?"

"No slight one!" he said. "There's something in that diagram. But what?"

Miss Raven, timid, and a little shy of concentrated attention, laid the photograph again on the table.

"Don't...don't you think there may be some explanation of this in what Salter Quick said to Mr. Middlebrook when they met on the cliffs?" she asked. "He told Mr. Middlebrook that he wanted to find a churchyard where there were graves of people named Netherfield, but he didn't know exactly where it was, though it was somewhere in this locality. Now supposing this is a rough outline of that churchyard? These outer lines may be the wall...then these little marks may show the situation of the Netherfield graves. And that cross in the corner...perhaps there is something buried, hidden, there, which Salter Quick wanted to find?"

The detective uttered a sharp exclamation and snatched up the photograph again.

"Good! Good!" he said. "Upon my word, I shouldn't wonder! To be sure, that may be it. What's against it?"

"This," remarked Mr. Cazalette solemnly. "That there isn't anybody of the name of Netherfield buried between Alnmouth and Budle Bay! That's a fact."

"Established," added the police inspector, "by as an exhaustive inquiry as anybody could make. It is a fact as Mr. Cazalette says."

"Well," observed Scarterfield, "but Salter Quick may have been wrong in his locality. You can be sure of this...

whatever secret he held was got from somebody else. He may have been twenty, thirty, even fifty miles out. But we know something, the Netherfield who was with him on the *Elizabeth Robinson* hailed from Blyth, in this county. I'm going to Blyth tomorrow and I'll find out if there are Netherfields buried about there. Personally, I believe Miss Raven's hit the nail on the head. This is a rough chart of a spot Salter Quick wanted to find...where, no doubt, something is hidden. What? Who knows? But judging from the fact two men have been murdered for the secret of it...something of great value. Buried treasure, no doubt."

"That's precisely what I've been thinking from the very first," murmured Mr. Cazalette. "And you'll have to go back...to go back, my man!"

"It's certainly the only way of going forward," agreed Scarterfield with a laugh. "But now, before we part, gentlemen, let us see where we've got to. I, for myself, have drawn five distinct conclusions about this affair:

First; That the Quicks, Noah and Salter, were in possession of a secret, which was probably connected with their shipmate of the *Elizabeth Robinson*, Netherfield, who hailed from Blyth.

Second; That certain men knew the Quicks to be in possession of that secret and murdered both to get hold of it.

Third; That they failed to get it from either Noah or Salter.

Fourth; That Mr. Cazalette's zeal about the tobacco box, publicly expressed, put the criminals on a new scent, and they, in pursuance of it, stole both the tobacco box and Mr. Cazalette's pocket-book.

Fifth; That the criminals are or were very recently, in fact, this very morning in the vicinity of this place.

"So," he continued, looking round, "the thing's narrowing. Let Mr. Wing there help by getting some news of Chuh Fen, if possible; as for me, I'm going to follow up the Netherfield line. I think we shall track these fellows yet...you never know how unexpectedly a clue may turn up."

"You've not said anything about the handkerchief that I found," observed Mr. Cazalette. "There's a clue, surely!"

"Difficult to follow up, sir," replied Scarterfield. "There is such a thing as little articles of that sort being lost at the laundry, put into the wrong basket, and so on. Now if we could trace the owner of the handkerchief and find where he gets his washing done, and a great deal more...you see? But we'll not lose sight of it, Mr. Cazalette...only, there are more important clues than that to go on in the meantime. The great thing is... what was this precious secret that the Quicks shared, and that certainly had to do with some place here in Northumberland? Let's get at that...if we can."

The two police officials went away with Dr. Lorrimore and his servant, all in deep converse, and the four of us who were left behind endeavored to settle our minds for the repose of the night. But I saw Mr. Raven had been upset by the recent talk: he had got it firmly fixed in his consciousness the murderer of Salter Quick was, as it were, in our very midst.

"How do I know the guilty man mayn't be one of my own servants?" he muttered, as Mr. Cazalette and I took up our candles. "There are six men in the house...all strangers to me and several employed outside. The idea's deucedly unpleasant!"

"You may put it clear away from you, Raven," said Mr. Cazalette. "The murderer may be within bow-shot, but he's none of yours. You'll look deeper, far, far deeper than that... this is no ordinary affair, and no ordinary men at the bottom of it." Then, when he and I had left our host, and were going along one of the upstairs passages towards our own rooms, he added. "No ordinary man, Middlebrook! but you see how ordinary folk are suspicioned! Raven will be doubting the *bona fides* of his own footmen and his own garden lads next. No... no! it'll be deeper down than that, my lad!"

"The mystery is deep," I agreed.

"Aye and I'm wondering if it was well to let the Chinese fellow into all of it," he muttered significantly. "I'm no great believer in Orientals, Middlebrook."

"Lorrimore answers for him," I said.

"And who answers for Lorrimore?" he demanded. "What do you or I know of Lorrimore? I'm thinking yon Lorrimore was far too glib of his tongue and maybe I was too ready myself and talked beyond reason to strangers. I don't know Lorrimore...nor his China-man."

From which I gathered Mr. Cazalette was not superior to suspicions.

Chapter 12

However Mr. Raven's nerves may have been wrung by the mysterious events which found place around his recently acquired possessions, nothing untoward or disturbing occurred at Ravensdene Court itself at that time. Indeed, had it not been for what we heard from outside, and for such doings as the visit of the inspector and Scarterfield, the daily life under Mr. Raven's roof would have been regular and decorous almost to the point of monotony. We were all engaged in our respective avocations...Mr. Cazalette with his coins and medals; I with my books and papers; Mr. Raven with his steward, his gardeners, and his various pottering's about the estate; Miss Raven with her flowers and her golf.

Certainly there was relaxation and in taking it, we sorted out each other. Mr. Raven and Mr. Cazalette made common cause of an afternoon; they were of that period of life despite the gulf of twenty years between them...when lounging in comfortable chairs under old cedar trees on a sunlit lawn is preferable to active exercise; Miss Raven and I being younger, found our diversion in golf and in occasional explorations of the surrounding country.

She had a touch of the nomadic instinct in her; so had I; the neighborhood was new to both; we began to find great pleasure in setting out on some excursion as soon as lunch was over and prolonging our wanderings until the falling shadows warned us that it was time to make for home. What these pilgrimages led to in more ways than one...will eventually appear. We heard nothing of Scarterfield, the detective, nor of Wing, pressed into his service, for some days after the consultation in Mr. Raven's dining-room.

Then, as we were breakfasting one morning, the post-bag was brought in, and Mr. Raven, opening it, presently handed me a letter in an unfamiliar handwriting, the envelope of which bore the post-mark Blyth. I guessed, of course, it was from Scarterfield, and immediately began to wonder what on earth made him write to me. But there it was...he had written, and here is what he wrote:

NORTH SEA HOTEL,
BLYTH, NORTHUMBERLAND
April 23, 1912
Dear Sir:
You will remember when we were discussing matters the other night round Mr. Raven's table I mentioned that I intended visiting this town in order to make some inquiries about the man Netherfield who was with the brothers Quick on the *Elizabeth Robinson*. I have been here two days, and I have made some very curious discoveries. And I am now writing to ask you if you could so far oblige and help me in my investigations as to join me here for a day or two, at once? The fact is, I want your assistance...I understand you are an expert in deciphering documents and the like, and I have come across certain things here in connection with this case which are beyond me. I can assure you that if you could make it convenient to spare me even a few hours of your valuable time you would put me under great obligations to you.
Yours truly,
Thomas Scarterfield

I read this letter twice over before handing it to Mr. Raven. Its perusal seemed to excite him.

"Bless me!" he exclaimed. "How very extraordinary! What strange mysteries we seem to be living among? You'll go, of course, Middlebrook?"

"You think I should?" I asked.

"Oh, certainly, certainly!" he said with emphasis. "If any of us can do anything to solve this strange problem, I think we should. Of course, one hasn't the faintest idea what it is that the man wants. But from what I observed of him the other evening, I should say Scarterfield is a clever fellow...a very clever fellow who should be helped."

"Scarterfield," I remarked, glancing at Miss Raven and at Mr. Cazalette, who were manifesting curiosity, "has made some discoveries at Blyth...about the Netherfield man and he wants me to go over there and help him...to elucidate something, I think, but what it is, I don't know."

"Oh, of course, you must go!" exclaimed Miss Raven. "How exciting! Mr. Cazalette! Aren't you jealous already?"

"No, but I'm curious," answered Mr. Cazalette, to whom I had passed the letter. "I see the man wants something deciphered...aye, that'll be in your line, Middlebrook. Didn't I tell all of you, all along, there'd be more in this business than met the eye? Well, I'll be inquisitive to know what new developments have arisen! It's a strange fact, but it is a fact, that in affairs of this sort there's often evidence, circumstantial, strong, lying ready to be picked up. Next door, as it were and as it is evidently in this case, for Blyth's a town that's not so far away."

Far away or near away, it took me some hours to get to Blyth, for I had to drive to Alnwick, and later to change at Morpeth, and again at Newsham. But there I was at last, in the middle of the afternoon, and there, on the platform to meet me was the detective, as rubicund and cheerful as ever, and full of gratitude for my speedy response to his request.

"I got your telegram, Mr. Middlebrook," he remarked as we walked away from the station, "and I've booked you the most comfortable room I could get in the hotel, which is a nice quiet house where we'll be able to talk in privacy, for barring you and myself there's nobody staying in it, except a few commercial travelers, and to be sure, they've their own quarters. You'll have had your lunch?"

"While I waited at Morpeth," I answered.

"Aye," he said, "I figured on that. So we'll just get into a corner of the smoking-room and have a quiet glass over a cigar, and I'll tell you what I've made out here and a very strange and queer tale it is, and one that's worth hearing, whether it really has to do with our affair or not!"

"You're not sure that it has?" I asked.

"I'm as sure as may be that it probably has!" he replied. "But still, there's a gulf between extreme probability and absolute certainty that's a bit wider than the unthinking reckon for. However, here we are and we'll just get comfortable."

Scarterfield's ideas of comfort, I found, were to dispose himself in the easiest of chairs in the quietest of corners with whiskey and soda on one hand and a box of cigars on the other. This sort of thing he evidently regarded as a proper relaxation from his severe mental labors.

I had no objection to it myself after four hours slow traveling...yet I confess I felt keenly impatient until he had mixed our drinks, lighted his cigar and settled down at my elbow.

"Now," he said confidentially, "I'll set it all out in order what I've done and found out since I came here two days ago. There's no need, Mr. Middlebrook, to go into detail about how I set to work to get information: we've our own ways and methods of getting hold of stuff when we strike a strange town. But you know what I came here for. There's been talk, all through this case, of the name Netherfield. From the questions that Salter Quick put to you when you met him on the cliffs, and from what was said at the Mariner's Joy. Very good...now I fell across that name, too, in my investigations in London, as being the name of a man who was on the *Elizabeth Robinson*, of uncertain memory, lost or disappeared in the year 1907, with the two Quicks. He was set down, that Netherfield, as being of Blyth, Northumberland. Clearly, then, Blyth was a place to get in touch with and here in Blyth we are!"

"A clear bit of preface, Scarterfield," I said approvingly. "Go ahead! I'm bearing in mind that you've been here forty-eight hours."

"I've made good use of my time!" he chuckled, with a knowing grin. "Although I say it myself, Mr. Middlebrook, I'm a bit of a hustler. Well, self-praise, they say, is no recommendation, though to be sure I'm no believer in that old proverb, for, after all, who knows a man better than himself? So we'll get to the story. I came here, of course, to see if I could learn anything of a man of this place who answered to what I had already learnt about Netherfield of the *Elizabeth Robinson.* I went to the likely people for news, and I very soon found out something. Nobody knew anything of any man, old or young, named William Netherfield, belonging, present or past, to this town. But a good many people...most, if not all people do know of a man who used to be in much evidence here some years ago; a man of the name of Netherfield Baxter."

"Netherfield Baxter," I repeated. "Not a name to be readily forgotten...once known."

"He's not forgotten," said Scarterfield, grimly, "and he was well enough known, here, once upon a time, and not so long since, either. And now, who was Netherfield Baxter? Well, he was the only child of an old tradesman of this town, whose wife died when Netherfield was a mere boy, and who died himself when his son was only seventeen years of age. Old Baxter was a remarkably foolish man. He left all he had to this lad...some twelve thousand pounds...in such a fashion that he came into absolute, uncontrolled possession of it on attaining his twenty-first birthday.

Now then you can imagine what happened! My young gentleman, nobody to say him nay, no father, mother, sister, brother, to restrain him or give him a word in season or a hearty kicking, which would have been more to the purpose... went the pace, pretty considerably. Horses, cards, champagne you know! The twelve thousand began to melt like wax in a fire. He carried on longer than was expected, for now and then he had luck on the race-course; won a good deal once, I heard, on the big race at Newcastle...what they call the Pitman's Darby. But it went...all of it went and by the beginning of the year 1904...bear the date in mind, Mr. Middlebrook... Netherfield Baxter was just about on his last legs, he was, in fact, living from hand to mouth.

He was then...I've been particular about collecting facts and statistics just twenty-nine years of age, so, one way or another, he'd made his little fortune last him eight years; he still had good clothes...a very taking, good-looking fellow he was, they say and he'd a decent lodging. But in spring 1904 he was living on the proceeds of chance betting, and was sometimes very low down, and in May of that year he disappeared, in startlingly sudden fashion, without saying a word to anybody, and since then nobody has ever seen a vestige or ever heard a word of him."

Scarterfield paused, looking at me as if to ask what I thought of it. I thought a good deal of it.

"A very interesting bit of life-drama, Scarterfield," I said. "And there have been far stranger things than it would be if this Netherfield Baxter of Blyth turned out to be the William Netherfield of the *Elizabeth Robinson*. You haven't hit on anything in the shape of a bridge, a connecting link between the two?"

"Not yet, anyway," he answered. "And I don't think it's at all likely that I shall, for, as I said just now, nobody in this place has ever heard of Netherfield Baxter since he walked out of his lodging one evening and clean vanished. To be sure, there's been nobody at all anxious to hear of him. For one thing, he left no near and dear relations or friends...for another, he left no debts behind him. The last fact, of course," added Scarterfield, with a wink, "was due to another, very pertinent fact...nobody, to be sure, in his latter stages, would give him credit!"

"You've more to tell," I suggested.

"Oh, much more!" he acquiesced. "We're about half-way through the surface matters. Now then...you're bearing in mind that Netherfield Baxter disappeared, very suddenly, in May 1904. Perhaps the town didn't make much to do over his disappearance for a good reason...it was just then in the very midst of what we generally call a nine days wonder. For some months the Old Alliance Bank here had been in charge of a temporary manager, in consequence of the regular manager's long-continued illness. This temporary manager was a chap named Lester...John Martindale Lester, who had come here from a branch of the same bank at Hexham, across country. Now, this Lester was a young man who was greatly given to going about on a motor-cycle...not so many of those things about, then, as we see now; he was always tearing about the country, they say, on half-holidays, and Saturdays and Sundays. And one evening, careering round a sharp corner, somewhere just outside the town, in the dark, he ran full tilt into a cart that carried no tail-light, and broke his neck! They picked him up dead."

"Well?" I said.

"You're wondering if that's anything to do with Netherfield Baxter's disappearance?" said Scarterfield. "Well... it's an odd thing, but out of all the folk that I've made inquiry of in the town, I haven't come across one yet who voluntarily suggested that it had! But I do! And you'll presently see why I think so. Now, this man, John Martindale Lester, was accidentally killed about the beginning of the first week in May 1904. Three or four days later, Netherfield Baxter cleared out. I've been careful, in my conversations with the town folk officials, mostly...not to appear to connect Lester's death with Baxter's departure. But there was a connection, I'm dead certain. Baxter hooked it, Mr. Middlebrook, because he knew Lester's sudden death would lead to an examination of things at the Old Alliance Bank!"

"Ah!" I said. "I begin to see things!"

"So do I...through smoked glass, though, as yet," assented Scarterfield. "But...it's getting clearer. Now, things at the bank were examined and some nice revelations came forth! To begin with, there was a cash deficiency...not a heavy one, but quite heavy enough. In addition to that, certain jewels were missing, which had been deposited with the bankers for security by a lady in this neighborhood...they were worth some thousands of pounds. And, to add to this, two chests of plate were gone which had been placed with the bank some years before by the executors of the will of the late Lord Forestburne, to be kept there till the coming of age of his heir, a minor when his father died. Altogether, Mr. John Martindale Lester and his accomplices, or accomplice, had helped themselves very freely to things until then safe in the vaults and strong room."

"Have you found out if Netherfield Baxter and the temporary bank-manager were acquainted?" I asked.

"No, that's a matter I've very carefully refrained from inquiring into," answered Scarterfield. "So far, no one has mentioned their acquaintanceship or association to me, and I haven't suggested it, for I don't want to raise suspicions. I want to keep things to myself, so that I can play my own game. No... I've never heard the two men spoken of in connection with each other."

"What is thought in the town about Lester and the valuables?" I inquired. "They must have some theory?"

"Oh, of course, they have," he replied. "The theory is Lester had accomplices in London, he shipped these valuables off there, and when his accomplices heard of his sudden death they...why, they just held their tongues. But my notion is that the only accomplice Lester had was our friend Netherfield Baxter."

"You've some ground?" I asked.

"Yes or I shouldn't think so," said Scarterfield. "I'm now coming to the reason of my sending for you, Mr. Middlebrook. I told you this fellow Baxter had a decent lodging in the town. Well, I made it my business to go there yesterday morning, and finding the landlady was a sensible woman and likely to keep a quiet tongue I just told her a bit of my business and asked her some questions. Then I found out that Baxter left various matters behind him, which she still had clothes, books...he was evidently a chap for reading, and of superior education, which probably accounts for what I'm going to tell you, papers, and the like. I got her to let me have a sight of them. And among the papers I found two, which seem to me to have been written hundreds of years ago and to be lists with names and figures in them. My impression is that Lester found them in those chests of plate, couldn't make them out, and gave them to Netherfield Baxter, as being a better educated man...Baxter, I found out, did well at school and could read and write two or three languages. Well, now, I persuaded the landlady to lend me these documents for a day or two, and I've got them in my room upstairs, safely locked up. I'll fetch them down presently and you shall see if you can decipher them...very old they are, and the writing crabbed and queer...but Lord bless you, the ink's as black as jet!"

"Scarterfield!" I said. "It strikes me you've possibly hit on a discovery. Supposing this stolen stuff is safely hidden somewhere about? Supposing Netherfield Baxter knew where, and he's the William Netherfield of the *Elizabeth Robinson*? Supposing he let the Quicks into the secret? Supposing...but, bless me! there are a hundred things one can suppose! Anyhow, I believe we're getting at something."

"I've been supposing a lot of what you've just suggested ever since yesterday morning," he answered quietly. "Didn't I say we should have to hark back? Well, I'll fetch down these documents."

He went away, and while he was absent I stood at the window of the smoking-room, looking out on the life of the little town and wondering. There, across the street, immediately in front of the hotel was the bank of which Scarterfield had been telling me...an old-fashioned, gray-walled, red-roofed place, the outer door of which was just then being closed for the day by a white-whiskered old porter in a sober-hued uniform.

Was it possible...could it really be the story which had recently ended in a double murder had begun in that quiet-looking house, through the criminality of an untrustworthy employee? But did I say ended...for all I knew the murderers of the Quicks were only an episode, a chapter in the story...the end was...where?

Then Scarterfield came back and from a big envelope drew forth and placed in my hands two folded pieces of old, time-yellowed parchment.

Chapter 13

Until that moment I had not thought much about the reason of my presence at Blyth. I had at any rate, thought, no more than Scarterfield had merely come across some writing which he found it hard to decipher. But one glance at the documents which he placed in my hands showed me that he had accidentally come across a really important find; within another moment I was deeply engrossed, and he saw that I was. He sat silently watching me; once or twice, looking up at him, I saw him nod as if to imply he had felt sure of the importance of the things he had given me. And presently, laying the documents on the table between us, I smiled at him.

"Scarterfield!" I said. "Are you at all up in the history of your own country?"

"Couldn't say that I am, Mr. Middlebrook," he answered with a shake of his head. "Not beyond what a lad learns at school and I dare say I've forgotten a lot of that. My job, you see, has always been with the hard facts of the actual present... not with what took place in the past."

"But you're up to certain notable episodes?" I suggested. "You know, for instance, when the religious houses were suppressed...abbeys, priories, convents, hospitals in the reign of Henry the Eighth, a great deal of their plate and jewels were confiscated to the use of the King?"

"Oh, I've heard that!" he admitted. "Nice haul the old chap got, too, I'm given to understand."

"He didn't get all," I said. "A great deal of the monastic plate disappeared...clean vanished. It used to be said that a lot of it was hidden away or buried by its owners, but it's much more likely that it was stolen by the covetous and greedy folk of the neighborhood...the big men, of course. Anyway, while a great deal was certainly sent by the commissioners to the king's treasury in London, a lot more...especially in out-of-the-way places and districts...just disappeared and was never heard of again. Up here in the North of England that was very often the case. And all this is merely a preface to what I'm going to tell you. Have you the least idea of what these documents are?"

"No," he replied. "Unless they're lists of something...I did make out that they might be, by the way the words and figures are arranged. Like...inventories."

"They are inventories!" I exclaimed. "Both. Written in crabbed calligraphy, too, but easy enough to read if you're acquainted with sixteenth century penmanship, spelling and abbreviations. Look at the first one. It is here described as an inventory of all the jewels, plate, et cetera, appertaining and belonging unto the Abbey of Forestburne, and it was made in the year 1536...this abbey, therefore, was one of the smaller houses that came under the £200 limit and was accordingly suppressed in the year just mentioned. Now look at the second. It also is an inventory of the jewels and plate of the Priory of Mellerton, made in the same year, and similarly suppressed. But though both these houses were of the smaller sort, it is quite evident, from a cursory glance at these inventories they were pretty rich in jewels and plate. By the term jewels is meant plate wherein jewels were set; as to the plate it was, of course, the sacramental vessels and appurtenances. And judging by these entries the whole mass of plate must have been considerable!"

"Worth a good deal, eh?" he asked.

"A great deal! and if it's in existence now, much more than a great deal," I replied. "But I'll read you some of the items set down here...I'll read a few haphazard. They are set down, you see, with their weight in ounces specified, and you'll observe what a number of items there are in each inventory. We'll look at just a few. A chalice, twenty-eight ounces. Another chalice, thirty-six ounces. A mazer, forty-seven ounces. One pair candlesticks, fifty-two ounces. Two cruets, thirty-one ounces. One censer, twenty-eight ounces. One cross, fifty-eight ounces. Another cross, forty-eight ounces. Three dozen spoons, forty-eight ounces. One salt, with covering, twenty-eight ounces. A great cross, seventy-two ounces. A paten, sixteen ounces. Another paten, twenty ounces. Three tablets of proper gold work, eighty-five ounces in all. And so on and so on...a very nice collection, Scarterfield, considering these are only a few items at random, out of some seventy or eighty altogether. But we can easily reckon up the total weight...indeed, it's already reckoned up at the foot of each inventory. At Forestburne, you see, there was a sum total of two thousand two hundred and thirty-eight ounces of plate; at Mellerton, one thousand eight hundred and seventy ounces, so these two inventories represent a mass of about four thousand ounces. Worth having, Scarterfield...in either the sixteenth or the twentieth century."

"And, in the main, it would be...what?" asked Scarterfield. "Gold, silver?"

"Some of it gold, some silver, a good deal of it silver-gilt," I replied. "I can tell all that by reading the inventories more attentively. But I've told you what a mere, cursory glance shows."

"Four thousand ounces of plate...some of it jeweled!" he said. "Whew! And what do you make of it, Mr. Middlebrook? I mean...of all that I've told you?"

"Putting everything together that you've told me," I answered, with some confidence, "I make this of it. This plate, originally church property, came...we won't ask how...into the hands of the late Lord Forestburne, and may have been in possession of his family, hidden away, perhaps, for four centuries. But at any rate, it was in his possession, and he deposited it with his bankers across the way. He may, indeed, not have known what was in it...again, he may have known. Now I take it the dishonest temporary manager you told me of examined those chests, decided to appropriate their valuable contents, and enlisted the services of Netherfield Baxter in his nefarious labors. I think these inventories were found in the chests...one, probably, in each and Baxter kept them out of sheer curiosity...you say he was a fellow of some education. As for the plate, I think he and his associate hid it somewhere and, if you want my honest opinion, it was for it that Salter Quick was looking."

Scarterfield clapped his hand on the table.

"That's it!" he exclaimed. "Hanged if I don't think that myself! It's my opinion this Netherfield Baxter, when he hooked it out of here, got into far regions and strange company, came into touch with those Quicks and told them the secret of this stolen plate...he was, I'm sure, the Netherfield of that ship the Quicks were on. Yes, sir...I think we may safely bet on it Salter Quick, as you say, was looking for this plate!"

"And so was somebody else," I said. "And it was that somebody else who murdered Salter Quick."

"Aye!" he assented. "Now...who? That's the question. And what's the next thing to do, Mr. Middlebrook?"

"It seems to me the next thing to do is to find out all you can about this plate," I replied. "If I were you, I should take two people into your confidence...the head man, director, chairman, or whatever he is, at the bank and the present Lord Forestburne."

"I will!" he agreed. "I'll see them both, first thing tomorrow morning. Will you go with me, Mr. Middlebrook? You'll explain these old papers better than I should."

So Scarterfield and I spent the evening together in the little hotel, and after dinner I explained the inventories more particularly. I came to the conclusion if the four thousand ounces of plate specified in them were in the chests which the dishonest temporary bank-manager had stolen, he had got a very fine haul: the value, of course, of the plate, was not so much intrinsic as extrinsic: there were collectors, English and American, who would cheerfully give vast sums for pre-Reformation sacramental vessels.

Transactions of this kind, I fancied, must have been in the minds of the thieves. There were features of the whole affair which puzzled me...not the least important was my wonder this plate, undeniably church property, should have remained so long in the Forestburne family without being brought into the light of day. I hoped our inquiries next morning would bring some information on that point. But we got no information...at least, none of any consequence. All that was known by the authorities at the bank was the late Lord Forestburne had deposited two chests of plate with them years before, with instructions they were to remain in the bank's custody until his son succeeded him...even then they were not to be opened unless the son had already come of age. The bank people had no knowledge of the precise contents of the chests. All they knew was they contained plate.

As for the present Lord Forestburne, a very young man, he knew nothing, except that his father's mysterious deposit had been burgled by a dishonest custodian. He expressed no opinion about anything, therefore. But the chief authority at the bank, a crusty and self-sufficient old gentleman, who seemed to consider Scarterfield and myself as busybodies, the notion the inventories which we showed him had anything to do with the rifled Forestburne chests, and scorned the notion the family had ever been in possession of goods obtained by sacrilege.

"Preposterous!" he said, with a sniff of contempt. "What the chests contained was, of course, superfluous family plate. As for these documents, that fellow Baxter, in spite of his loose manner of living, was, I remember, a bit inclined to scholarship, and went in for old books and things...a strange mixture altogether. He probably picked up these parchments in some book-seller's shop in Durham or Newcastle. I don't believe they've anything to do with Lord Forestburne's stolen property, and I advise you both not to waste time in running after mare's nests."

Scarterfield and I got ourselves out of this starchy person's presence and confided to each other our private opinions of him and his intelligence. For to us the theory which we had set up was unassailable: we tried to reduce it to strict and formal precision as we ate our lunch in a quiet corner of the hotel coffee-room, previous to parting.

"More than one of us, Scarterfield, who have taken part in this discussion, have said if we are going to get at the truth of things we shall have to go back," I observed. "Well, what you have found out here takes us back some way. Let us suppose we can't do anything without a certain amount of supposition... let us, I say, for the sake of argument, suppose the man Netherfield of Blyth, who was with Noah and Salter Quick on the ship *Elizabeth Robinson*, bound from Hong-Kong to Chemulpo is the same person as Netherfield Baxter, who certainly lived in this town a few years ago. Very well...now then, what do we know of Baxter? We know this...that a dishonest bank-manager stole certain valuables from the bank, died suddenly just afterwards, and Baxter disappeared just as suddenly. The supposition is Baxter was concerned in that theft. We'll suppose more...Baxter knew where the stolen goods were; had, in fact, helped to secrete them. Well, the next we hear of him is...supposing him to be Netherfield on this ship, which, according to the reports you got at Lloyds, was lost with all hands in the Yellow Sea. But...a big but, we know

112

now that whatever happened to the rest of those on board her, three men at any rate saved their lives....Noah Quick, Salter Quick and the Chinese cook, whose exact name we've forgotten, but one of whose patronymics was Chuh. Chuh turns up at Lloyds, in London, and asks a question about the ship. Noah Quick materializes at Devonport, and runs a public-house. Salter joins him there. And presently Salter is up on the Northumbrian coast, professing great anxiety to find a churchyard, or churchyards wherein are graves with the name Netherfield on them...he makes the excuse that is the family name of his mother's people. Now we know what happened to Salter Quick, and we also know what happened to Noah Quick. But now I'm wondering if something else had happened before that?"

"Aye, Mr. Middlebrook?" said Scarterfield. "And what, now?"

"I'm wondering," I answered, leaning nearer to him across the little table at which we sat, "if Noah and Salter, severally, or conjointly, had murdered this Netherfield Baxter before they were murdered? They or somebody who was in with them, who afterwards murdered them? Do you understand?"

"I'm afraid I don't," he said. "No, I don't quite see things."

"Look here, Scarterfield," I said. "Supposing a gang of men...men of no conscience, desperate, adventurous men gets together, as men were together on that ship, the doings and fate of which seem to be pretty mysterious. They're all out for what they can get. One of them is in possession of a valuable secret, and he imparts it to the others, or to some of them...a chosen lot. There have been known such cases...where a secret is shared by say five or six men in which murder after murder occurs until the secret is only held by one or two. A half-share in a thing is worth more than one-sixth, Scarterfield and a secret of one is far more valuable than a secret shared with three. Do you understand now?"

"I see!" he answered slowly. "You mean Salter and Noah may have got rid of Netherfield Baxter and somebody has got rid of them?"

"Precisely!" I said. "You put it very clearly."

"Well," he said, "if that's so, there are...as has been plain all along, two men concerned in putting the Quicks out of the way. For Noah was finished off on the same night saw Salter finished and there was four hundred miles distance between the scenes of their respective murders. The man who killed Noah was not the man who killed Salter, to be sure."

"Of course!" I agreed. "We've always known there were two. There may be more...a gang of them, and remarkably clever fellows. But I'm getting sure the desire to recover some hidden treasure, valuables, something of that sort, was at the bottom of it, and now I'm all the surer because of what we've found out about this monastic spoil. But there are things that puzzle me."

"Such as what?" he asked.

"Well, that eagerness of Salter Quick's to find a churchyard with the name Netherfield on the stones," I replied. "And his coming to that part of the Northumbrian coast expecting to find it. Because, so far as the experts know, there is no such name on any stone, nor in any parish register, in all that district. Who, then, told him of the name? You see, if my theory is correct, and Baxter told him and Noah, he'd tell them the exact locality."

"Ah, but would he?" said Scarterfield. "He mightn't. He might only give them a general notion. Still...Netherfield it was that Salter asked for."

"That's certain," I said. "And I'm puzzled why. But I'm puzzled still more about another thing. If the men who murdered Noah and Salter Quick were in possession of the secret as well, why did they rip their clothes to pieces, searching for something? Why, later, did somebody steal that tobacco box from under the very noses of the police?"

Scarterfield shook his head. The shake meant a great deal.

"That fairly settles me!" he remarked. "Why, the murderer must have been actually present at the inquest."

But at that I shook my head.

"Oh, dear me, no!" I said. "Not at all! But the agent of his was certainly there. My own impression is that Mr. Cazalette's eagerness about that box gave the whole show away. Shall I tell you how I figure things out? Well, I think there were men...we don't know who...that either knew with absolute certainty, or were pretty sure Noah and Salter Quick were in possession of a secret and one or the other and perhaps both carried it on him, in the shape of papers. Each was killed for that secret. The murderers found nothing, in either case. But Mr. Cazalette's remarks, made before a lot of men, drew attention to the tobacco box, and the murderer determined to get it. And what was easier than to abstract it, at the inquest, where it was exhibited in company with several other things of Salter's?"

"I can't say if it was easy or not, Mr. Middlebrook," observed Scarterfield. "Were you there...present?"

"I was there," I said. "So were most people of the neighborhood...as many as could get into the room, anyway. A big room...there'd be a couple of hundred people in it. And many of them were strangers. When the proceedings were over, men were crowding about the table on which Quick's things had been laid out, for exhibition to the coroner and the jury...what easier than for someone to pick up that box? The place was so crowded that such an action would pass unnoticed."

"Very evident it did!" observed Scarterfield.

"But I've heard of such things being taken out of sheer curiosity...morbid desire to get hold of something that had to do with a murder. However, if this particular thing was abstracted by the murderer, or by somebody acting on his behalf it looks as if he, or they, were on the spot. And then that affair of Mr. Cazalette's pocket-book!"

"Well, Scarterfield," I said. "There's another way of regarding both these thefts. Supposing tobacco box and pocket-book were stolen, not as means of revealing a secret, but so that no one else...Cazalette or anybody should get at it!"

"There's something in that," he admitted thoughtfully. "You mean the murderers had already gotten rid of the Quicks so there should be two less in the secret, and these things stolen lest outsiders should get any inkling of it?"

"Precisely!" I answered. "Closeness and secrecy that's been at the back of everything so far. I tell you...you're dealing with unusually crafty brains!"

"I wish I could get the faintest idea of whose brains they were!" he sighed. "A direct clue, now..."

Before he could say any more one of the hotel servants came into the coffee-room and made for our table.

"There's a man in the hall asking for Mr. Scarterfield," he announced. "Looks like a seafaring man, sir. He says Mrs. Ormthwaite told him he'd find you here."

"Woman with whom Baxter used to lodge," muttered Scarterfield, in an aside to me. "Come along, Mr. Middlebrook, you never know what you may hear."

We went out into the hall. There, twisting his cap in his hands, stood a big, brown-bearded man.

Chapter 14

It needed but one glance at Scarterfield's visitor to assure me he was a person who had used the sea. There was the suggestion of salt water and strong winds all over him, from his grizzled hair and beard to his big, brawny hands and square set build. He looked the sort of man who all his life had been looking out across wide stretches of ocean and battling with the forces of Nature in her roughest moods. Just then there was questioning in his keen blue eyes...he was obviously wondering, with all the native suspicion of a simple soul, what Scarterfield might be after.

"You're asking for me?" said the detective.

The man glanced from one to the other of us; then jerked a big thumb in the direction of some region beyond the open door behind his burly figure.

"Mrs. Ormthwaite," he said, bending a little towards Scarterfield. "She said as how there was a gentleman staying in this here house as was making inquiries, about Netherfield Baxter, as used to live hereabouts. So I come along."

Scarterfield contrived to jog my elbow. Without a word, he turned towards the door of the smoking room, motioning his visitor to follow. We all went into the corner wherein, on the previous afternoon, Scarterfield had told me of his investigations and discoveries at Blyth. Evidently I was now to hear more. But Scarterfield asked for no further information until he had provided our companion with refreshment in the shape of a glass of rum and a cigar, and his first question was of a personal sort.

"What's your name, then?" he inquired.

"Fish," replied the visitor, promptly. "Solomon. As everybody is aware."

"Blyth man, no doubt," suggested Scarterfield.

"Born and bred," said Fish. "And lived here always... excepting when I been away, which, to be sure, has been considerable. But whether north or south, east or west, always

117

make for the old spot when on dry land. That is to say...when in this here country."

"Then you'd know Netherfield Baxter?" asked Scarterfield.

Fish waved his cigar. "As a baby...as a boy...as a young man," he declared. "Cut many a toy boat for him at one stage, taught him to fish at another, went sailing with him in a bit of a yawl that he had when he was grown up. Know him? Did I know my own mother!"

"Just so," said Scarterfield, understandingly. "To be sure! You know Baxter quite well, of course." He paused a moment, and then leaned across the table round which the three of us were sitting. "And when did you see him last?" he asked.

Fish, to my surprise, laughed. It was a queer laugh. There was incredulity, uncertainty, a sense of vagueness in it; it suggested that he was puzzled.

"Aye, once?" he said. "That's just it And I asks you and this other gent, which I takes him to be a friend of yours, and confidential, I asks you, can a man trust his own eyes and his own ears? Can he now, solemn?"

"I've always trusted mine, Fish," answered Scarterfield.

"Same here, till a while ago," replied Fish. "But now I ain't so mortal sure of that matter as I was! Because, according to my eyes, and according to my ears, I see Netherfield Baxter, and I hear Netherfield Baxter, inside of three weeks ago!"

He brought down his big hand on the table with a hearty smack as he spoke the last word or two; the sound of it was followed by a dead silence, in which Scarterfield and I exchanged quick glances. Fish picked up his tumbler, took a gulp at its contents, and set it down with emphasis.

"Gospel truth!" he exclaimed.

"That you did see him?" asked Scarterfield.

"Gospel truth, that if my eyes and ears is to be trusted I see him and I hear him!" declared Fish. "Only," he continued, after a pause, during which he stared fixedly, first at me, then at Scarterfield. "Only...he said as how he wasn't he! Do you understand? Denied himself!"

"What you mean is the man you took for Baxter said you were mistaken, and he wasn't Baxter," suggested Scarterfield. "That it?"

"You puts it very plain," assented Fish. "That is what did happen. But if the man I refers to wasn't Netherfield Baxter, then I've no more eyes than this here cigar, and no more ears than that glass! Fact!"

"But you've never had reason to doubt either before, I suppose," said Scarterfield. "And you're not inclined to doubt them now. Now then, let's get to business. You really believe, Fish, that you met Netherfield Baxter about three weeks ago? That's about it, isn't it? Never mind what the man said...you took him to be Baxter. Now, where was this?"

"Hull!" replied Fish. "Three weeks ago come Friday."

"Under what circumstances?" asked Scarterfield. "Tell us about it."

"Ain't such a long story, neither," remarked Fish. "And seeing as how, according to Widow Ormthwaite, you're making some inquiries about Baxter, I don't mind telling, because I been mighty puzzled ever since I see this chap. Well, you see, I landed at Hull from my last voyage...been out Eastward and back with a trading vessel what belongs to Hull owners. And before coming home here to Blyth, knocked about a day or two in that port with an old messmate of mine that I chanced to meet there. Now then one morning...as I say, three weeks ago it is, come this Friday...me and my mate, which his name is Jim Shanks, of Hartlepool, and can corroborate, as they call it, what I says...we turns into a certain old-fashioned place there is there in Hull, in a bit of an alley off High Street...you'll know Hull, no doubt, you gentlemen?"

"Never been there," replied Scarterfield.

"I have," I said. "I know it well...especially the High Street."

"Then you'll know, that all round about that High Street there's still a lot of queer old places as ancient as what it is," continued Fish. "Me and my mate, Shanks, knew one, what we'd oft used in times past...the Goose and Crane, as snug a spot as you'll find in any shipping-town in this here country. Maybe you'll know it?"

"I've seen it from outside, Fish," I answered. "A fine old front half-timber."

"That's it, guv'nor and as pleasant inside as it's remarkable outside," he said. "Well, my mate and me we goes in there for a morning glass, and into a room where you'll find

119

some interesting folk about that time of day. There's a sign on the door of that room, gentlemen, what reads 'For Master Mariners Only,' but it's an old piece of work, and you don't want to take no heed of it...me and Shanks we ain't master mariners, though we may look it in our shore rig-out, and we've used that room whenever we've been in Hull.

Well, now we gets our glasses, and our cigars, and we sits down in a quiet corner to enjoy ourselves and observe what company drops in. Some queer old birds there is comes in to that place, I do assure you, gentlemen, and some strange tales of seafaring life you can hear. However, there wasn't nothing particular struck me that morning until it was getting on to dinner-time, and me an Shanks was thinking of laying a course for our lodgings, where we'd ordered a special bit of dinner to celebrate our happy meeting, like when in, comes the man I'm a talking about. And if he wasn't Netherfield Baxter, what I'd known ever since he was the height of six-pen north of copper, then, says I, a man's eyes and a man's ears isn't to be trusted!"

"Fish!" said Scarterfield, who was listening intently. "It'll be best if you give us a description of this man. Tell us, as near as you can, what he's like...I mean, of course the man you saw at the Goose and Crane."

Our visitor seemed to pull his mental faculties together. He took another pull at his glass and several at his cigar.

"Well," he said, "that ain't much in my line, that, me not being a scholar, but I can give a general idea. A tall, good-looking chap, as the women would call handsome, sort of rakish fellow, you understand. Dressed very smart. Blue serge suit...good stuff, new. Straw hat...black band. Brown boots... polished and shining. Quite the swell...as Netherfield always was, even when he'd got through his money. The gentleman! Lord bless your souls, I knew him, for all that I hadn't seen him for several years, and that he'd grown a beard!"

"A beard, eh..." interrupted Scarterfield.

"Beard and moustache," assented Fish.

"What color?" asked Scarterfield.

"What you might call a golden-brown," replied Fish. "Cut...the beard was to a point. Suited him."

Scarterfield drew out his pocket-book and produced a slightly-faded photograph...that of a certain good-looking, rather young man, taken in company with a fox-terrier. He handed it to Fish.

"Is that Baxter?" he asked.

"Aye! as he was, years ago," said Fish. "I know that well enough...used to be one of them in the photographer's window down the street, outside here. But now, he's grown a beard. Otherwise...the same!"

"Well?" said Scarterfield, "What happened? This man came in. Was he alone?"

"No," replied Fish. "He'd two other men with him. One was a chap about his own age, just as smart as what he was, and dressed similar. The other was an older man, in his shirt sleeves and without a hat...seemed to me he'd brought Baxter and his friend across from some shop or other to stand them a drink. Anyways, he did call for drinks...whisky and soda and the three of them stood together talking. And as soon as I heard Baxter's voice, I was dead sure about him...he'd always a high voice, talked as gentlemen talks, of course, he was brought up that way...high educated, you understand?"

"What were these three talking about?" asked Scarterfield.

"Far as I could make out about ship's fittings," answered Fish. "Something of that sort, anyway, but I didn't take much notice of their talk; I was too much taken up watching Baxter, and growing more certain every minute, that it was him. And excepting that a few of years does make a bit of difference, and he's grown a beard, I didn't see no great alteration in him. Yet I see one thing."

"Aye?" asked Scarterfield. "What, now?"

"A scar on his left cheek," replied Fish. "What begun underneath his beard, as covered most of it, and went up to his cheek-bone. Just an inch or so showing, you understand? That's been knife's work!' thinks I to myself. You've had your cheek laid open with a knife, my lad, somewhere and somehow! Struck me, then, he'd grown a beard to hide it."

"Very likely," assented Scarterfield. "Well, and what happened? You spoke to this man?"

"I waited and watched," continued Fish. "I'm one as has been trained to use his eyes. Now, I see two or three little things about this man as I remembered about Baxter. There was a way he had of chucking up his chin...there it was! Another of playing with his watch-chain when he talked...it was there! And of slapping his leg with his walking-stick...that was there, too! 'Jim!' I says to my mate, 'if that ain't a man I used to know, I'm a Dutchman!' Which, of course, I ain't. And so, when the three of them sets down their glasses and turns to the door, I jumps up and makes for my man, holding out a hand to him, friendly. And then, of course, come all the surprise!"

"Didn't know you, I suppose?" suggested Scarterfield.

"I tell you what happened," answered Fish. "Morning, Mr. Baxter! says I. It's a long time since I had the pleasure of seeing you, sir! and as I say, shoves my hand out, hearty. He turns and gives me a hard, keen look...not taken aback, mind you, but searching-like. 'You're mistaken, my friend,' he says, quiet, but pleasant. 'You're taking me for somebody else.' What! says I, all of a heap. Ain't you Mr. Netherfield Baxter, what I used to know at Blyth, away up North? 'That I'm certainly not,' says he, as cool as the North Pole. 'Then I ask your pardon, sir, says I, and all I can say is that I never see two gentlemen so much alike in all my born days, and hoping no offence. 'None at all!' says he, as pleasant as might be. 'They say everybody has a double.' And at that he gives me a polite nod, and out he goes with his pals, and I turns back to Shanks. 'Jim!' says I. 'Don't let me ever trust my eyes and ears no more, Jim!' I says. 'I'm a breaking-up, Jim! That's what it is. Thinking I sees things when I don't.' 'Stow all that!' says Jim, what's a practical sort of man. 'You was only mistook' says he. 'I've been in that case more than once,' he says. 'Wherever there's a man, there's another somewhere that's as like him as two peas is like each other; let's go home to dinner,' he says. So we went off to the lodgings, and at first I was sure I'd been mistaken. But later, and now...well, I ain't. That there man was Netherfield Baxter!"

"You feel sure of it?" suggested Scarterfield.

"Aye, certain," declared Fish. "I've had time to think it over, and to reckon it all up, and now I'm sure it was him...only he wasn't going to let out that it was. Now, if I'd only chanced on him when he was by himself, what?"

"You'd have got just the same answer," said the detective laconically. "He didn't want to be known. You saw no more of him in Hull, of course..."

"Yes, I did," answered Fish. "I saw him again that night.

And as regards one of them at any rate, in queer company."

"What was that?" asked Scarterfield.

"Well," replied Fish, "me and Jim Shanks, we went home to dinner...couple of roast chickens, and a nice bit of sirloin to follow. And after that we had a nice comfortable sleep for the rest of the afternoon, and then, after a wash-up and a drop of tea, we went out to look round the town a bit for an evening's diversion. Not to any particular place, but just strolling round, like, as sailor-men will, being ashore and stretching their legs. And it so came about that late in the evening we turned into the smoking-room of the Cross Keys, in the Market Place...maybe this here friend of yours, seeing as he's been in Hull, knows that!"

"I know it, Fish," I said.

"Then you'll know that you goes in at an archway, turns in at your right, and there you are," he said. "Well, Shanks and me, we goes in, casual like, not expecting anything that you wouldn't expect. But we'd no sooner sat us down in that smoking-room and taken an observation that I sees the very man that I'd seen at the Goose and Crane, him that I'd taken for Baxter. There he was, in a corner of the room, and the other smart-dressed man with him, their glasses in front of them, and their cigars in their mouths. And with them there was something else that I certainly didn't go for to expect to see in that place."

"What?" asked Scarterfield.

"What I seen plenty of, time and again, in various parts of this here world, and ain't so mighty fond of seeing," answered Fish, with a scowl. "A chink!"

"A...what?" demanded the detective. "A...chink?"

"He means a China-man," I said. "That's it, isn't it, Fish?"

"That's it," assented Fish. "A yellow-skinned, slit-eyed, thin-fingered Chinese, with a face like an image and a voice like silk...which," he added, scowling more than ever, "is poison that I can't abide, no how, having seen more than enough of."

I looked at Scarterfield. He had been attentive enough all through the course of our visitor's story, but I saw that his attention had redoubled since the last few words.

"A China-man!" he said in a low voice. "With him!"

123

"As I say, a Chinese, and with that there man, what, when all's said and done, I'm certain was and is Netherfield Baxter," reiterated Fish. "But mind you, and here's the queer part of it, he wasn't no common China-man. Not the sort that you'll see by the score down in Lime-house way, or in Liverpool, or in Cardiff...not at all. Lord bless you, this here chap was smarter dressed than the other two! Swell-made dark clothes, gold-handled umbrella, kid gloves on his blooming hands, and a silk top hat...a regular dude! But a chink!"

"Well?" said Scarterfield, after a pause, during which he seemed to be thinking a good deal. "Anything happen?"

"Nothing happened...what should happen?" replied Fish. "Them here were in their corner, and Jim Shanks and me, we was in ours. They were busied talking among themselves...of course, we heard nothing. And at last all three went out."

"Did the man you take to be Baxter look at you?" asked Scarterfield.

"Never showed a sign of it!" declared Fish. "Him and the other passed us on their way to the door, but he took no notice."

"See him again anywhere?" inquired Scarterfield.

"No, I didn't" replied Fish. "I left Hull early next morning, and went to see relatives of mine at South Shields. Only came home a day or two since, and happening to pass the time of day with widow Ormthwaite this morning, I told her what I've told you. Then she told me that you was inquiring about Baxter...so I comes along here to see you. What might you be wanting with my gentleman, now?"

Scarterfield told Fish enough to satisfy and quieten him; and presently the man went away, having first told us that he would be at home for another month. When he had gone Scarterfield turned to me.

"There!" he said. "What do you think of that, Mr. Middlebrook?"

"What do you think of it?" I suggested.

"I think Netherfield Baxter is alive and active and up to something," he answered. "And I'd give a good deal to know who that China-man is who was with him. But there's ways of finding out a lot now that I've heard all this, Mr. Middlebrook! I'm off to Hull. Come with me!"

Until that instant such an idea had never entered my head. But I made up my mind there and then.

"I will!" I said. "We'll see this through, Scarterfield. Get a time-table."

Chapter 15

There were reasons, other than the suddenly excited desire to follow this business out to whatever end it might come at, which induced me to consent to the detective's suggestion that I should go to Hull with him. As I had said to Solomon Fish, I knew Hull...well enough. In my very youthful days I had spent an annual holiday there, with relatives, and I had vivid recollections of the place. Already, in those days, they had begun to pull Hull to pieces, laying out fine new streets and open spaces where there had been old-fashioned, narrow alleys and not a little in the slum way.

But then, as happily now, there was still the old Hull of the ancient High Street, and the Market Place, and the Land of Green Ginger, and the older docks, wharves, and quays; it had been among these survivals of antiquity, and in the great church of Holy Trinity and its scarcely less notable sister of St. Mary in Lowgate that I had loved to wander as a boy.

There was a peculiar smell of the sea in Hull, and an atmosphere of seafaring life that I have never met with elsewhere, neither in Wapping nor in Bristol, in South Hampton nor in Liverpool. One felt in Hull that one was already half-way to Bergen or Stockholm or Riga...there was something of North Europe about you as soon as you crossed the bridge at the top of Whitefriargate and plunged into masts and funnels, stacks of fragrant pine, and sheds bursting with foreign merchandise. And I had a sudden itching and half-sentimental desire to see the old seaport again, and once more catch up its appeal and its charm.

"Yes, I'll certainly go with you, Scarterfield!" I repeated. "In for a penny, in for a pound, they say. I wonder, though, what we are in for! You think, really, we're on the track of Netherfield Baxter?"

"Haven't a doubt of it!" asserted Scarterfield, as he turned over the pages of the railway guide. "That man who's just gone was right...that was Baxter he saw. With who knows what of mystery and crime and all sorts of things behind him!"

"Including the murder of one of the Quicks?" I suggested.

"Including some knowledge of it, anyway," he said. "It's a clue, Mr. Middlebrook, and I'm on it. As this man was in Hull, there'll be news of him to be picked up there...very likely in plenty."

"Very well," I said. "I'm with you. Now let's be off."

Going southward by way of Newcastle and York, we got to Hull that night, late...too late to do more than eat our suppers and go to bed at the Station Hotel. And we took things leisurely next morning, breakfasting late and strolling through the older part of the town before, as noon drew near, we approached the Goose and Crane. We had an object in selecting time and place. Fish had told us the man whom he had seen in company with our particular quarry, the supposed Baxter, had come into the queer old inn in his shirt-sleeves and without his hat. He was therefore probably some neighboring shop or store-keeper, and in the habit of turning into the ancient hostelry for a drink about noon. Such a man...that man Scarterfield hoped to encounter. Out of him, if he met him, he could hope to get some news.

Although, as a boy, I had often seen the street front of the Goose and Crane, I had never passed its portals. Now, entering it, we found it to be even more curious inside than it was out. It was a fine relic of Tudor days...a rabbit warren of snug rooms, old furniture, wide chimney places, tiled floors; if the folk who lived in it and the men who frequented it had only worn the right sorts of costume, we might easily have thought ourselves to be back in "Elizabethan times." We easily found the particular room of which Solomon Fish had spoken...there was the door, half open, with its legend on an upper panel in faded gilt letters, "For Master Mariners Only." But, as we had inferred, that warning had been set up in the old days, and was no longer a strict observance; we went into the room unquestioned by guardians or occupants, and calling for refreshments, sat ourselves down to watch and wait.

There were several men in this quaint old parlor; all seemed, in one degree or another, to be connected with the sea. Men, thick-set, sturdy, bronzed, branded in solid suits of good blue cloth, all with that look in the eye which stamps the seafarer. Other men whom one supposed to have something to do with sea-trade...ship's chandlers, perhaps, or shipping-agents. We caught stray whiffs of talk...it was all about the life of the port and of the wide North Sea that stretches away from the Humber. And in the middle of this desultory and apparently aimless business in came a man who, I am sure from my first glimpse of him, was the very man we wanted. A short, stiffly-built, paunchy man, with a beefy face, shrewd eyes, and a bristling, iron-gray moustache; a well-dressed man, and sporting a fine gold chain and a diamond pin in his cravat. But...in his shirt sleeves, and without a hat. Scarterfield leaned nearer to me.

"Our man for a million!" he muttered.

"I think so," I said.

The new-comer, evidently well-known from the familiar way in which nods and brief salutations were exchanged for him, bustled up to the bar, called for a glass of bitter beer and helped himself to a crust of bread and a bit of cheese from the provender at his elbow. Leaning one elbow on the counter and munching his snack he entered into conversation with one or two men near him; here, again, the talk as far as we could catch it, was of seafaring matters. But we did not catch the name of the man in the shirt-sleeves, and when, after he had finished his refreshment, he nodded to the company and bustled out as quickly as he had entered, Scarterfield gave me a look, and we left the room in his wake, following him.

Our quarry bustled down the alley and turned the corner into the old High Street. He was evidently well known there; we saw several passers-by exchange greetings with him. Always bustling along, as if he were a man whose time was precious, he presently crossed the narrow roadway and turned into an office, over the window of which was a sign "Jallanby, Ship Broker." He had only got a foot across his threshold, however, when Scarterfield was at his elbow.

"Excuse me, sir," he said politely. "May I have a word with you?"

The man turned, stared, evidently recognized Scarterfield as a stranger he had just seen in the Goose and Crane, and turned from him to me.

"Yes?" he answered questionably. "What is it?"

Scarterfield pulled out his pocket-book and produced

his official card.

"You'll see who I am from that," he remarked. "This gentleman's a friend of mine...just now giving me some professional help. I take it you're Mr. Jallanby?"

The ship-broker started a little as he glanced at the card and realized Scarterfield's calling. "Yes, I'm Mr. Jallanby," he answered. "Come inside, gentlemen." He led the way into a dark, rather dismal and dusty little office, and signed to a clerk who was writing there to go out. "What is it, Mr. Scarterfield?" he asked. "Some information?"

"You've hit it sir," replied Scarterfield. "That's just what we do want; we came here to Hull on purpose to find you, believing you can give it. From something we heard only yesterday afternoon, Mr. Jallanby, a long way from here, we believe that one morning about three weeks ago, you were in the Goose and Crane in that very room where we saw you just now, in company with two men...smartly dressed men, in blue serge suits and straw hats; one of them with a pointed, golden-brown beard. Do you remember?"

I was watching the ship-broker's face while Scarterfield spoke, and I saw that deep interest, wonder, perhaps suspicion was being aroused in him.

"Bless me!" he exclaimed. "You don't mean to say they're...wanted?"

"I mean to say that I want to get some information about them, and very particularly," answered Scarterfield. "You do remember that morning, then?"

"I remember a good many mornings," said Jallanby, readily enough. "I went across there with those two several times while they were in the town. They were doing a bit of business with me...we often dropped in over yonder for a glass before dinner. But I'm surprised that...well, to put it plainly that detectives should be inquiring after them! I am, indeed."

"Mr. Jallanby," said Scarterfield, "I'll be plain with you. This is, so far, merely a matter of suspicion. I'm not sure of the identity of one of these men...its but one I want to trace at present, though I should like to know who the other is. But...if my man is the man I believe him to be, there's a matter of robbery, and possibly of murder. So you see how serious it is! Now, I'll jog your memory a bit. Do you remember one morning, as you and these two men were leaving the Goose and Crane, a big seafaring-looking man stepped up to the bearded man you were with and claimed acquaintance with him as being one Netherfield Baxter?"

Jallanby started. It was plain that he remembered.

"I do!" he exclaimed. "Well enough! I stood by. But...he said he wasn't. There was a mistake."

"I believe there was no mistake," said Scarterfield. "I believe that man is Netherfield Baxter, and...it's Netherfield Baxter I want. Now, Mr. Jallanby, what do you know of those two? In confidence!"

We had all been standing until then, but at this invitation to disclosure the ship-broker motioned us to sit down, he was turning the stool which the clerk had just vacated.

"This is a queer business, Mr. Scarterfield," he said. "Robbery? Murder? Nasty things, nasty terms to apply to folk that one's done business with. And that, of course, was all that I did with those two men, and all I know about them. Pleasant, good-mannered, gentlemanly chaps I found them...why, Lord bless me, I dined with them one night at their hotel!"

"Which hotel?" asked Scarterfield.

"Station Hotel," replied Jallanby. "They were there for ten days or so, while they did their business with me. I never saw anything wrong about them either...seemed to be what they represented themselves to be. Certainly they'd plenty of money...for what they wanted here in Hull, anyway. But of course, that's neither here nor there."

"What names did you know them under?" inquired Scarterfield. "And where did they profess to come from?"

"Well, the man with the brownish beard called himself Mr. Norman Belford," answered Jallanby. "I gathered he was from London. The other man was a Frenchman...some French lord or other, from his name, but I forget it. Mr. Belford always called him Vicomte...which I took to be French for our Viscount."

Scarterfield turned and looked at me. And I, too, looked at him. We were thinking of the same thing...old Cazalette's find on the bush in the scrub near the beach at Ravensdene Court. And I could not repress an exclamation.

"The handkerchief!"

Scarterfield coughed. A dry, significant cough...it meant

a great deal.

"Aye!" he said. "Just so...the handkerchief! Um!" He turned to the ship-broker. "Mr. Jallanby," he continued, "what did these two want of you? What was their business here in Hull?"

"I can tell you that in a very few words," answered Jallanby. "Simple enough and straight enough, on the surface. So far as I was concerned, anyhow. They came in here one morning, told me they were staying at the Station Hotel, and said they wanted to buy a small craft of some sort that a small crew could run across the North Sea to the Norwegian fiords... the sort of thing you can manage with three or four, you know. They said they were both amateur yachtsmen, and, of course, I very soon found out they knew what they were talking about... in fact, between you and me, I should have said they were as experienced in sea-craft as any man could be! I soon detected that."

"Aye!" said Scarterfield, with a nod at me. "I dare say you would."

"Well, it so happened that I'd just the very thing they seemed to want," continued the ship-broker. "A vessel that had recently been handed over to me for disposal, and then lying in the Victoria Dock, just at the back here, beyond the old harbor: just the sort of craft that they could sail themselves, with say a man, or a boy or two...I can tell you exactly what she was, if you like."

"It might be very useful to know that," remarked Scattered, with emphasis on the last word. "We may want to identify her."

"Well," said Jallanby, "she was a yawl about eighteen tons register; thirty tons yacht measurement; length forty-two feet; beam thirteen; draught seven and a half feet; square stern; coppered above the water-line; carried main, jib-headed mizen, fore-staysail, and jib, and in addition had a sliding gunter gaff-topsail, and..."

"Here!" interrupted Scarterfield with a smile. "That's all too technical for me to carry in my head! If we want details, I'll trouble you to write them down later. But I take it this vessel was all ready for going to sea."

"Ready any day," asserted Jallanby. "Only just wanted tidying up and storing. As a matter of fact, she'd been in use, quite recently, but she was a bit too solid for her late owner's tastes...the truth was, she'd been originally built for a Penzance fishing-lugger...splendid sea-going boats, those!"

"Do I understand this vessel could undertake a long voyage?" asked Scarterfield. "For instance, could they have crossed, say, the Atlantic in her?"

"Atlantic? Lord bless you, yes!" replied the ship broker. "Or Pacific, either. Go tens of thousands of miles in a craft of that soundness, as long as you'd got provisions on board"

"Did they buy her?" asked Scarterfield.

"They did...at once," replied Jallanby. "And paid the money for her...in cash, there and then."

"Check?" inquired Scarterfield, laconically.

"No, sir...good Bank of England notes," answered Jallanby. "Oh, they were all right as regards money...in my case, anyway. And you'll find the same as regards the tradesmen they dealt with here...cash on the spot. They fitted her out with provisions as soon as they'd got her, of course, took a few days."

"And then went off...to Norway?" asked Scarterfield.

"So I understand," assented Jallanby. "That's what they said. They were going, first of all, to Stavanger...then to Bergen...then further north."

"Just the two of them?" asked Scarterfield.

"Why, no," replied Jallanby. "They were joined, a day or two before they sailed, by a friend of theirs...a Chinaman. Queer combination...Englishman, Frenchman, Chinaman. But this Chinaman, he was a swell...what we should call a gentleman, you know...Mr. Belford told me, in private, that he belonged to the Chinese Ambassador's suite in London."

"Oh!" said Scarterfield. "Just so! A diplomat. And where did he stop...here?"

"Oh, he joined them at the hotel," answered Jallanby. "He'd come there the night I dined with them. Quiet, very gentlemanly little chap...quite the gentleman, you know."

"And his name?" asked Scarterfield.

But the ship-broker held up a deprecating hand.

"Don't ask me!" he said. "I heard it, but I'm not up to those Chinese names. Still, you'd find it in the hotel register, no doubt. But really, gentlemen, you surprise me! I should never have thought...yet, you never know who people are, do you? Nice, pleasant, well-behaved fellows these were, and..."

"Ah!" said Scarterfield, with deep significance. "It's a queer world, Mr. Jallanby. Now then, for the moment, oblige me by keeping all this to yourself. But two questions...first, how long since is it these chaps sailed for Bergen; second, what is the name of this smart little vessel?"

"They sailed precisely three weeks ago next Monday," answered the ship-broker, "and the name of the vessel is the *Blanchflower.*"

We left Mr. Jallanby then, promising to see him again, and went away. I was wondering what the detective made out of all this, and I waited with some curiosity for him to speak. But we had got half way up the old High Street before Scarterfield opened his lips. And then his tone was a blend of speculation and distrust.

"Now, I wonder where those chaps have gone?" he muttered. "Of course they haven't gone to Norway! Of course that Chinese chap wasn't from the Chinese Legation in London! The whole thing's a bluff. By this time they'll have altered the name of that yawl, and gone...where? In search of that buried stuff, to be sure!"

"If the man who called himself Belford is really Baxter, he'll know precisely where it is," I said.

"Aye, just so, Mr. Middlebrook," assented Scarterfield. "But...there's been time in all these years to shift that stuff from one place to another! I haven't the slightest doubt that Belford is Baxter, and he and his associates bought that vessel as the easiest way of getting the stuff from wherever it's hid... but where are we to look for them and their craft? Have they gone north or south! It would be waste of time and money to cable to the Norwegian ports for news of them...they're not gone there, that I'll swear."

"Scarterfield," I said, feeling convinced on the matter. "If the man's Baxter, and he's after that stuff, he's gone north. The stuff is near Blyth! Dead certain!"

"I dare say you're right," he said slowly. "And as I've found out all there is to find out here in Hull, I suppose a return to Blyth is the most advisable thing. After all, we know what to look out for on that coast...a twenty-ton yawl, with an Englishman, a Frenchman, and a Chinaman aboard her. Very well."

So that afternoon, after seeing the ship-broker again, and making certain arrangements with him in case he heard anything of the *Blanchflower* and her crew of three queerly-assorted individuals, we retraced our steps northward. But while Scarterfield turned off at Newcastle for Tynemouth and Blyth, I went forward alone, for Alnwick and Ravensdene Court.

Chapter 16

Being very late in the evening when I arrived at Alnwick, I remained there for that night, and it was not until noon of the next day that I once more reached Ravensdene Court. Lorrimore was there, he had come over to lunch, and for the moment I hoped that he had brought some news from his Chinese servant. But he had heard nothing of Wing since his departure: it would scarcely be Wing's method, he said, to communicate with him by letter; when he had anything to tell, he would either return or act, of his own initiative, upon his acquired information: the way of the China-man, he remarked with a knowing look at Mr. Raven, was dark, subtle, and not easily understandable to Western minds.

"And yourself, Middlebrook?" asked Mr. Raven. "What did the detective want, and what have you found out?"

I told them the whole story as we sat at lunch. They were all deeply absorbed, but no one so much as Mr. Cazalette, who, true to his principle of doing no more than crumbling a dry biscuit and sipping a glass or two of sherry at that hour, gave my tale of the doings at Blyth and Hull his undivided attention. And when he had heard me out, he slipped away in silence, evidently very thoughtful, and disappeared into the library.

"So there it all is," I said in conclusion, "and if anybody can make head or tail of it and get a definite and dependable theory, I am sure Scarterfield, from a professional standpoint, will be glad to hear whatever can be said."

"It seems to me Scarterfield is on the high road to a very respectable theory already," remarked Lorrimore. "So are you! The thing to me it appears to be fairly plain. It starts out with the association of Baxter and the dishonest bank-manager. The bank-manager, left in charge of this old-fashioned bank at Blyth, where any supervision of his doings was no doubt pretty slack, and where he was, of course, fully trusted, examines the nature of the various matters committed to his care, and finds out the contents of those Forestburne chests. He then enters into a conspiracy with Baxter for purloining them and some other valuables...those jewels you mentioned, Middlebrook. It would not be a difficult thing to get them away from the bank premises without anyone knowing.

Then the two conspirators secrete them in a safe and unlikely place, easily accessible, I take it, from the sea. Probably, they meant to remove them for good and all, just before the dishonest bank-manager's temporary residence in the town came to an end. But his fatal accident occurs. Then Master Baxter is placed in a nice fix! He knows that his fellow-criminal's sudden death will necessarily lead to some examination, more or less thorough, of the effects at the bank. That examination, to be sure, was made. But Baxter has gone, cleared out, vanished, before the result is known. He may have had an idea...we can only guess at it...that suspicion would fall on him. Anyway, he leaves the town, and is never seen in or near it again. If this theory is a true one, things seem pretty clear up to this point."

"Of course," I said, "it is theory! All supposition, you know."

"Right!" assented Lorrimore. "But let us theorize a bit further...I am, you see, merely following out the train of thought which seems to have been set up in you and in Scarterfield. Baxter disappears. Nobody knows where he's gone. There is a veil drawn over a certain period...pretty thickly. But we, who have had occasion to try to pierce it, have seen, so we think, through certain tears and rifts in it. We know that a certain number of years ago there was a trading ship in the Yellow Sea, the *Elizabeth Robinson*, concerning the fate of which there is more mystery than is quite in accordance with either safety or respectability. She was bound from Hong-Kong to Chemulpo, and she never reached Chemulpo. But we also know that on her, when she left Hong-Kong there were two men, presumably brothers, whose names were Noah and Salter Quick, set down, mind you, not as members of the crew, but as passengers. Also there was a Chinese cook, of the name of Lo Chuh Fen. And there was another man, who called himself Netherfield, and who hailed from Blyth, in Northumberland."

He looked round the table, evidently bent on securing

our attention to their particular point. We were all, of course, fully acquainted with the details he was unfolding, but he was summing things up in quite judicial fashion, and there was a certain amount of intellectual satisfaction in listening to a succinct résumé. One of us, at any rate, was following him with rapt attention...Miss Raven. I fancied I saw why Baxter, or Netherfield, had already presented himself to her as a personage of a dark and romantic, if deeply-wicked and even blood-stained sort.

"Now," continued Lorrimore, becoming more judicial than ever, "according to the official accounts, as shown at Lloyds, the *Elizabeth Robinson* never reached Chemulpo, and she is...officially believed to have been lost, with all hands, during a typhoon, in the Yellow Sea. All hands! But we know that, whatever happened to the *Elizabeth Robinson*, and to the rest of the crew, certain men who were on board her when she left Hong-Kong, for Chemulpo, did escape whatever catastrophe occurred. The *Elizabeth Robinson* may be at the bottom of the Yellow Sea, and most of her folk with her.

But in course of time Noah Quick turns up at Devonport in England, in possession, evidently, of plenty of money. He takes a licensed house, runs it on highly respectable lines, and comports himself as a decent member of society; also he prospers, and has a very good balance at his bankers. So there is one man who certainly did not go down with the *Elizabeth Robinson*. And now to keep matters in chronological order...we hear of another. A Chinaman, undoubtedly Lo Chuh Fen, turns up at Lloyds and endeavors to find out if this *Elizabeth Robinson* ever did reach Chemulpo.

There is a strange point here...Lo Chuh Fen certainly sailed out of Hong-Kong with the *Elizabeth Robinson*, bound for Chemulpo, yet, some years later, he is inquiring in London, if the *Elizabeth Robinson* ever reached her destination. Why? Did the *Elizabeth Robinson* touch at any port after leaving Hong-Kong? Did Lo Chuh Fen leave her at any such port? We don't know and for the moment it is not material; what is material is that a second member of the company on board the *Elizabeth Robinson* did not go down with her in the Yellow Sea if, as is said, she did go. So there are two survivors...Noah Quick and Lo Chuh Fen. And now a third is added in the person of another Quick...Salter, who turns up at Devonport as the guest of Noah, and who, like his brother, is evidently in possession of a plenitude of this world's goods. He has money in the bank, is a gentleman of leisure, and, like Noah, a person of reserved speech."

Lorrimore was now fairly into his stride, and becoming absorbed in his summing-up. He pushed aside his glass and other table impediments, and leaning forward spoke more earnestly, emphasizing his words with equally emphatic gestures.

"A person of reserved speech!" he continued. "But on one occasion, at any rate, so eager to get hold of information, that he casts his habitual reserve aside. On a certain day in March of this year, Salter Quick, with a handsome amount of ready money in his pocket, leaves Devonport, saying that he is going away for a few days. We next hear of him at an hotel in Alnwick, where he is asking for information about certain churchyards on this Northumbrian coast wherein he will find the graves of people of the name of Netherfield...the name of a man, be it remembered, who was with him and his brother Noah Quick, on board the *Elizabeth Robinson*.

Next morning he meets with Mr. Middlebrook on the headlands between Alnmouth and Ravensdene Court and taking him for an inhabitant of these parts, he puts the same question to him. He accompanies Mr. Middlebrook to an inn on the cliffs; he asks the same question there and there, evidently to his great discomfiture, he hears that another man, whose identity did not then appear, but who, we now know, was only a casual traveler who was merely repeating Salter Quick's own questions of the previous evening which he had overheard at Alnwick, had been asking similar questions.

Why had Salter Quick travelled all the way from Devonport to Northumberland to find the graves of some people named Netherfield? We don't know, but we do know that on the very night of the day on which he had asked his questions of Mr. Middlebrook and of Claigue, the landlord, Salter Quick was murdered. And on that same night, at Devonport, four hundred miles away, his brother, Noah Quick, met a similar fate."

Mr. Cazalette came back into the room. He was carrying a couple of fat quarto books under one arm, and a large folio under the other, and he looked as if he had many important things to communicate. But Miss Raven smilingly motioned him to be seated and silent, and Lorrimore, with a glance at him which a judge might have bestowed on some belated counsel who came tip-toeing into his court, went on.

"Now," he said, "there were certain similarities in these two murders which lead to the supposition that, far apart as they were, they were the work of a gang, working with common purpose. There was no robbery from the person in either instance, though each victim had money and valuables on him to a considerable amount. But each man had been searched. Pockets had been turned out...clothing ripped up.

In the case of Salter Quick, we are familiar with the details of the tobacco box, on the inner lid of which there was a roughly-scratched plan of some place, and of the handkerchief bearing a monogram which Mr. Cazalette discovered near the scene of the murder. These are details of great importance...the true significance of which does not yet appear. But the real, prime detail is the curious, mysterious connection between the name Netherfield, which Salter Quick was so anxious to find on gravestones in some Northumbrian churchyard or other, and the man of that name who was with him on the *Elizabeth Robinson*. And we are at once faced with the question...was the man, Netherfield Baxter, who left Blyth some years ago, the man Netherfield, described as of Blyth, whose name was on the *Elizabeth Robinson's* list?"

Mr. Raven treated us to one of his characteristic sniffs. He had a way, when he was stating what he considered to be a dead certainty, or when he was assenting to one, of throwing up his head and sniffing, with a somewhat cynical smile as accompaniment. He sniffed now, and Lorrimore went on...to a peroration.

"There can be no doubt about it!" he said with emphasis. "A Blyth man, a seafarer, named Solomon Fish, chances to be in Hull and, in a tavern there which is evidently the resort of seafaring folk, sees a man whom he instantly recognizes as Netherfield Baxter, whom he had known as child, boy and young man. He accosts him...the man denies it. We need pay no attention whatever to that denial: we may be quite sure from the testimony of Fish the man is Baxter. Now then, what is Baxter doing? He is evidently in possession of ample funds...he and his companions buy a small vessel, a twenty-ton yawl, in which, they said, they want to cross the North Sea to the Norwegian fiords. And who are his companions? One is a Chinaman. Probably Lo Chuh Fen. The other is a Frenchman, who, says Mr. Jallanby, the Hull ship-broker, was addressed as Vicomte. He, probably, is an adventurer, and a criminal one, like Baxter, and he is also probably the owner of the handkerchief which Mr. Cazalette found, stained with Salter Quick's blood!"

Lorrimore paused a moment, looking round to see how this impressed us. The last suggestion was new to me, but I saw its reasonableness and nodded. Lorrimore nodded back, and continued.

"Now a last word," he said. "I, personally, haven't a doubt these three, one or other of them, murdered the Quicks, and they're now going to take up that swag which Baxter and the dishonest bank-manager safely planted somewhere. But...I don't believe it's buried or secreted in any out-of-the-way place on the coast. I know where I should look for it, and where Scarterfield ought to search for it."

"Where, then?" I exclaimed.

"Well," he answered, "the thing is to consider what those fellows were likely to do with the old monastic plate and the jewels and so on when they'd got them. They probably knew the ancient chalices, reliquaries, and that sort of thing would fetch big prices, sold privately to collectors...especially to American collectors, who, as everybody knows, are not at all squeamish or particular about the antecedents of property so long as they secure it. I should say that Baxter, acting for his partner in crime, stored these things, and has waited for a favorable, opportunity to resume possession of them. I incline to the opinion that he stored them at Hartlepool, or at Newcastle, or at South-Shields...at any place when they could easily be transferred by ship. He may, indeed, have stored them at Liverpool, for easy transit across the Atlantic. I don't believe in the theory they're planted in some hole-and-corner of the coast."

"In that case, what becomes of Salter Quick's search for the graves of the Netherfields?" I suggested.

"Can't say," replied Lorrimore, with a shrug of his shoulders. "But Salter Quick may have got hold of the wrong tale, or half a tale, or mixed things up. Anyway, that's my opinion...this stolen property is not cached anywhere, but is somewhere within four respectable walls, and if I were Scarterfield, I should communicate with stores and repositories asking for information about goods left with them some time ago and not yet reclaimed."

"Good idea!" agreed Mr. Raven. "Much more likely than the buried treasure notion."

"To which, however, I incline," I said stubbornly. "When Salter Quick sought for the graves of the Netherfields, he had a purpose."

Mr. Cazalette came nearer the table with his big volumes. It was very evident that he had made some discovery and was anxious to tell us of it.

"Before you go any further into that matter," he said, laying down his burdens, "there are one or two things I should like to draw your attention to in connection with what Middlebrook told us before I left the room just a while since. Now about that monastic plate, Middlebrook, of which you've seen the inventories...you may not be aware of it, but there's a reference to that matter in Dryman's 'History of the Religious Foundations of Northumberland' which I will now read to you. Hear you this, now:

"*Abbey of Forestburne.* It is well known the altar vessels, plate, and jewels of this house were considerable in number and in value, but were never handed over to the custodians of the King's Treasury House in London. They were duly inventoried by the receivers in these parts, and there are letters extant recording their dispatch to London. But they never reached their destination, and it is commonly believed that like a great deal more of the monastic property of the Northern districts these valuables were appropriated by high-placed persons of the neighborhood who employed their underlings, marked and disguised, to waylay and despoil the messengers entrusted to carry them Southward. N. B. These foregoing remarks apply to the plate and jewels which appertained to the adjacent Priory of Mellerton, which were also of great value."

"So," continued Mr. Cazalette, "there's no doubt, in my mind, anyway, the plate of which Middlebrook saw the inventories is just what they describe it to be, and that it came, in course of time, into the hands of the Lord Forestburne who deposited it in the bank. And now," he went on, opening the biggest of his volumes, "here's the file of a local paper which your respected predecessor, Mr. Raven, had the good sense to keep, and I've turned up the account of the inquest that was held at Blyth on the dishonest bank-manager. And there's a bit of evidence here that nobody seems to have drawn Scarterfield's attention to. 'The deceased gentleman,' it reads, 'was very fond of the sea, and frequently made excursions along our beautiful coast in a small yacht which he hired from Messrs. Capsticks, the well-known boat-builders of the town.

It will be remembered that he had a particular liking for night-sailing, and would often sail his yacht out of harbor late of an evening in order, as he said, to enjoy the wonderful effects of moonlight on sea and coast.' That, you'll bear in mind," concluded Mr. Cazalette, with a more than usually sardonic grin, "was penned by some fatuous reporter before they knew the deceased gentleman had robbed the bank.

And no doubt it was on those night excursions that he, and this man Baxter that we've heard of, carried away the stolen valuables, and safely hid them in some quiet spot on this coast and there you'll see, they'll be found all in good time. And as sure as my name is what it is, Dr. Lorrimore, it was that spot Salter Quick was after...only he wasn't exactly certain where it was, and had somehow got mixed about the graves of the Netherfields. Man alive! the plate of the old monks is buried under some Netherfield headstone at this minute!"

"Don't believe it, sir!" said Lorrimore. "It's much more likely to be stored in some handy seaport where it can be easily called for without attracting attention. And if Middlebrook will give me Scarterfield's address that's what I'm going to suggest to him."

I suppose Lorrimore wrote to the detective. But during the next few days I heard nothing from Scarterfield; indeed nobody heard anything new from anywhere. I believe that Scarterfield from Blyth, gave some hints to the coastguard people about keeping a look-out for the *Blanchflower*, but I am not sure of it. However, two of us at Ravensdene Court took a mutual liking for walks along the loneliest stretches of the coast...myself and Miss Raven. Before my journey to Blyth and Hull, she and I had already taken to going for afternoon excursions together; now we lengthened them, going out after

142

lunch and remaining away until we had only just time to return home by the dinner-hour. I think we had some vague idea that we might possibly discover something...perhaps find some trace, we knew not of what. Then we were led, unexpectedly, as such things always do happen, to the threshold of our great and perilous adventure. Going further afield than usual one day, and, about five o'clock of a spring afternoon, straying into a solitary ravine that opened up before us on the moors that stretched to the very edge of the coast, we came upon an ancient wood of dwarf oak, so venerable and time-worn in appearance that it looked like a survival of the Druid age. There was not an opening to be seen in its thick undergrowth, nor any sign of path or track through it, but it was with a mutual consent and understanding that we made our way into its intense silence.

Chapter 17

In order to arrive at a proper understanding of the peculiar circumstances and position in which Miss Raven and myself very shortly found ourselves placed, it is necessary to give some information as to the geographical situation of the wood into which we plunged, more I think, out of a mingled feeling of curiosity and mystery than of anything else. We had then walked several miles from Ravensdene Court in a northerly direction, but instead of keeping to the direct line of the cliffs and headlands we had followed an inland track along the moors, which, however, was never at any point of its tortuous way more than a mile from the coast.

The last mile or two of this had been through absolute solitudes...save for a lonely farmstead, or shepherd's cottage, seen far off on the rising ground, further inland, we had not seen a sign of human habitation. Nor that afternoon did we see any sail on the broad stretch of sea at our right, nor even the smoke-trail of any passing steamer on the horizon. Yet the place we now approached seemed even more solitary.

We came to a sort of ravine, a deep fissure in the line of the land, on the south side of which lay the wood of ancient oak of which I have spoken. Beyond it, on the northern side, the further edge of this ravine rose steeply, masses of scarred limestone jutting out of its escarpments; it seemed to me that at the foot of the wood and in the deepest part of this natural declension, there would be a burn, a stream, that ran downwards from the moor to the sea.

I think we had some idea of getting down to this, following its course to its outlet on the beach, and returning homeward by way of the sands. The wood into which we made our way was well-nigh impregnable; it seemed to me that for age upon age its undergrowth had run riot, untrimmed, unchecked, until at last it had become a matted growth of interwoven, strangely twisted boughs and tendrils. It was only by turning in first one, then another direction through it that we made any progress in the downward direction we desired; sometimes it was a matter of forcing one's way between the thickly twisted obstacles. We exchanged laughing remarks about our having found the forest primeval; before long each was plentifully adorned with scratches and tears. All around us the silence was intense; there was no singing of birds nor humming of insects in that wood.

But more than once we came across bones...the whitened skeletons of animals that had sought these shades and died there or had been dragged into them and torn to pieces by their fellow beasts. Altogether there was an atmosphere of eeriness and gloom in that wood, and I began... more for my companion's sake than my own...to long for a glimpse of some outlet, a sight of the sunlit sea beyond, and for the murmur of the burn which I felt sure, ran rippling coast-wards beneath the fringes of this almost impassable thicket.

And then at the end of quite half-an-hour's struggling, borne, I must say, by Miss Raven, with the truly sporting spirit which was a part of her general character, a sudden exclamation from her, as she pushed her way through a clump of wilding a little in advance of me, caused me to look ahead.

"There's some building just in front of us!" she said. "See...grey stones...a ruin!"

I looked in the direction she indicated, and through the interstices of the thickly-leaved branches, just then prodigal of their first spring foliage, saw, as she said, a grey wall, venerable and time-stained, rising in front. I could see the topmost stones, a sort of broken parapet, ivy clustering about it, and beneath the green of the ivy, a fragment of some ornamentation and the cavernous gloom of a window place from which glass and tracery had long since gone.

"That's something to make for, anyway," I said. "Some old tower or other. Yet I don't remember anything of the sort, marked on the maps."

We pushed forward, and came out on a little clearing. Immediately in front of us stood the masonry of which we had caught glimpses; a low, squat, square tower, some forty feet in height, ruinous as to the most part, but having the side facing us nearly perfect and still boasting a fine old doorway which I set down as of Norman architecture. North of this lay a mass of fallen masonry, a long line of grass-grown, weed-encumbered stone, which was evidently the ruin of a wall; here and there in the clearing were similar smaller masses. Rank weed, bramble bush, beds of nettles, encumbered the whole place; it was a scene of ruin and desolation. But a mere glance was sufficient to show me that we had come by accident on a once sacred spot.

"Why this," I said, as we paused at the edge of the wood, "this is the ruin of some ancient church, or perhaps of a religious house! Look at the niche there above the arch of the door...there's been an image in that and at the general run of the stone lying about. Certainly this is an old church! Why have we never heard of it?"

"Utterly forgotten, I should think," said Miss Raven. "It must be a long time since there were people about here to come to it."

"Probably a village down on the coast...now swept away," I remarked. "But we must look this place out in the local books. Meanwhile let's explore it."

We began to look about the clearing. The tower was almost gone as to three sides of it; the fourth was fairly intact. A line of fallen masonry lay to the north and was continued a little on the east, where it rose into a higher, ivy-covered mass. Within this again was another, less obvious line, similar in plan, and also covered with unchecked growth: within the uneven surface of the ground was thickly encumbered with rank weeds, beds of thistle, beds of nettle, and a plenitude of bramble and gorse; in one place towards the eastern mass of overgrown wall, a great clump of gorse had grown to such a height and thickness as to form an impenetrable screen. And, peering and prying about, suddenly we came, between this screen and the foot of the tower on signs of great slabs of stone, over the edges of which the coarse grass had grown, and whose surfaces were thickly encumbered with moss and lichen.

"Gravestones!" said Miss Raven. "But...I suppose they're quite worn and illegible."

I got down on my knees at one of the slabs less encumbered than the others and began to tear away the grass and weed. There was a rich, thick carpet of moss on it, and a fringe of grey, clinging lichen, but by the aid of a stout pocket-knife I forced it away, and laid bare a considerable surface of the upper half of the stone. And now that the moss, which had formed a sort of protecting cover, was removed, we saw lettering, worn and smoothed at its edges in common with the rest of the slab, but still to be made out with a little patience. There may be...probably is a certain density in me, a slowness of intuition and perception, but it is the fact that at this time and for some minutes later, I had not the faintest suspicion that we had accidentally lighted upon something connected with the mystery of Salter Quick.

All I thought of, I think, just then was that we had come across some old relic of antiquity...the church of some coast hamlet or village which had long been left to the ruinous work of time, and my only immediate interest was in endeavoring to decipher the half-worn-out inscription on the stone by which I was kneeling. While my companion stood by me, watching with eager attention, I scraped out the earth and moss and lichen from the lettering...fortunately, it had been deeply incised in the stone...a hard and durable sort and much of it remained legible, once the rubbish had been cleared from it. Presently I made out at any rate several words and figures:

Hic jacet dominus ...Humfrey de Knaythville ...quond' vicari huius ...ecclie qui obéit ...anno dei mccccxix.

Beneath these lines were two or three others, presumably words of scripture, which had evidently become worn away before the moss spread its protecting carpet over the others. But we had learnt something.

"There we are!" I said, regarding the result of my labors with proud satisfaction. "There it runs 'Here lies the lord, or master, Humphrey de Knaythville, sometime vicar of this church, who died in the year of our Lord one thousand four hundred and nineteen' nearly six hundred years ago! A good find!"

"Splendid!" exclaimed Miss Raven, already excited to enthusiasm by these antiquarian discoveries. "I wonder if there are inscriptions on the other tombs?"

"No doubt," I assented, "and perhaps some, or things of interest, on this fallen masonry. This place is well worth careful examination, and I'm wondering how it is that I haven't come across any reference to it in the local books. But to be sure, I haven't read them very fully or carefully...Mr. Cazalette may know of it. We shall have something to tell him."

We began to look round again. I wandered into the base

of the tower; Miss Raven began to explore the weed-choked ground towards the east end. Suddenly I heard a sharp, startled exclamation from her. Turning, I saw her standing by the great clump of overgrown gorse of which I have already spoken. She glanced at me; then at something behind the gorse.

"What is it?" I asked.

Unconsciously, she lowered her voice, at the same time glancing, half-nervously, at the thick undergrowth of the wood.

"Come here!" she said. "Come!"

I went across the weed-grown surface to her side. She pointed behind the gorse-bush.

"Look there!" she whispered.

I knew as soon as I looked that we were not alone in that wild, solitary-seeming spot; there were human ears listening, and human eyes watching; we were probably in danger. There behind the yellow-starred clump of green was what at first sight appeared to be a newly-opened grave, but was in reality a freshly-dug excavation; a heap of soil and stone, just flung out, lay by it; on this some hand had flung down a mattock; near it rested a pick. And suddenly, as by a heaven-sent inspiration, I saw things. We had stumbled on the graveyard which Salter Quick had wished to find; de Knaythville and Netherfield were identical terms which had got mixed up in his uneducated mind; here the missing treasure was buried, and we had walked into this utterly deserted spot to interrupt...what, and who? Before I could say a word, I heard Miss Raven catch her breath; then another sharp exclamation came from her lips... stifled, but clear.

"Oh, I say!" she cried. "Who...who are these...these men?"

Her hand moved instinctively towards my arm as she spoke, and as I drew it within my grasp I felt that she was trembling a little. And in that same instant, turning quickly in the direction she indicated, I became aware of the presence of two men who had quietly stepped out from the shelter of the high undergrowth on the landward side of the clearing and stood silently watching us. They were attired in something of the fashion of seamen, in rough trousers and jerseys, but I saw at first glance they were not common men.

Indeed, I saw more, and realized with a sickening

feeling of apprehension that our wandering into that place had brought us face to face with danger. One of the two, a tall, slender-built, good-looking man, not at all unpleasant to look on if it had not been for a certain sinister and cold expression of eye and mouth, I recognized as a stranger whom I had noticed at the coroner's inquest on Salter Quick and had then taken for some gentleman of the neighborhood.

The other, I felt sure, was Netherfield Baxter. There was the golden-brown beard of which Fish had told me and Scarterfield; there, too, was the half-hidden scar on the left cheek. I had no doubt whatever that Miss Raven and myself were in the hands of the two men who had bought the *Blanchflower* from Jallanby, the ship-broker of Hull. The four of us stood steadily gazing at each other for what seemed to be a long and to me a painful minute. Then the man whom I took to be Baxter moved a little nearer to us; his companion, hands in pockets, but watchful enough, lounged after him.

"Well, sir?" said Baxter, lifting his cap as he glanced at Miss Raven. "Don't think me too abrupt, nor intentionally rude, if I ask you what you and this young lady are doing here?"

His voice was that of a man of education and even of refinement, and his tone polite enough; there was something of apology in it. But it was also sharp, business-like, compelling; I saw at once that this was a man whose character was essentially matter-of-fact, and who would not allow himself to stick at trifles, and I judged it best to be plain in my answer.

"If you really want to know," I replied, "we are here by sheer accident. Exploring the wood for the mere fun of the thing, we chanced upon these ruins and have been examining them, that's all?"

"You didn't come here with any set purpose?" he asked, looking from one to the other. "You weren't seeking this place?"

"Certainly not!" I said. "We hadn't the faintest notion that such a place was to be found."

"But here it is, anyway," he said. "And there you are! In the possession of the knowledge of it. And so...you'll excuse me...I must ask a question. Who are you? Tourists? Or do you live hereabouts?"

The other man made a remark under his breath, in some foreign language, eyeing me the while. And Baxter spoke again watching me.

"I think you, at any rate, are a resident?" he said. "My friend has seen you before in these parts."

"I have seen him," I said unthinkingly. "I saw him amongst the people at Salter Quick's inquest."

The faintest shadow of an understanding glance passed between the two men, and Baxter's face grew stern.

"Just so!" he remarked. "That makes it all the more necessary to repeat my question. Who are you...both?"

"My name is Middlebrook, if you must know," I answered. "And I am not a resident of these parts. I am visiting here. As for this lady, she is Miss Raven, the niece of Mr. Francis Raven, of Ravensdene Court. And really..." He waved his hand as if to deprecate any remonstrance or threat on my part, and bowed as politely to my companion as if I had just given him a formal introduction to her.

"No harm shall come to you, Miss Raven," he said, with evidently honest assurance. "None whatever!"

"Nor to Mr. Middlebrook, either, I should hope!" exclaimed Miss Raven, almost indignantly.

He smiled, showing a set of very white, strong teeth.

"That depends on Mr. Middlebrook," he said. "If he behaves like a good and reasonable boy...Mr. Middlebrook," he went on, interrupting himself and turning on me with a direct look, "a plain question? Are you armed?"

"Armed!" I retorted scornfully. "Do you think I carry a revolver on an innocent country stroll?"

"We do!" he answered with another smile. "You see, we don't know with whom we may meet. It was a million to one... perhaps more...against our meeting anybody this afternoon, yet...we've met you."

"We are sorry to have interrupted you," I said, not without a touch of satirical meaning. "We won't interrupt any longer if you will permit us to say good day."

I motioned to Miss Raven to follow me, and made to move. But Baxter laughed a little and shook his head.

"I'm not sure that we can allow that, just yet," he said. "It is unfortunate...I offer a thousand apologies to Miss Raven, but business is business, and..."

"Do you mean to tell me that you intend to interfere with our movements, just because you chance to find us here?" I demanded. "If so..."

"Don't let us quarrel or get excited," he said, with another wave of his hand. "I have said that no harm shall come to you...a little temporary inconvenience, perhaps, but...however, excuse me for a moment."

He stepped back to his companion; together they began to whisper, occasionally glancing at us.

"What does he mean?" murmured Miss Raven. "Do they want to keep us...here?"

"I don't know what they intend," I said. "But don't be afraid."

"I'm not afraid," she answered. "Only I've a pretty good idea of who it is that we've come across! And so have you?"

"Yes," I replied. "Unfortunately, I have. And we're at their mercy. There's nothing for it but to obey, I think."

Baxter suddenly turned back to us. It was clear that his mind was made up.

"Miss Raven...Mr. Middlebrook," he said. "I'm sorry, but we can't let you go. The fact is, you've had the bad luck to light on a certain affair of ours about which we can't take any chances. We have a yacht lying outside here...you'll have to go with us on board and to remain there for a day or two. I assure you, no harm shall come to either of you. And as we want to get on with our work here...will you please to come, now?"

We went silently. There was nothing else to do. In a similar silence they led us through the rest of the wood, along the side of the stream which I had expected to find there, and to a small boat that lay hidden by the mouth of the creek. As they rowed us away in it, and rounded a spit of land, we saw the yacht, lying under a bluff of the cliffs. Ten minutes' stiff pulling brought us alongside and for a moment, as I glanced up at her rail, I saw the yellow face of a China-man looking down on us. Then it vanished.

Chapter 18

In the few moments which elapsed between my catching sight of that yellow face peering at us from the rail and our setting foot on the deck of what was virtually a temporary prison, I had time to arrive at a fairly conclusive estimate of our situation. Without doubt we were in the hands of Netherfield Baxter and his gang; without doubt this was the craft which they had bought from the Hull ship broker; without doubt the reason of its presence on this lonely stretch of the coast lay in the proceedings among the ruins beneath whose walls we had come face to face with our captors. I saw or believed that I saw through the whole thing.

Baxter and his accomplices had bought the yawl, ostensibly for a trip to the Norwegian fjords, but in reality that they might sail it up the coast, in the capacity of private yachtsmen, recover the treasure which had been buried near the tombs of the de Knaythevilles, and then go elsewhere. Miss Raven and I had broken in upon their operations, and we were to pay for the accident with our liberty. I was not concerned about myself...I fancied that I saw a certain amount of honesty in Baxter's assurances, but I was anxious about my companion, and about her uncle's anxiety. Miss Raven was not the sort of girl to be easily frightened, but the situation, after all, was far from pleasant...there we were, defenseless among men who were engaged in a dark and desperate adventure, whose hands were probably far from clean in the matter of murder, and who, if need arose, would doubtless pay small regard to our well-being or safety. Yet there was nothing else for it but to accept the situation.

We went on deck. The vessel was at anchor; she lay, a thing of idleness, quiet and peaceful enough, in a sheltered cove, wherein, I saw at a glance, she was lost to sight from the open sea outside the bar at its entrance, and hid from all but the actual coastline of the land. And all was quiet on her clean, freshly-scoured decks. She looked, seen at close quarters, just

152

what her possessors, of course, desired her to be taken for...a gentleman's pleasure yacht, the crew of which had nothing to do but keep her smart and bright. No one stepping aboard her would have suspected piracy or nefarious doings. And when we boarded her, there was nobody visible. The Chinaman whom I had seen looking over the side had disappeared, and from stem to stern there was not a sign of human life. But as Miss Raven and I stood side by side, glancing about us with curiosity, a homely-looking gray cat came rubbing its shoulder against the woodwork and from somewhere forward, where a wisp of blue smoke escaped from the chimney of the cook's galley, we caught a whiff of a familiar sort...somebody, somewhere, was toasting bread or tea-cakes.

We stood idle, like prisoners awaiting orders, while our captors transferred from the boat to the yawl two big, iron-hooped chests, the wood of which was stained and discolored with earth and clay. They were heavy chests, and they used tackle to get them aboard, setting them down close by where we stood. I looked at them with a good deal of interest; then, remembering that Miss Raven was fully conversant with all that Scarterfield had discovered at Blyth, I touched her elbow, directing her attention to the two bulky objects before us.

"Those are the chests that disappeared from the bank at Blyth," I whispered. "Now you understand?"

She gave me a quick, comprehending look.

"Then we are in the hands of Netherfield Baxter?" she murmured. "That man...there."

"Without a doubt," I answered. "And the thing is...show no fear."

"I'm not a scrap afraid," she answered. "It's exciting! And he's rather interesting, isn't he?"

"Gentlemen of his kidney usually are, I believe," I replied. "All the same, I should much prefer his room to his company."

Baxter just then came over to us, rubbing from his fingers the soil which had gathered on them from handling the chests. He smiled politely, with something of the air of a host who wants to apologize for the only accommodation he can offer.

"Now, Miss Raven," he said, with an accent of almost benevolent indulgence, "as we shall be obliged to inflict our hospitality upon you for a day or two...I hope it won't be for longer, for your sake...let me show you what we can give you in the way of quarters to yourself. We can't offer you the services of a maid, but there is a good cabin, well fitted, in which you'll be comfortable, and you can regard it as your own domain while you're with us. Come this way."

He led us down a short gangway, across a sort of small saloon evidently used as common-room by himself and his companion, and threw open the door of a neat though very small cabin.

"Never been used," he said with another smile. "Fitted up by the previous owner of this craft, and all in order, as you see. Consider it as your own, Miss Raven, while you're our guest. One of my men shall see that you've whatever you need in the way of towels, hot water, and the like. If you'll step in and look round, I'll send him to you now. As he's a China-man, you'll find him as handy as a French maid. Give him any orders or instructions you like. And then come on deck again, if you please, and you shall have some tea."

He beckoned me to follow him as Miss Raven walked into her quarters, and he gave me a reassuring look as we crossed the outer cabin.

"She'll be perfectly safe and secluded in there," he said. "You can mount guard here if you like, Mr. Middlebrook...in fact, this is the only place I can offer you for quarters for yourself...I dare say you can manage to make a night's rest on one of these lounges, with the help of some rugs and cushions, and we've plenty of both."

"I'm all right, thank you," I said. "Don't trouble about me. My only concern is about Miss Raven."

"I'll take good care that Miss Raven is safe in everything," he answered. "As safe as if she were in her uncle's house. So don't bother your head on that score...I've given my word."

"I don't doubt it," I said. "But as regards her uncle...I want to speak to you about him."

"A moment," he replied. "Excuse me." We were on deck again, and he went forward, poked his head into an open hatchway, and gave some order to an unseen person. A moment later a Chinaman, the same whose face I had seen as we came aboard, shot out of the hatchway, glided past me as he crossed the deck with silent tread, and vanished into the cabin we had just left. Baxter came back to me, pulling out a cigarette case. "Yes?" he said, offering it. "About Mr. Raven?"

"Mr. Raven," I said, "will be in great anxiety about his niece. She is the only relative he has, I believe, and he will be extremely anxious if she does not return this evening. He is a nervous, highly-strung man..."

He interrupted me with a wave of his cigarette.

"I've thought of all that," he said. "Mr. Raven shall not be kept in anxiety. As a matter of fact, my friend, whom you met with me up there at the ruins, is going ashore again in a few minutes. He will go straight to the nearest telegraph office, which is a mile or two inland, and there he will send a wire to Mr. Raven...from you. Mr. Raven will get it by, say, seven o'clock. The thing is...how will you word it?"

We looked at each other. In that exchange of glances, I could see that he was a man who was quick at appreciating difficulties and he saw the peculiar niceties of the present one.

"That's a pretty stiff question!" I said.

"Just so!" he agreed. "It is. So take my advice. Instead of having the wire sent from the nearest office, do this...my friend, as a matter of fact, is going on by rail to Berwick. Let him send a wire from there: it will only mean Mr. Raven will get it an hour or so later. Say that you and Miss Raven find you cannot get home tonight, and she is quite safe...word it in any reassuring way you like."

I gave him a keen glance.

"The thing is," I said. "Can we get home tomorrow?"

"Well...possibly tomorrow night...late," he answered. "I will do my best. I may be...I hope to be through with my business tomorrow afternoon. Then..."

At that moment the other man appeared on deck, emerging from somewhere. He had changed his clothes...he now presented himself in a smart tweed suit, Homburg hat, polished shoes, gloves, walking cane. Baxter signed to him to wait, turning to me.

"That's the wisest thing to do," he remarked. "Draft your wire."

I wrote out a message which I hoped would allay Mr. Raven's anxieties and handed it to him. He read it over, nodded as if in approbation, and went across to the other man.

For a moment or two they stood talking in low tones; then the other man went over the side, dropped into the boat which lay there, and pulled himself off shore-wards. Baxter came back to me.

"He'll send that from Berwick railway station as soon as he gets there, at six-thirty," he said. "It should be delivered at Ravensdene Court by eight. So there's no need to worry further, you can tell Miss Raven. And when all's said and done, Mr. Middlebrook, it wasn't my fault that you and she broke in upon very private doings up there in the old churchyard nor, I suppose, yours either. Make the best of it! It's only a temporary detention."

I was watching him closely as he talked, and suddenly I made up my mind to speak out. It might be foolish, even dangerous, to do it, but I had an intuitive feeling that it would be neither.

"I believe," I said, brusquely enough, "that I am speaking to Mr. Netherfield Baxter?"

He returned me a sharp glance which was half-smiling. Certainly there was no astonishment in it.

"Aye!" he answered. "I thought, somehow, you might be thinking that! Well, and suppose I admit it, Mr. Middlebrook? What then? And what do you...a Londoner, I think you told me...know of Netherfield Baxter?"

"You wish to know?" I asked. "Shall I be plain?"

"As a pike-staff, if you like," he replied. "I prefer it."

"Well," I said, "a good many things recently discovered by accident. That you formerly lived at Blyth, and had some association with a certain temporary bank-manager there, about whose death and the disappearance of some valuable portable property...there was a good deal of concern manifested about the time that you left Blyth. That you were never heard of again until recently, when a Blyth man recognized you in Hull, where you bought a yawl...this yawl, I believe and said you were going to Norway in her. And that... but am I to be still more explicit?"

"Why not?" said he with a laugh. "Forewarned is forearmed. You're giving me valuable information."

"Very well, Mr. Baxter," I continued, determined to show him my cards. "There's a certain detective, one Scarterfield, a sharp man, who is very anxious to make your

156

acquaintance. For if you want the plain truth, he believes you, or some of your accomplices, or you and they together, to have had a hand in the murders of Noah and Salter Quick. And he's on your track."

I was watching him still more closely as I spoke the last sentence or two. He remained as calm and cool as ever, and I was somewhat taken aback by the collected fashion in which he not only replied to my glance, but answered my words.

"Scarterfield of whose doings I've heard a bit...has got hold of the wrong end of the stick there, Mr. Middlebrook," he said quietly. "I had no hand in murdering either Noah Quick or his brother Salter. Nor had my friend...the man who's just gone off with your telegram. I don't know who murdered those men. But I know there have always been men who were ready to murder them if they got the chance, and I wasn't the least surprised to hear they had been murdered. The wonder is that they escaped murder as long as they did! But beyond the fact they were murdered, I know nothing nor does anybody on board this craft. You and Miss Raven are amongst...well, you can call us pirates if you like, buccaneers, adventurers, anything! but we're not murderers. We know nothing whatever about the murders of Noah and Salter Quick except what we've read in the papers."

I believed him. And I made haste to say so out of a sheer relief to know Miss Raven was not among men whose hands were stained with blood.

"Thank you," he said, as coolly as ever. "I'm obliged to you. I've been anxious enough to know who did murder those two men. As I say, I felt no surprise when I heard of the murders."

"You knew them...the Quicks?" I suggested.

"Did I?" he answered with a cynical laugh. "Didn't I? They were a couple of rank bad ones! I have never professed sanctity, Mr. Middlebrook, but Noah and Salter Quick were of a brand that's far beyond me...they were bad men. I'll tell you more of them, later...here's Miss Raven."

"I may as well tell you," I murmured hastily, "Miss Raven knows as much as I do about all that I've just told you."

"That so?" he said. "Um! And she looks a sensible sort of lass, too...well, I'll tell you both what I know...as I say, later. But now some tea!"

While he went forward to give his orders, I contrived to inform Miss Raven of the gist of our recent conversation, and to assert my own private belief in Baxter's innocence. I saw that she was already prejudiced in his favor.

"I'm glad to know that," she said. "But in that case...the mystery's all the deeper. What is it, I wonder, that he can tell."

"Wait till he speaks," I said. "We shall learn something."

Baxter came back, presently followed by the little China-man whom I had seen before, who deftly set up a small table on deck, drew chairs round it, and a few minutes later spread out all the necessaries of a dainty afternoon tea. And in the center of them was a plum cake. I saw Miss Raven glance at it; I glanced at her; I knew of what she was thinking.

Her thoughts had flown to the plum cake at Lorrimore's, made by Wing, his Chinese servant. But whatever we thought, we said nothing. The situation was romantic, and not without some attraction, even in those curious circumstances. Here we were, prisoners, first-class prisoners, if you will, but still prisoners, and there was our jailer; he and ourselves sat round a tea-table, munching toast, nibbling cakes and dainties, sipping fragrant tea, as if we had been in any lady's drawing-room.

I think it speaks well for all of us that we realized the situation and made the most of it by affecting to ignore the actual reality. We chatted, as well-behaved people should under similar conditions, about anything but the prime fact of our imprisonment. Baxter, indeed, might have been our very polite and attentive host and we his willing guests. As for Miss Raven, she accepted the whole thing with hearty good humor and poured out the tea as if she had been familiar with our new quarters for many a long day; moreover, she adopted a friendly attitude towards our captors which did much towards smoothing any present difficulties.

"You seem to be very well accommodated in the matter of servants, Mr. Baxter," she observed. "That little China-man, as you said, is as good as a French maid, and you certainly have a good cook...excellent pastry cook, anyway."

Baxter glanced lazily in the direction of the galley.

"Another China-man," he answered. He looked significantly at me. "Mr. Middlebrook," he continued, "is aware that I bought this yawl from a ship-broker in Hull, for a special purpose..."

"Not aware of the special purpose," I interrupted, with a purposely sly glance at him.

"The special purpose is a run across the Atlantic, if you want to know," he answered carelessly. "Of course, when I'd got her, I wanted a small crew. Now, I've had great experience of China-men...best servants on earth, in my opinion so I sailed her down to the Thames, went up to London Docks, and took in some Chinese chaps that I got in Lime-house. Two men and one cook...man cook, of course. He's good...I can't promise you a real and proper dinner tonight, but I can promise a very satisfactory substitute which we call supper."

"And you're going across the Atlantic with a crew of three?" I asked.

"As a matter of fact," he answered candidly, "there are six of us. The three Chinese; myself; my friend who was with me this afternoon, and who will join us again tomorrow, and another friend who will return with him, and who, like the crew, is a China-man. But he's a China-man of rank and position."

"In other words, the Chinese gentleman who was with you and your French friend in Hull?" I suggested.

"Just so...since we're to be frank," he answered. "The same." Then, with a laugh, he glanced at Miss Raven. "Mr. Middlebrook," he said, "considers me the most candid desperado he ever met!"

"Your candor is certainly interesting," replied Miss Raven. "Especially if you really are a desperado. Perhaps you'll give us more of it?"

"I'll tell you a bit later on,' he said. "That Quick business, I mean."

Suddenly, setting down his tea-cup, he got up and moved away towards the galley, into which he presently disappeared. Miss Raven turned sharply on me.

"Did you eat a slice of that plum-cake?" she whispered. "You did?"

"I know what you're thinking," I answered. "It reminds you of the cake that Lorrimore's man, Wing, makes."

"Reminds!' she exclaimed. "There's no reminding about it! Do you know what I think? That man Wing is aboard this yacht! He made that cake!"

Chapter 19

There was so much of real importance, not only to us in our present situation, but to the trend of things in general, in Miss Raven's confident suggestion that her words immediately plunged me into a thoughtful silence. Rising from my chair at the tea-table, I walked across to the landward side of the yawl, and stood there, reflecting. But it needed little reflection to convince me that what my fellow-prisoner had just suggested was well within the bounds of possibility.

I recalled all that we knew of the recent movements of Dr. Lorrimore's Chinese servant. Wing had gone to London, on the pretext of finding out something about that other problematical Chinese, Lo Chuh Fen. Since his departure, Lorrimore had had no tidings of him and his doings...in Lorrimore's opinion, he might be still in London, or he might have gone to Liverpool, or to Cardiff, to any port where his fellow-countrymen are to be found in England.

Now it was well within probabilities that Wing, being in Lime-house or Poplar, and in touch with Chinese sailor-men, should, with others, have taken service with Baxter and his accomplice, and, at that very moment there, in that sheltered cove on the Northumbrian coast, be within a few yards of Miss Raven and myself, separated from us by a certain amount of deck-planking and a few bulkheads.

But why? If he was there, in that yawl, in what capacity...real capacity was he there? Ostensibly, as cook, no doubt...but that, I felt sure, would be a mere blind. Put plainly, if he was there, what game was that bland, suave, obsequious, soft-tongued China-man playing? Was this his way of finding out what all of us wanted to know? If it came to it, if there was occasion...such occasion as I dared not contemplate could Miss Raven and myself count on Wing as a friend, or should we find him an adherent of the strange and curious gang, which, if the truth was to be faced, literally held not only our liberty, but our lives at its disposal? For we were in a tight place...of that there was no doubt. Up to that moment I was not unfavorably impressed by Netherfield Baxter, and, whether against my better judgment or not, I was rather more than inclined to believe him innocent of actual share or complicity in the murders of Noah and Salter Quick.

But I could see that he was a queer mortal; odd, even to eccentricity; vain, candid and frank because of his very vanity; given, I thought, to talking a good deal about himself and his doings; probably a megalomaniac. He might treat us well so long as things went well with him, but supposing any situation to arise in which our presence, nay, our very existence, became a danger to him and his plans...what then? He had a laughing lip and a twinkle of sardonic humor in his eye, but I fancied the lip could settle into ruthless resolve if need be and the eye become more stony than would be pleasant.

And we were at his mercy; the mercy of a man whose accomplice might be of a worse kidney than himself, and whose satellites were yellow-skinned slant-eyed Easterners, pirates to a man, and willing enough to slit a throat at the faintest sign from a master. As I stood there, leaning against the side, gloomily staring at the shore, which was so near, and yet so impossible of access, I reviewed a point which was of more importance to me than may be imagined the point of our geographical situation. I have already said that the yawl lay at anchor in a sheltered cove.

The position of that cove was peculiar. It was entered from seawards by an extremely narrow inlet, across the mouth of which stretched a bar, I could realize that much by watching the breakers rolling over it; it was plain to me, a landsman, that even a small vessel could only get in or out of the cove at high water. But once across the bar, and within the narrow entry, any vessel coming in from the open sea would find itself in a natural harbor of great advantages; the cove ran inland for a good mile and was quite another mile in width; its waters were deep, rising some fifteen to twenty feet over a clear, sandy bottom, and on all sides, right down to the bar at its entrance, it was sheltered by high cliffs, covered from the tops of their headlands to the thin, pebbly stretches of shore at their feet by thick wood, mostly oak and beech.

The cove was known to the folk of that neighborhood it was impossible to doubt, but I felt sure that any strange craft passing along the sea in front would never suspect its existence, so carefully had Nature concealed the entrance on the landward side of the bar. And there were no signs within the cove itself that any of the shore folk ever used it. There was not a vestige of a human dwelling-place to be discovered anywhere along its thickly-wooded banks; no boat lay on its white beach; no fishing-net was stretched out there to dry in the sun and wind; the entire stretch was desolate. And I knew that an equal desolation lay all over the land immediately behind the cove and its sheltering woods. That was about the loneliest part of a lonely coast and by that time I had become well acquainted with it.

For some miles, north and south of that exact spot, there were no coast villages...there was nothing, save an isolated farmstead, set in deep ravines at wide distances. The only link with busier things lay in the railway that, as I also knew, lay about two or two-and-a-half miles inland; as far as I could recollect the map which lay in my pocket, but which I did not dare to pull out, there was a small wayside station on this line, immediately behind the woods through which Miss Raven and I had unthinkingly wandered to our fate; from it, doubtless, the Frenchman, Baxter's accomplice, had taken train for Berwick, some twenty miles northward. Everything considered, Miss Raven and I were as securely trapped and as much at our captor's mercy as if we had been immured in a twentieth-century Bastille.

I went back, presently, to the tea-table and dropped into my deck-chair again. Baxter was still away from us; as far as I could see, there was no one about. I gave her a look which was intended to suggest caution, but I spoke in a purposely affected tone of carelessness.

"I shouldn't wonder if you are right in your suggestion," I said. "In that case, I think we should have a friend on board in case we need one."

"But you don't anticipate any need?" she asked quickly.

"I don't," I said. "No don't think I do."

"What do you suppose is going to happen to us?" She asked, glancing over her shoulder at the open door of the galley into which Baxter had vanished.

"I think they'll detain us until they're ready to depart, and then they'll release us," I answered. "Our host, or jailor, or whatever you like to call him, is a queer chap...he'll probably make us give him our word of honor that we'll keep close tongues."

"He could have done that without bringing us here," she remarked.

"Ah, but he wanted to make sure!" I said. "He's taking no risks. However, I'm sure he means no harm to us. Under other conditions, I shouldn't have objected to meeting him. He's...a character."

"Interesting, certainly," she agreed. "Do you think he really is a...pirate?"

"I don't think he'll have any objection to making that quite clear to us if he is," I replied, cynically. "I should say he'd be rather proud of it. But I think we shall hear a good deal of him before we get our freedom."

I was right there. Baxter seemed almost wistfully anxiously to talk with us. He behaved like a man who for a long time had small opportunity of conversation with the people he would like to converse with, and he kept us both talking as the afternoon faded into evening and the evening fell towards night. He was a good talker, too, and knew much of books and politics and of men, and could make shrewd remarks, tinged, it seemed to me, with a little cynicism that was more good-humored than bitter. The time passed rapidly in this fashion; supper-time arrived; the meal, as good and substantial as any dinner, was served in the little saloon-like cabin by the soft-footed Chinaman who, other than Baxter, was the only living soul we had seen since the Frenchman went away in the boat; all through it Baxter kept up his ready flow of talk while punctiliously observing his duties as host. Until then, the topics had been of a general nature, such as one might have heard dealt with at any gentleman's table, but when supper was over and the Chinaman had left us alone, he turned on us with a queer, inquisitive smile.

"You think me a strange fellow," he said. "Don't deny it! I am, and I don't mind who thinks it. Or who knows it."

I made no reply beyond an acquiescent nod, but Miss Raven...who, all through this adventure, showed a coolness and resourcefulness which I can never sufficiently praise... looked steadily at him.

"I think you must have seen and known some strange

things," she said quietly.

"Aye and done some!" he answered, with a laugh that had more of harshness in it than was usual with him. Then he glanced at me. "Mr. Middlebrook, there, from what he told me this afternoon, knows a bit about me and my affairs," he said. "But not much. Sufficient to whet your curiosity, eh, Middlebrook?"

"I confess I should like to know more," I replied. "I agree with Miss Raven you must have seen a good deal of the queer side of life."

There was some fine old claret on the table between us; he pushed the bottle over to me, motioning me to refill my glass. For a moment he sat, a cigar in the corner of his lips, his hands in the armholes of his waistcoat, silently reflecting.

"What's really puzzling you this time," he said suddenly, "is that Quick affair...I know because I've not only read the newspapers, but I've picked up a good deal of local gossip... never mind how. I've heard a lot of your goings-on at Ravensdene Court, and the suspicions, and so on. And I knew the Quicks...no man better, at one time, and I'll tell you what I know. Not a nice story from any moral point of view, but though it's a story of rough men, there's nothing in it at all that need offend your ears, Miss Raven...nothing. It's just a story... an instance of some of the things that happen to Ishmaels, outcasts, like me."

We made no answer, and he refilled his own glass, took a mouthful of its contents, and glancing from one to the other of us, went on.

"You're both aware of my youthful career at Blyth?" he said. "You, Middlebrook, are, anyway, from what you told me this afternoon, and I gather you put Miss Raven in possession of the facts. Well, I'll start out from there...when I made the acquaintance of that temporary bank-manager chap. Mind you, I'd about come to the end of my tether at that time as regards money. I'd been pretty well fleeced by one or another, largely through carelessness, largely through sheer ignorance. I didn't lose all my money on the turf, Middlebrook, I can assure you...I was robbed by more than one worthy man of my native town...legally, of course, bless them! And it was that, I think, turned me into the Ishmael I've been ever since...as men had robbed me, I thought it a fair thing to get a bit of my own back.

164

Now that bank-manager chap was one of those fellows who are born with predatory instincts...my impression of him, from what I recollect, is that he was a born thief. Anyway, he and I, getting pretty thick with each other, found out that we were just then actuated by similar ambitions...I from sheer necessity, he, as I tell you, from temperament.

And to cut matters short, we determined to help ourselves out of certain things of value stored in that bank, and to clear out to far-off regions with what we got. We discovered that two chests deposited in the bank's vaults by old Lord Forestburne contained a quantity of simply invaluable monastic spoil, stolen by the good man's ancestors four centuries before: we determined to have that and to take it over to the United States, where we knew we could realize immense sums on it, from collectors, with no questions asked. There were other matters, too, which were handy...we carefully removed the lot, brought them along the coast to this very cove, and interred them in those ruins where we three fore-gathered this afternoon."

"And when, I take it, you have just removed them to the deck above our heads?" I suggested.

"Right, Middlebrook, quite right...there they are!" he admitted with a laugh. "A grand collection, too...chalices, patens, reliquaries, all manner of splendid medieval craftsmanship and certain other more modern things with them...all destined for the other side of the Atlantic...the market's sure and safe and ready..."

"You think you'll get them there?" I asked.

"I shall be more surprised than I ever was in my life if I don't," he answered readily, and with that note of dryness which one associates with certainty. "I'm a pretty good hand at making and perfecting and carrying out a plan. Yes, sir, they'll be there, in good time and they'd have been there long since if it hadn't been for an accident which I couldn't foresee...that bank-manager chap had the ill-luck to break his neck. Now that put me in a fix. I knew the abstraction of these things would soon be discovered, and though I'd exercised great care in covering up all trace of my own share in the affair, there was always a bare possibility of something coming out. So, knowing the stuff was safely planted and very unlikely to be disturbed, I cleared out, and determined to wait a fitting opportunity of regaining possession of it. My notion at that time, I remember, was to get hold of some American millionaire collector who would give me facilities for taking up the stuff, to be handed over to him. But I didn't find one, and for the time being I had to keep quiet. Inquiries, of course, were set afoot about the missing property, but fortunately I was not suspected. And if I had been, I shouldn't have been found, for I know how to disappear as cleverly as any man who ever found that convenient."

He threw away the stump of his cigar, deliberately lighted another, and leaned across the table towards me in a more confidential manner.

"Now we're coming to the more immediately interesting part of the story," he said. "All that I've told you is, as it were, ancient history. We'll get to more modern times, affairs of yesterday, so to speak. After I cleared out of Blyth...with a certain amount of money in my pocket. I knocked about the world a good deal, doing one thing and another. I've been in every continent and in more sea-ports than I can remember. I've taken a share in all sorts of queer transactions from smuggling to slave-trading. I've been rolling in money in January and shivering in rags in June. All that was far away, in strange quarters of the world, for I never struck this country again until comparatively recently. I could tell you enough to fill a dozen fat volumes, but we'll cut all that out and get on to a certain time, now some years ago, where in Hong-Kong, I and the man you saw with me this afternoon, who, if everybody had their own, is a genuine French nobleman, came across those two particularly precious villains, the brothers Noah and Salter Quick."

"Was that the first time of your meeting with them?" I asked. Now that he was evidently bent on telling me his story, I, on my part, was bent on getting out of him all that I could. "You'd never met them before...anywhere?"

"Never seen nor heard of them before," he answered. "We met in a certain house-of-call in Hong-Kong, much frequented by Englishmen and Americans; we became friendly with them; we soon found out that they, like ourselves, were adventurers, would-be pirates, buccaneers, ready for any game; we found out, too, they had money, and could finance any desperate affair that was likely to pay handsomely. My friend and I, at that time, were also in funds...we had just had a very paying adventure in the Malay Archipelago, a bit of illicit trading, and we had got to Hong-Kong on the look-out for another opportunity. Once we had got thoroughly in with the Quicks, that was not long in coming. The Quicks were as sharp as their name...they knew the sort of men they wanted.

And before long they took us into their confidence and told us what they were after and what they wanted us to do, in collaboration with them. They wanted to get hold of a ship, and to use it for certain nefarious trading purposes in the China seas...they had a plan by which the lot of us could have made a lot of money. Needless to say, we were ready enough to go in with them. Already they had a scheme of getting a ship such as they particularly needed. There was at that time lying at Hong-Kong a sort of tramp steamer, the *Elizabeth Robinson*, the skipper of which wanted a crew for a trip to Chemulpo, up the Yellow Sea. Salter Quick got himself into the confidence and graces of this skipper, and offered to man his ship for him, and he packed her as far as he could with his own brother, Noah, myself, my French friend, and a certain Chinese cook of whom he knew and who could be trusted...trusted, that is, to fall in whatever we wanted."

"Am I right in supposing the name of the Chinese cook to have been Lo Chuh Fen?" I asked.

"Quite right...Lo Chuh Fen was the man," answered Baxter. "A very handy man for anything, as you'll admit, for you've already seen him...he's the man who attended on Miss Raven and who served our supper. I came across him again, in Lime-house, recently, and took him into my service once more. Very well...now you understand there were five of us all in for the Quick's plan, and the notion was that when we'd once got safely out of Hong-Kong, Salter, who had a particularly greasy and insinuating tongue, should get round certain others of the crew by means of promises helped out by actual cash bribes. That done, we were going to put the skipper, his mates, and such of the men as wouldn't fall in with us, in a boat with provisions and let them find their way wherever they liked, while we went off with the steamer. That was the surface plan...my own belief is that if it had come to it, the two Quicks would have been quite ready to make skipper and men walk the plank, or to have settled them in any other way...both Noah and Salter, for all their respectable appearance, were born out of their due time...they were admirably qualified to have been lieutenants to Paul Jones or any other eighteenth-century pirate! But in this particular instance, their schemes went all wrong. Whether it was the skipper of the *Elizabeth Robinson*, who was an American and cuter than we fancied, got wind of something, or whether somebody spilt to him, I don't know, but the fact is that one fine morning when we were in the Yellow Sea he and the rest of them set on the Quicks, my friend, myself, and the China-man, bundled us into a boat and landed us on a miserable island, to fend for ourselves. There we were, the five of us...a precious bad lot, to be sure... marooned!"

Chapter 20

At that last word, spoken with an emphasis which showed that it awoke no very pleasant memories in the speaker, Miss Raven looked questioningly from one to the other of us.

"Marooned?" she said. "What is that, exactly?"

Baxter gave her an indulgent and me a knowing look.

"I daresay Mr. Middlebrook can give you the exact etymological meaning of the word better than I can, Miss Raven," he answered. "But I can tell you what the thing means in actual practice! It means to put a man, or men, ashore, preferably on a desert island, leaving him, or them, to fend for himself, or themselves, as best he, or they, can! It may mean slow starvation...at best it means living on what you can pick up by your own ingenuity, on shell-fish and that sort of thing, even on edible sea-weed. Marooned? Yes! that was the only experience I ever had of that...it's all very well talking of it now, as we sit here on a comfortable little vessel, with a bottle of good wine before us, but at the time...ah!"

"You'd a stiff time of it?" I suggested.

"Worse than you'd believe," he answered. "That old Yankee skipper was a vindictive chap, with method in him. He'd purposely gone off the beaten track to land us on that island, and he played his game so cleverly that not even the Quicks...who were as subtle as snakes knew anything of his intentions until we were all marched over the side at the point of ugly-looking revolvers.

If it hadn't been for that little Chinese whom you've just seen we would have starved, for the island was little more than a reef of rock, rising to a sort of peak in its center worn-out volcano, I imagine and with nothing eatable on it in the way of flesh or fruit. But Chuh was a God-send! He was clever at fishing, and he showed us an edible sea-weed out of which he made good eating, and he discovered a spring of water... altogether he kept us alive. All of which," he suddenly added, with a darkening look, "made the conduct of these two Quicks not merely inexcusable, but devilish!"

"What did they do?" I asked.

"I'm coming to it," he said. "All in due order. We were on that island several weeks, and from the time we were flung unceremoniously upon its miserable shores to the day we left it we never saw a sail nor a wisp of smoke from a steamer. And it may be that this, and our privations, made us still more birds of a feather than we were. Anyway, you, Middlebrook, know how men, thrown together in that way, will talk...must talk unless they'd go mad...talk about themselves and their doings and so on. We all talked...we used to tell tales of our doubtful pasts as we huddled together under the rocks at nights, and some nice, lurid stores there were, I can assure you. The Quicks had seen about as much of the doubtful and seamy side of seafaring life as men could, and all of us could contribute something. Also, the Quicks had money, safely stowed away in banks here and there...they used to curse their fate, left there apparently to die, when they thought of it. And it was that, I think, that led me to tell, one night, about my adventure with the naughty bank-manager at Blyth, and of the chests of old monastic treasure which I'd planted up here on this Northumbrian coast."

"Ah!" I exclaimed. "So you told Noah and Salter Quick that?"

"I told Noah and Salter Quick that," he replied slowly. "Yes and I can now explain to you what Salter was after when he appeared in these parts. I read the newspaper accounts, of the inquest and so on, and I saw through everything, and could have thrown a lot of light on things, only I wasn't going to. But it was this way, I told the Quicks all about the Blyth affair...the truth was, I didn't believe we should ever get away from that cursed island...but I told them in a fashion which, evidently, afterwards led to considerable puzzlement on their part. I told them that I buried the chests of old silver, and the other valuables taken from the vaults of the bank, in a churchyard on this coast, close to the graves of my ancestors. I described the spot and the lie of the ruins pretty accurately. Now where the Quicks...Salter, at any rate got puzzled and mixed was over my use of the word ancestors. What I meant...but never said was that I had planted the stuff near the graves of my maternal ancestors, the old De Knaythevilles, who were once great folk

170

in these parts, and of whose name my own Christian name, Netherfield, is, of course, a corruption. But Salter Quick, to be sure, thought the graves would bear the name Netherfield, and when he came along this coast, it was that name he was hunting for. Do you see?"

"Then Salter Quick was after that treasure?" I said.

"Of course he was!" replied Baxter. "The wonder to me is that he and Noah hadn't been after it before. But they were men who had a good many irons in the fire. Too many and some of them far too hot, as it turned out and I suppose they left this little affair until an opportune moment. Without a doubt, not so long after I'd told them the story, Salter Quick scratched inside the lid of his tobacco box a rough diagram of the place I'd mentioned, with the latitude and longitude approximately indicated...that's the box there's been so much fuss about, I read in the papers, and I'll tell you more about it in due process. But now about that island and the Quicks, and how they and the rest of us got out of it.

I told you that the center of this island rose to a high peak, separating one coast from the other...well, one day, when we'd been marooned for several weary weeks and there didn't seem the least chance of rescue, I, my French friend, and the China-man crossed the shoulder of that peak and went along the other coast, prospecting...more out of sheer desperation than in the hope of finding anything. We spent the next night on the other side of the island, and it was not until late on the following afternoon that we returned to our camp, if you can call that a camp which was nothing but a hole in the rocks. And we got back to find Noah and Salter Quick gone and we knew how they had gone when the China-man's sharp eyes made out a sail vanishing over the horizon. Some Chinese fishing-boat had made that island in our absence, and these two skunks had gone away in her and left us, their companions, to shift for ourselves. That's the sort the Quicks were! Those were the sort of tricks they'd play off on so called friends! Do you wonder, either of you, that both Noah and Salter eventually got what they got?"

We made no answer to that beyond, perhaps, a shake of our heads. Then Miss Raven spoke.

"But you got away, in the end?" she suggested.

"We got away in the end...some time later, when we

were about done for," assented Baxter, "and in the same way... a Chinese fishing-boat that came within hail. It landed us on the Kiang-Su coast, and we had a pretty bad time of it before we made our way to Shanghai. From that port we worked our passage to Hong-Kong. I had an idea that we might strike the Quicks there, or get news of them. But we heard nothing of those two villains, at any rate. But we did hear that the *Elizabeth Robinson* had never reached Chemulpo...she'd presumably gone down with all hands, and we were supposed, of course, to have gone down with her. We did nothing to disabuse anybody of the notion; both I and my friend had money in Hong Kong, and we took it up and went off to Singapore. As for our China-man, Chuh, he said farewell to us and vanished as soon as we got back to Hong-Kong, and we never set eyes on him again until very recently, when I ran across him in a Chinese eating-house in Poplar."

"From that meeting, I suppose, the more recent chapters of your story begin?" I suggested. "Or do they begin somewhat earlier?"

"A bit earlier," he said. "My friend and I came back to England a little before that with money in our pockets. We'd been very lucky in the East and with a friend of ours, a Chinese gentleman, mind you, we decided to go in for a little profitable work of another sort, and to start out by lifting my concealed belongings up here. So we bought this craft in Hull, then ran her down to the Thames, then, as I say, I came across Lo Chuh Fen and got his services and those of two other compatriots of his, then in London, and here we are! You see how candid I am...do you know why?"

"It would be interesting to know, Mr. Baxter," said Miss Raven. "Please tell us."

"Well," he said, with a queer deliberation. "Some men in my position would have thought nothing about putting bullets through both of you when we met this afternoon...you hit on our secret. But I'm not that sort...I treat you as what you are, a gentlewoman and a gentleman, and no harm whatever shall come to you. Therefore, I feel certain that all I've said and am saying to you will be treated as it ought to be by you. I daresay you think I'm an awful scoundrel, but I told you I was an Ishmael and I certainly haven't got the slightest compunction about appropriating the stuff in those chests on deck...one of the Forestburnes stole it from the monks...why shouldn't I steal it from his successor? It's as much mine as his...perhaps more so, for one of my ancestors, a certain Geoffrey de Knaytheville, was at one time Lord Abbot of the very house that the Forestburnes stole that stuff from! I reckon I've a prior claim, Middlebrook?"

"I should imagine," I answered, guardedly, "it would be very difficult for anybody to substantiate a claim to ecclesiastical property of that particular nature which disappeared in the sixteenth century. What is certain, however, is that you've got it. Take my advice...hand it over to the authorities!"

He looked at me in blank astonishment for a moment; then laughed as a man laughs who is suddenly confronted by a good joke.

"Hah! hah! hah!" he let out at the top of his voice. "Good! You're a born humorist, friend Middlebrook!" He pushed the claret nearer. "Fill your glass again! Hand it over to the authorities? Why, that would merit a full-page cartoon in the next number of *Punch*. Good, good! but," he went on, suddenly becoming grave again, "we were talking of those scoundrels Quicks. Of course we...that is, my French friend and I have been, and are, suspected of murdering them?"

"I think that is so," I answered.

"Well, that's a very easy point to settle, if it should ever come to it," he replied. "And I'll settle it, for your edification, just now. Noah and Salter Quick were done to death, one near Saltash, in Cornwall, the other near Alnwick, in Northumberland, several hundreds of miles apart, about the same hour of the same evening. Now, my friend and I, so far from being anywhere near either Saltash or Alnwick on that particular evening and night, spent them together at the North Eastern Railway Hotel at York. I went there that afternoon from London; he joined me from Berwick. We met at the hotel about six o'clock; we dined in the hotel; we played billiards in the hotel; we slept in the hotel; we breakfasted in the hotel; the hotel folks will remember us well, and our particulars are duly registered in their books on the date in question. We had no hand whatever in the murders of Noah and Salter Quick, and I give you my word of honor...being under the firm impression that though I am a pirate, I am still a gentleman...that neither of us have the very slightest notion who had!"

Miss Raven made an involuntary murmur of approval, and I was so much convinced of the man's good faith that I stretched out my hand to him.

"Mr. Baxter!" I said, "I'm heartily glad to have that assurance from you! And whether I'm a humorist or not, I'll beg, you once more to take my advice and give up that loot to the authorities...you can make a plausible excuse, and throw all the blame on that bank-manager fellow, and take my word for it, little will be said and then you can devote your undoubtedly great and able talents to legitimate ventures!"

"That would be as dull as ditch-water, Middlebrook," he retorted with a grin. "You're tempting me! But those Quicks... I'll tell you in what fashion there is a connection between their murder and ourselves, and one that would need some explanation. Bear in mind that I've kept myself posted in those murders through the newspapers, and also by collecting a certain amount of local gossip. Now you've a certain somewhat fussy and garrulous old gentleman at Ravensdene Court..."

"Mr. Cazalette!" exclaimed Miss Raven.

"Mr. Cazalette is the name," said Baxter. "I have heard much of him, through the sources I've just referred to. Now, this Mr. Cazalette, going to or coming from a place where he bathed every morning, which place happened to be near the spot whereat Salter Quick was murdered, found a blood-stained handkerchief?"

"He did," I said. "And a lot of mystery attaches to it."

"That handkerchief belongs to my French friend," said Baxter. "I told you that he joined me at York from Berwick. As a matter of fact, for some little time just before the Salter Quick affair, he was down on this coast, posing as a tourist, but really just ascertaining if things were as I'd left them at the ruins in the wood above this cove and what would be our best method of getting the chests of stuff away. For a week or so, he lodged at an inn somewhere, I think, near Ravensdene Court, and he used sometimes to go down to the shore for a swim. One morning he cut his foot on the pebbles, and staunched the blood with his handkerchief, which he carelessly threw away and your Mr. Cazalette evidently found it. That's the explanation of that little matter. And now for the tobacco box."

"A much more important point," I said.

"Just so," agreed Baxter. "Now, my friend and I first heard of the murder while we were at York. In the newspapers that we read, there was an account of a conversation which took place in, I believe, Mr. Raven's coach-house, or some out-building, whither the dead man's body had been carried, between this old Mr. Cazalette and a police inspector, regarding a certain metal tobacco box found on Salter Quick's body. Now I give you my word that news was the first intimation we had ever had that the Quicks were in England! Until then we hadn't the slightest idea they were in England but we knew what those mysterious scratches in the tobacco box signified. Salter had made a rude plan of the place I had told him of, and was in Northumberland to search for it. Then, later, we read your evidence at the opening of the inquest, and heard what you had to tell about his quest of the Netherfield graves, and just to satisfy ourselves we determined to get hold of that tobacco box, don't you see, as long as it was about, a possible clue, there was a danger of somebody discovering our buried chests of silver and valuables. So my friend came down again, in his tourist capacity; put up at the same quarters, strolled about, fished a bit, botanized a bit, attended the adjourned inquest as a casual spectator, and abstracted the tobacco box under the very noses of the police! It's in that locker now," continued Baxter, with a laugh, pointing to a corner of the cabin, "and with it are the handkerchief, your old friend Mr. Cazalette's pocket-book..."

"Oh! your friend got that, too, did he?" I exclaimed. "I see!"

"He abstracted that, too, easily enough, one morning when the old fellow was bathing," assented Baxter. "Naturally, we weren't going to take any chances about our hidden goods being brought to light. We're highly indebted to Mr. Cazalette for making so much fuss about the tobacco box, and we're glad there was so much local gossip about it. Eh?"

I remained silent awhile, reflecting.

"It's a very fortunate thing for both of you that you could, if necessary, prove your presence at York on the night of the murder," I remarked at last. "Your doings about the tobacco box and the other things might otherwise wear a very suspicious look. As it is, I'm afraid the police would probably say...granted they knew what you've just told us so frankly...

that even if you and your French friend didn't murder Salter Quick and his brother, you were probably accessory to both murders. That's how it strikes me, anyway."

"I think you're right," he said calmly. "Probably they would. But the police would be wrong. We were not accessory, either before or since. We haven't the ghost of a notion as to the identity of the Quicks murderers. But since we're discussing that, I'll tell you both of something that seems to have completely escaped the notice of the police, the detectives, and of yourself, Middlebrook. You remember in both cases the clothing of the murdered men had been literally ripped to pieces?"

"Very well," I said. "It had in Salter's, anyway, to my knowledge."

"And so, they said, it had in Noah's," replied Baxter. "And the presumption, of course, was the murderers were searching for something?"

"Of course," I said. "What other presumption could there be?"

Baxter gave us both a keen, knowing look, bent across the table, and tapped my arm as if to arrest my closer attention.

"How do you know the murderers didn't find what they were seeking for?" he asked in a low, forceful voice. "Come, now!"

I stared at him; so, too, did Miss Raven. He laughed.

"That, certainly, doesn't seem to have struck anybody," he said. "I'm sure, anyway, it hasn't struck you before. Does it now?"

"I'd never thought of it," I admitted.

"Exactly! Nor, according to the papers and to my private information...had anybody," he answered. "Yet it would have been the very first thought that would have occurred to me. I should have said to myself, seeing the ripped-up clothing, whoever murdered these men was in search of something that one or other of the two had concealed on him, and the probability is, he's got it. Of course!"

"I'm sure nobody...police or detectives ever did think of that," I said. "But perhaps with your knowledge of the Quicks antecedents and queer doings, you have some knowledge of what they might be likely to carry about them?"

176

He laughed at that, and again leaned nearer to us.

"Aye, well!" he replied. "As I've told you so much, I'll tell you something more. I do know of something the two men had on them when they were on that miserable island and they of course, carried away with them when they escaped. Noah and Salter Quick were then in possession of two magnificent rubies...worth no end of money!"

Chapter 21

I could not repress an unconscious, involuntary start on hearing this remarkable declaration; it seemed to open, as widely as suddenly, an entirely new field of vision; it was as if some hand had abruptly torn aside a veil and shown me something that I had never dreamed of. And Baxter laughed, significantly.

"That strikes you, Middlebrook?" he said.

"Very forcibly, indeed!" I said. "If what you say is true...I mean, if one of those two men had such valuables on him, then there's a reason for the murder of both that none of us knew of. But is it probable the Quicks would still be in possession of jewels that you saw some years ago?"

"Not so many years ago, when all is said and done," he answered. "And you couldn't dispose of things like those very readily, you know. You can take it from me, knowing what I did of them, neither Noah nor Salter Quick would sell anything unless at its full value, or something like it. They weren't hard up for money, either of them; they could afford to wait, in the matter of a sale of anything, until they found somebody who would give their price."

"You say these things...rubies, I think were worth a lot of money?" I asked.

"Heaps of money!" he affirmed. "Do you know anything about rubies? Not much? Well, the ruby, I daresay you do know, is the most precious of precious stones. The real true ruby, the Oriental one, is found in greatest quantity in Burma and Siam, and the best are those that come from Mogok, which is a district lying northward of Mandalay. These rubies that the Quicks had come from there...they were remarkably fine ones. And I know how and where those precious villains got them!"

"Yes?" I said, feeling that another dark story lay behind this declaration. "Not honestly, I suppose?"

"Far from it!" he replied, with a grim smile. "Those two rubies formed the eyes of some ugly god or other in a heathen temple in the Kwang-Tung province of Southern China where the Quicks carried on more nefarious practices than that. They gouged them out...according to their own story. Then, of course, they cleared off."

"You saw the rubies?" I asked.

"More than once...on that island in the Yellow Sea," he answered. "Noah and Salter would have bartered either, or both, for a ship at one period. But!" he added, with a sneering laugh, "you may lay your life that when they boarded that Chinese fishing-boat on which they made their escape they'd pay for their passage as meanly as possible. No...my belief is they still had those rubies on them when they turned up in England again, and as likely as not, they were murdered for them. Take all the circumstances of the murder into consideration...in each case the dead man's clothing was ripped to pieces, the linings examined, even the padding at chest and shoulder torn out and scattered about.

What were the murderers seeking for? Not for money... as far as I remember, each man had a good deal of money on him, and not a penny was touched. What was it, then? My own belief is that after Salter Quick joined Noah at Devonport, both brothers were steadily watched by men who knew what they had on them, and when Salter came North he was followed, just as Noah was tracked down at Saltash. And I should say that whoever murdered them got the rubies. They may have been on Noah; they may have been on Salter; one may have been in Salter's possession; one in Noah's. But there in the rubies lies, in my belief, the secret of those murders."

I felt that here, in this lonely cove, we were probably much nearer the solution of the mystery that had baffled Scarterfield, ourselves, the police, and everybody that we knew. And so, apparently, did Miss Raven, who suddenly turned on Baxter with a look that was half an appeal.

"Mr. Baxter!" she said, coloring a little at her own temerity. "Why don't you follow Mr. Middlebrook's advice... give up the old silver and the rest of it to the authorities and help them to track down those murderers? Wouldn't that be better than whatever it is that you're doing?"

But Baxter laughed, flung away his cigar, and rose to his feet.

"A deal better from many standpoints, my dear young

lady!" he exclaimed. "But too late for Netherfield Baxter. He's an Ishmael...a pirate...a highwayman and it's too late for him to do anything but gang his own gait. No! I'm not going to help the police...not I! I've enough to do to keep out of their way."

"You'll get caught, you know," I said, as good-humoredly as possible. "You'll never get this stuff that's upstairs across the Atlantic and into New York or Boston or any Yankee port without detection. As you are treating us well, your secret's safe enough with us...but think, man, of the difficulties of taking your loot across an ocean...to say nothing of Customs officers on the other side."

"I never said we were going to take it across the Atlantic," he answered coolly and with another of his cynical laughs. "I said we were going to sail this bit of a craft across there...so we are. But when we strike New York or New Orleans or Pernambuco or Buenos Ayres, Middlebrook, the stuff won't be there...the stuff, my lad, won't leave British waters! Deep, deep, is your queer acquaintance, Netherfield Baxter, and if he does run risks now and then, he always provides for them."

"Evidently you intend to trans-ship your precious cargo?" I suggested.

"The door of its market is yawning for it, Middlebrook, and not far away," he answered. "If this craft drops in at Aberdeen, or at Thurso, or at Moville, and the Customs folks or any other such-like hawks and kites come aboard, they'll find nothing but three innocent gentlemen and their servants a-yachting it across the free seas. *Verbum sapienti*, Middlebrook, as we said in my Latin days...far off, now! But wouldn't Miss Raven like to retire...it's late. I'll send Chuh with hot water...if you want anything, Middlebrook, command him. As for me, I shan't see you again tonight, I must keep a watch for my pal coming aboard from his little mission ashore."

Then, with curt politeness, he bade us both good night, and went off on deck, and we two captives looked at each other.

"Strange man!" murmured Miss Raven. She gave me a direct glance that had a lot of meaning in it. "Mr. Middlebrook," she went on in a still lower voice, "let me tell you that I'm not afraid. I'm sure that man means no personal harm to us. But...is there anything you want to say to me before I go?"

"Only this," I answered. "Do you sleep very soundly?"

"Not so soundly that I shouldn't hear if you called me," she replied.

"I'm going to mount guard here," I said. "I, too, believe in what Baxter says. But...if I should, for any reason, have occasion to call you during the night, do at once precisely what I tell you to do."

"Of course," she said.

The China-man who had been in evidence at intervals since our arrival came into the little saloon with a can of hot water and disappeared into the inner cabin which had been given up to Miss Raven. She softly said goodnight to me, with a reassurance of her confidence that all would be well, and followed him. I heard her talking to this strange makeshift for a maid for a moment or two; then the man came out, grinning as if well-pleased with himself, and she closed and fastened the door on him. The China-man turned to me, asking in a soft voice if there was anything I pleased to need.

"Nothing but the rugs and pillows that your master spoke of," I answered.

He opened a locker on the floor of the place and producing a number of cushions and blankets from it made me up a very tolerable couch. Then, with a polite bow, he, too, departed, and I was left alone. Of one thing I was firmly determined...I was not going to allow myself to sleep. I firmly believed in Baxter's good intentions...in spite of his record, strange and shady by his own admission, there was something in him that won confidence; he was unprincipled, without doubt, and the sort of man who would be all the worse if resisted, being evidently naturally wayward, headstrong, and foolishly obstinate, but like all bad men, he had good points, and one of his seemed to be a certain pride in showing people like ourselves that he could behave himself like a gentleman. That pride...a species of vanity, of course would, I felt sure, make him keep his word to us and especially to Miss Raven. But he was only one among a crowd. For anything I knew, his French friend might be as consummate a villain as ever walked, and the Chinese in the galley cut-throats of the best quality. And there, behind a mere partition, was a helpless girl and I was unarmed. It was a highly serious and unpleasant situation, at the best of it, and the only thing I could do was to keep awake and remain on the alert until morning came. I took off coat and waistcoat, folded a blanket shawl-wise around my shoulders, wrapped another round my legs, and made myself fairly comfortable in the cushions which the China-man had deftly arranged in an angle of the cabin. I had directed him to settle my night's quarters in a corner close to Miss Raven's door, and immediately facing the half-dozen steps which led upwards to the deck. At the head of those steps was a door; I had bade him leave it open, so that I might have plenty of air; when he had gone I had extinguished the lamp which swung from the roof. And now, half-sitting, half-lying among my cushions and rugs, I faced the patch of sky framed in that open doorway and saw that the night was a clear one and that the heavens were full of glittering stars.

I had just refilled and lighted my pipe before settling down to my vigils, and for a long time I lay there smoking and thinking. My thoughts were somewhat confused...confused, at any rate, to the extent they ranged over a variety of subjects... our apprehension that afternoon; the queer, almost, if not wholly, eccentric character of Netherfield Baxter; his strange story of the events in the Yellow Sea; his frank avowal of his share in the theft of the monastic spoils; his theory about Noah and Salter Quick, and other matters arising out of these things.

The whirl of it all in my anxious brain made me more than once feel disposed to sleep; I realized in spite of everything, I should sleep unless I kept up a stern determination to remain awake. Everything on board that strange craft was as still as the skies above her decks; I heard no sound whatever save a very gentle lapping of the water against the vessel's timbers, and, occasionally, the far-off hooting of owls in the woods that overhung the cove; these sounds, of course, were provocative of slumber.

I had to keep smoking to prevent myself from dropping into a doze. And perhaps two hours may have gone in this fashion, and it was, I should think, a little after midnight, when I heard, at first far away towards the land, then gradually coming nearer, the light, slow plashing of oars that gently and leisurely rose and fell. This, of course, was the Frenchman, coming back from his mission to Berwick...he would, I knew, have gone there from the little wayside station that lay beyond the woods at the back of the cove and have returned by a late train to the same place. Somehow...I could not well account for it...the mere fact of his coming back made me nervous and uneasy. I was not so certain about his innocence in the matter of Salter Quick's murder. On Baxter's own showing the Frenchman had been hanging about that coast for some little time, just when Salter Quick descended upon it. He, like Baxter, if Baxter's story were true, was aware that one or other of the Quicks carried those valuable rubies; even if, the York episode being taken for granted, he had not killed Salter Quick himself he might be privy to the doings of some accomplice who had. Anyway, he was a doubtful quantity, and the mere fact that he was back again on that yawl made me more resolved than ever to keep awake and preserve a sharp look-out. I heard the boat come alongside; I heard steps on the deck just outside my open door; then, Baxter's voice.

Presently, too, I heard other voices...one that of the Frenchman, which I recognized from having heard him speak in the afternoon; the other a soft, gentle, laughing voice... without doubt that of an Eastern. This, of course, would be the Chinese gentleman of whom I had heard...the man who had been seen in company with Baxter and the Frenchman at Hull. So now the three principal actors in this affair were all gathered together, separated from me and Miss Raven by a few planks, and close by were three Chinese of whose qualities I knew nothing. Safe we might be...but we were certainly on the very edge of a hornet's nest.

I heard the three men talking together in low, subdued tones for a few minutes; then they went along the deck above me and the sound of their steps ceased. But as I lay there in the darkness, two round discs of light suddenly appeared on a mirror which hung on the boarding of the cabin, immediately facing me, and turning my head sharply, I saw that in the bulkhead behind me there were two similar holes, pierced in what was probably a door, which would, no doubt, be sunk flush with the boarding and was possibly the entrance to some other cabin that could be entered from a further part of the deck. Behind that, under a newly-lighted lamp, the three men were now certainly gathered.

I was desperately anxious to know what they were doing...anxious, to the point of nervousness, to know what they looked like, taken in bulk. I could hear them talking in there, still in very low tones, and I would have given much to hear even a few words of their conversation. And after a time of miserable indecision...for I was afraid of doing anything that would lead to suspicion or resentment on their part, and I was by no means sure that I might not be under observation of one of those silky-footed Chinese from the galley. I determined to look through the holes in the door and see whatever was to be seen. I got out of my wrappings and my corner so noiselessly that I don't believe anyone actually present in my cabin would have heard even a rustle, and tip-toeing in my stockinged feet across to the bulkhead which separated me from the three men, put an eye to one of the holes.

To my great joy, I then found that I could see into the place to which Baxter and his companions had retreated. It was a sort of cabin, rougher in accommodation than that in which I stood, fitted with bunks on three sides and furnished with a table in the center over which swung a lamp. The three men stood round this table, examining some papers...the lamp-light fell full on all three. Baxter stood there in his shirt and trousers; the Frenchman also was half-dressed, as if preparing for rest. But the third man was still as he had come aboard...a little, yellow-faced, dapper, sleek China-man, whose smart, velvet-collared overcoat, thrown open, revealed an equally smart dark tweed suit beneath it, and an elegant gold watch-chain festooned across the waistcoat.

He was smoking a cigar, just lighted; that it was of a fine brand I could tell by the aroma that floated to me. And on the table before the three stood a whiskey bottle, a syphon of mineral water, and glasses, which had evidently just been filled. Baxter and the Frenchman stood elbow to elbow; the Frenchman held in his hands a number of sheets of paper, foolscap size, to the contents of which he was obviously drawing Baxter's attention.

Presently they turned to a desk which stood in one corner of the place, and Baxter, lifting its lid, produced a big ledger-like book, over which they bent, evidently comparing certain entries in it with the papers in the Frenchman's hand. What book or papers might be, I of course, knew nothing, for all this was done in silence. But had I known anything, or heard anything, it would have seemed of no significance compared with what I just then saw...a thing that suddenly turned me almost sick with a nameless fear and set me trembling from toe to finger. The dapper and smug China-man, statuesque on one side of the table, immovable save for an occasional puff of his cigar, suddenly shot into silent activity as the two men turned their backs on him and bent, apparently absorbed, over the desk in the corner. Like a flash it reminded me of the lightning-like movement of a viper, his long, thin fingers went into a waistcoat pocket; like a flash emerged, shot to the glasses on the table and into two of them dropped something small and white...some tabloid or pellet that sank and dissolved as rapidly as it was put in.

It was all over, all done, within, literally, the fraction of a second; when, a moment or two later, Baxter and the Frenchman turned round again, after throwing the ledger-like book and the papers into the desk, their companion was placidly smoking his cigar and sipping the contents of his glass between the whiffs. I was by that time desperately careless as to whether I might or might not be under observation from the open door and stairway of my own cabin. I remained where I was, my eye glued to that ventilation hole, watching.

For it seemed to me that the China-man was purposely drugging his companions, for some insidious purpose of his own...in that case, what of the personal safety of Miss Raven and myself? For one moment I was half-minded to rush round to the other cabin and tell Baxter of what I had just seen...but I reflected that I might possibly bring about there and then an affair of bloodshed and perhaps murder in which there would be four Chinese against three others, one of whom...my miserable self...was not only unarmed, but like enough to be useless in a scene of violence.

No...the only thing was to wait, and wait I did, with a thumping heart and tingling nerves, watching. Nothing happened. Baxter gulped down his drink at a single draught; the Frenchman took his in two leisurely swallows; each flung himself on his bunk, pulled his blankets about him, and, as far as I could see, seemed to fall asleep instantly. But the China-man was more deliberate and punctilious. He took his time over his cigar and his whiskey; he pulled out a suit-case from some nook or other and produced from it a truly gorgeous sleeping-suit of gaily-striped silk; it occupied him quite twenty minutes to get undressed and into this grandeur, and even then he lingered, fiddling about in carefully folding and arranging his garment. In the course of this, and in moving about the narrow cabin, he took apparently casual glances at Baxter and the Frenchman, and I saw from his satisfied, quiet smirk that each was sound and fast asleep. And then he thrust his feet into a pair of bedroom slippers, as loud in their coloring as his pajamas, and suddenly turning down the lamp with a twist of his wicked-looking fingers, he glided out of the door into the darkness above. At that I, too, glided swiftly back to my blankets.

Chapter 22

I heard steps, soft as snowflakes, go along the deck above me; for an instant they paused by the open door at the head of my stairway; then they went on again and all was silent as before. But in that silence, above the gentle lapping of the water against the side of the yawl, I heard the furious thumping of my own heart and I did not wonder at it, nor was I then, nor am I now ashamed of the fear that made it thump. Clearly, whatever else it might mean, if Baxter and the Frenchman were, as I surely believed them to be, soundly drugged, Miss Raven and I were at the positive mercy of a pack of Chinese adventurers who would probably stick at nothing.

But my problem...one sufficient to wrack every fiber of my brain...was, what were they after? The Chinese gentleman in the flamboyant pajamas's had without doubt, repaired to his compatriots in the galley, forward: at that moment they were, of course, holding some unholy conference. Were they going to murder Baxter and the Frenchman for the sake of the swag now safely on board? It was possible: I had heard many a tale far less so. No doubt the supreme spirit was a man of subtlety and craft; so, too, most likely was our friend Lo Chuh Fen; the other two would not be wanting.

And if, of these other two, Wing, as Miss Raven had confidently surmised and as I thought it possible, was one, then, indeed, there would be brains enough and to spare for the carrying out of any adventure. It seemed to me as I lay there, quaking and sweating in sheer fright..I, a defenseless, quiet, peace-loving gentleman of bookish tastes, who scarcely knew one end of a revolver from the other...that what was likely was that the Chinese were going to round on their English and French associates, collar the loot for themselves, and sail the yawl...Heaven alone knew where! But in that case, what was going to become of me and my helpless companion? It was not likely that these Easterners would treat us with the consideration which we had received from the queer, eccentric, somewhat muddle-headed Netherfield Baxter, who...it struck me with odd in-consequence at that inopportune moment was certainly a combination of Dick Turpin, Gil Blas, and Don Quixote. I suppose it was nearly an hour that passed: it may have been more; it may have been less; what I know is that it gave me some idea of what an accused man may feel who, waiting in a cell below, wonders what the foreman of a jury is going to say when he is called upstairs once more to the dock which he has vacated pending that jury's deliberations.

Once or twice I thought of daring everything, rousing Miss Raven, and attempting an escape by means of the boat which no doubt lay at the side of the yawl. But reflection suggested that so desperate a deed would only mean getting a bullet through me, and perhaps through her as well. Then I speculated on my chances of making a sinuous way along the deck on my hands and knees, or on my stomach, snake-fashion, with the idea of listening at the hatch of the galley reflection, again, warned me that such an adventure would as likely as not end up with a few inches of cold steel in my side or through my gullet. So there I lay, sweating with fear, rapidly disintegrating as to nerve-power, becoming a lump of moral rag-and-bone and suddenly, unheralded by the slightest sound, I saw the figure of a man on my stairway, his outline silhouetted against the sky and the stars.

It was not because of any bravery on my part...I am sure of that...but through sheer fright that, before I had the least idea of what I was doing, I had thrown myself clear of rugs and pillows, sprung to my feet, made one frenzied leap across the bit of intervening space and clutched my intruder by his arms before his softly-padded feet touched the floor of the cabin. My own breath was coming in gasps...but the response to my frenzy was quiet and cool as an autumnal afternoon.

"Can you row a boat?"

I shall never forget the mental douche which dashed itself over me in that clear, yet scarcely perceptible whisper, accompanied as it was by a ghost-like laugh of sheer amusement. I released my grip, staring in the starlight at my visitor. Lo Chuh Fen!

"Yes!" I answered, steadying my voice and keeping it down to as low tones as his own. "Yes...I can!"

He pointed to the door behind which lay Miss Raven.

"Wake missy as quietly as possible," he whispered. "Tell her get ready...come on deck...make no noise. All ready for you...then you go ashore and away, see? Not good for you to be here longer."

"No danger to...her?" I asked him.

"No danger to anybody, you do as I say," he answered. "All ready for you...nothing to do but come on deck, forward; get into the boat, be off. Now!"

Without another word he glided up the stairway and disappeared. For a few seconds I stood irresolute. Was it a trick, a plant? Should we be safe on deck or targets for Chinese bullets, or receptacles for Chinese knives? Maybe...yet...

I suddenly made up my mind. It was but one step to the door of the little inner cabin...I scraped on its panels. It opened instantly...a crack.

"Yes?" whispered Miss Raven.

I remembered then that if need arose she was to do unquestioningly anything I told her to do.

"Dress at once and come out," I said. "Be quick!"

"I've never been undressed," she answered. "I lay down in my clothes."

"Then come, just now," I commanded. "Wait for nothing!"

She was out of the room at once and by my side in the gloom. I laid a hand on her arm, giving its plump softness a reassuring pressure.

"Don't be afraid!" I whispered. "Follow me on deck. We're going."

"Going!" she said. "Leaving?"

"Come along!" I said.

I went before her up the stairway and out on the open deck. The night was particularly clear; the stars very bright; the patch of water between the yawl and the shore lay before us calm and dark; we could see the woods above the cove quite plainly, and at the edge of them a ribbon of white, the silver-sanded beach. And also, at the forward part of the vessel we were leaving I saw, or fancied I saw, shadowy forms...the Chinese were going to see us off. But one form was not shadowy, nor problematical. Chuh was there, awaiting us, his arms filled with rugs. Without a word he motioned us to follow, preceded us along the side of the yawl to the boat, went before us into it, helped us down, settled us, put the oars into my hands, climbed out again, and leaned his yellow face down at me.

"You pull straight ahead," he murmured. "Good landing place straight before you: dry place on beach, too...morning come soon; you get away then through woods."

"The boat?" I asked him.

"You leave boat there...anywhere," he answered. "Boat not wanted again...we go, soon as high water over bar. Hope you get young missy safe home."

"Bless you!" I said under my breath. Then, remembering that I had some money in my pocket...three or four loose sovereigns as luck would have it, I thrust a hand therein, pulled them out, forced them into the man's claw-like fingers. I heard him chuckle softly...then his head disappeared behind the rail of the yawl, and I shoved the boat off, and for the next few minutes bent to those oars as I had certainly never bent to any previous labor, mental or physical, in my life. And Miss Raven, seeing my earnestness, said nothing, but quietly took the tiller and steered us in a straight line for the spot which the China-man had indicated. Neither of us...strange as it may seem...spoke one single word until, at the end of half an hour's steady pull, the boat's nose ran on to the shingly beach, beneath a fringe of dwarf oak that came right down to the edge of the shore. I sprang out, with a feeling of thankfulness that it would be hard to describe and for a good reason found my tongue once more.

"Great Scott!" I exclaimed. "I've left my boots in that cabin!"

Despite the strange situation in which we were still placed, Miss Raven's sense of humor asserted itself; she laughed.

"Your boots!" she said. "Whatever will you do? These stones and the long walk home?"

"There are things to be thought of before that," I said. "We're still in the middle of the night. But this boat...do you think you can help me to drag it up the beach?"

Between us, the boat being a light one, we managed to pull it across the pebbles and under the low cliff beneath the overhanging fringe of the wood. In the uncertain light...for there was no moon and since our setting out from the yawl masses of cloud had come up from the south-east to obscure the stars...the wood looked impenetrably black.

"We shall have to wait here until the dawn comes," I remarked. "We can't find our way through the wood in this darkness. I can't even recollect the path, if there was one, by which they brought us down here from the ruins. You had better sit in the boat and make yourself comfortable with those rugs. Considerate of them, at any rate, to provide us with those!"

She got into the boat again and I wrapped one rug round her knees and placed another about her shoulders.

"And you?" she asked.

"I must do a bit of amateur boot-making," I answered. "I'm going to cut this third rug into strips and bind them about my feet...can't walk over stones and thorns and thistles, to say nothing of the moorland track, without some protection."

I got out my pocket-knife and sitting on the side of the boat began my task; for a few minutes she watched me, in silence.

"What does all this mean!" she said at last, suddenly. "Why have they let us go?"

"No idea," I answered. "But...things have happened since Baxter said good-night to us." And I went on to tell her of all that had taken place on the yawl since the return of the Frenchman and his Chinese companion. "What does it look like?" I concluded. "Doesn't it seem as if the Chinese intend foul play to those two?"

"Do you mean...they intend to...to murder them?" she asked in a half-frightened whisper. "Surely not that?"

"I don't see that a man who has lived the life that Baxter has can expect anything but a violent end," I replied callously. "Yes, I suppose that's what I do mean. I think the Chinese mean to get rid of the two others and get away with the swag... cleverly enough, no doubt."

"Horrible!" she murmured.

"Inevitable!" I said. "To my mind, the whole atmosphere was one of...that sort of thing. We're most uncommonly lucky."

She became silent again, and remained so for some time, while I went on at my task, binding the strips of rug about my feet and ankles, and fastening them, puttee fashion, around my legs.

191

"I don't understand it!" she exclaimed, after several minutes had gone by. "Surely those men must know that we, once free of them, would be sure to give the alarm. We weren't under any promise to them, whatever we were to Baxter."

"I don't understand anything," I said. "All I know is the surface of the situation. But that gentle villain who saw us off the yawl said they were sailing at high water...only waiting until the tide was deep on the bar outside there. And they could get a long way, north or south or east, before we could set anybody on to them. Supposing they did get rid of Baxter and his Frenchman, what's to prevent them making off across the North Sea to, say, some port in the north of Russia? They've got stuff on board that would be sale-able anywhere... no doubt they'll have melted it all into shapeless lumps before many hours are out."

Once more she was silent, and when she spoke again it was in a note of decision.

"No, I don't think that's it at all," she said emphatically. "They're dependent on wind and weather, and the seas aren't so wide, but they'd be caught on our information. I'm sure that isn't it."

"What is it, then?" I asked.

"I've a sort of vague, misty idea," she answered, with a laugh that was plainly intended to be deprecatory of her own power. "Supposing these Chinese...you say they're awfully keen and astute...supposing they've got a plot among themselves for handing Baxter and the Frenchman over to the police...the authorities with their plunder? "

I had just finished the manufacture of my novel foot-wear, and I jumped to my padded feet with an exclamation that this time did not come from unpleasant contact with the sharp stones.

"By George!" I said. "There is an idea in that...there may be something in it!"

"We thought Wing was on board," she continued. "If so, I think I may be right in offering such a suggestion. Supposing that Wing came across these people when he went to London; took service with them in the hope of getting at their secret; supposing he's induced the other Chinese to secure Baxter and the Frenchman...that, in short, he's been playing the part of detective? Wouldn't that explain why they sent us away?"

"Partly...yes, perhaps wholly," I said, struggling with this new idea. "But where and when and how do they intend...if your theory's correct to do the handing over?"

"That's surely easy enough," she replied quickly. "There's nothing to do but sail the yawl into say Berwick harbor and call the police aboard. A very, very easy matter!"

"I wonder if it is so?" I answered, musingly. "It might be...but if we stay here until it's light and the tide's up, we shall see which way the yawl goes."

"It's high water between five and six o'clock," she remarked. "Anyway, it was between four and five yesterday morning at Ravensdene Court...which now seems to be far away, in some other world."

"Hungry?" I asked.

"Not a bit," she answered. "But it's a long way since yesterday afternoon. We've seen things."

"We've certainly seen Mr. Netherfield Baxter," I observed.

"A fascinating man!" she said, with a laugh. "The sort of man under other circumstances one would like to have to dinner."

"Um!" I said. "A ready and plausible tongue, to be sure. I dare say there are women who would fall in love with such a man."

"Lots!" she answered, with ready assent. "As I said just now, he's a very fascinating person."

"Ah!" I said, teasingly. "I had a suspicion last night that he was exciting your sympathetic interest."

"I'm much more sympathetic about your lack of boots and shoes," she retorted. "But as you seem to have rigged up some sort of satisfactory substitute, don't you think we might be making our way homewards? Is there any need to go through the woods? Why should we not follow the coast?"

"I'm doubtful about our ability to get round the south point of this cove," I answered. "I was looking at it yesterday afternoon from the deck of the yawl, and I saw that just there a sort of wall of rock runs right out into the sea. And if the tide's coming in..."

"Then, the woods," she interrupted. "Surely we can make our way through them, somehow. And it will begin to get light in another hour or so."

"If you like to try it," I answered. "But it's darker in there than you think for, and rougher going, too. However..." Just then, and before she had made up her mind, we were both switched off that line of action by something that broke out on another. Across the three-quarters of a mile of water which separated us from our recent prison came the sound, clear and unmistakable, of a revolver shot, followed almost instantly by another. Miss Raven, who had risen to her feet, suddenly sat down again. A third shot rang out...a fourth...a fifth; we saw the flashes of each; they came, without doubt, from the deck of the yawl.

"Firing!" she murmured.

"Fighting!" I said. "That's just...listen to that!"

Half a dozen reports, sharp, insistent, rang out in quick succession; then two or three, all mingling together; the echoes followed from wood and cliff. Rapidly as the flashes pierced the gloom, the sounds died out...a heavy silence followed.

"That's just what?" asked Miss Raven calmly.

"Well, if not just what I expected, it's at any rate partly what I expected," I said. "It had already struck me that if...well, supposing whatever it was that the Chinaman dropped into those glasses didn't act quite as soporifically as he intended it to, and Baxter and his companion woke up and found there was a conspiracy, a mutiny, going on, there'd be..."

"Fighting?" she suggested.

"You're not a squeamish girl," I answered. "There'd be bloody murder! Their lives or the others. And I should say that death's stalking through that unholy craft just now."

She made no answer and we stood staring at the black bulk lying motionless on the grey water; stood for a long time, listening. I, to tell the truth, was straining my ears to catch the plash of oars: I thought it possible that some of those on board the yawl might take a violent desire to get ashore.

But the silence continued. And now we said no more of setting out on our homeward journey: curiosity as to what had happened kept us there, whispering. The time passed...almost before we realized that night was passing, we were suddenly aware of a long line of faint yellow light that rose above the far horizon.

"Dawn," I muttered. "Dawn!"

And then, at that moment, we both heard something.

194

Somewhere outside the bar, but close to the shore, a steam-propelled vessel was tearing along at a break-neck speed.

Chapter 23

As we stood there, watching, the long line of yellow light on the eastern horizon suddenly changed in color...first to a roseate flush, then to a warm crimson; the scenes around us, sky, sea and land brightened as if by magic. And with equal suddenness there shot round the edge of the southern extremity of the cove, outlining itself against the red sky in the distance the long, low-lying hulk of a vessel...a dark, sinister-looking thing which I recognized, at once as a torpedo-destroyer.

It was coming along, about half a mile outside the bar, at a rare turn of speed which would, I knew, quickly carry it beyond our field of vision. And I was wondering whether from its decks the inside of the cove and the yawl lying at anchor there was visible when it suddenly slackened in its headlong career, went about, seaward, and describing the greater part of a circle, came slowly in towards the bar, nosing about there, beyond the line of white surf, for all the world like a terrier at the lip of some rat-hole.

Up to that moment Miss Raven and I had kept silence, watching this unexpected arrival in our solitude; now, turning to look at her, I saw the thought which had come into my mind had also occurred to hers.

"Do you think that ship is looking for the yawl?" she asked. "It's a gunboat or something of that sort, isn't it?"

"Torpedo destroyer...latest class, too," I answered.

"Rakish, wicked-looking things, aren't they? And that's just what I, too, was wondering. It" possible, some news of the yawl may have got to the ears of the authorities, and this thing may have been sent from the nearest base to take a look along the coast. Perhaps they've spotted the yawl. But they can't get over that bar, yet."

"The tide's rising fast, though," she remarked, pointing to the shore immediately before us. "It'll be up to this boat soon."

I saw that she was right, and presently the boat would

196

be floating. We made it fast, and retreated further up the beach, amongst the overhanging trees, and there, from beneath the shelter of a group of dwarf oaks, looked seaward again. The destroyer lay supine outside the bar, watching. Suddenly, right behind her, far across the grey sea, the sun shot up above the horizon...her long dark hull cut across his ruddy face. And we were then able to make out shapes that moved here and there on her deck. There were live men there....but on the yawl we saw no sign of life.

Yet, even as we looked, life sprang up there again. Once more a shot rang out, followed by two others in sharp succession. And as we stared in that direction, wondering what this new affray could be, we saw a boat shoot out from beneath the bows, with a low, crouching figure in it which was evidently making frantic efforts to get away. Somebody on board the yawl was just as eager to prevent this escape; three or four shots sounded...following one of them, the figure in the boat fell forward with a sickening suddenness.

"Got him!" I said involuntarily. "Poor devil...whoever he is."

"No!" exclaimed Miss Raven. "See! He's up again."

The figure was struggling to an erect position...even at that distance we could make out the effort. But the light of the newly-risen sun was so dazzling and confusing that we could not tell if the figure was that of an Englishman or a Chinaman...it was, at any rate, the figure of a tall man. And whoever he was, he managed to rise to his feet, and to lift an arm in the direction of the yawl, from which he was then some twenty yards away. Two more shots rang out...one from the yawl, another from the boat. It seemed to me that the man in the boat swayed...but a moment later he was again busy at his oars. No further shot came from the yawl, and the boat drew further and further away from it, in the direction of a spit of land some three or four hundred yards from where we stood. There were high rocks at the sea end of that spit...the boat disappeared behind them.

"There's one villain loose, at any rate," I muttered, not too well pleased to think he was within reach of ourselves. "I wonder which. But I'm sure he was winged...he fell in a heap, didn't he, at one of those shots? Of course, he'll take to these woods and we've got to get through them."

"Not yet!" said Miss Raven. "Look there!"

She pointed across the cove and beyond the bar, and I saw then that a boat had been put off from the destroyer and was being pulled at a rapid rate towards the line of surf which, under the deepening tide, was now but a thin streak of white. It seemed to me that I could see the glint of arms above the flash of the oars...anyway there was a boat's crew of blue-jackets there.

"They're going to board her!" I exclaimed. "I wonder what they'll find?"

"Dead men!" answered Miss Raven, quietly.

"What else? After all that shooting! I should think that man who's just got away was the last."

"There was a man left on board who fired at him and at whom he fired back," I pointed.

"Yes and who never fired again," she retorted. "They must all...oh!"

She interrupted herself with a sharp exclamation, and turning from watching the blue-jackets and their boat I saw that she was staring at the yawl. From its forecastle a black column of smoke suddenly shot up, followed by a great lick of flame.

"Good heavens!" I exclaimed. "The yawl's on fire!"

I guessed then at what had probably happened. The man who had just disappeared with his boat behind the spit of land further along the cove had in all likelihood been one of two survivors of the fight which had taken place in the early hours of the morning. He had wished to get away by himself, had set fire to the yawl, and sneaked away in the only boat, exchanging shots with the man left behind and probably killing him with the last one. And now...there was smoke and flame above what was doubtless a shambles. But by that time the boat's crew from the destroyer had crossed the bar and entered the cove and the vigorously impelled oars were flashing fast in the sheltered waters. The boat disappeared behind the drifting smoke that poured out of the yawl...presently we saw figures hurrying hither and thither about her deck.

"They may be in time to get the fire under," I said. "Better, perhaps, if they let the whole thing burn itself out. It would burn up a lot of villainy."

"Here are people coming along the beach," remarked

Miss Raven, suddenly. "Look! They must have seen the smoke rising."

I turned in the direction in which she was looking, and saw, on the strip of land and pebble, beneath the woods, a group of figures, standing at that moment and staring in the direction of the burning ship, which had evidently just rounded the extreme point of the cove at its southern confines. There were several figures in the group, and two were mounted. Presently these moved forward in our direction, at a smart pace; before they had gone far, I recognized the riders.

"A search party!" I exclaimed. "Look...that's Mr. Raven, in front, and surely that's Lorrimore, behind him. They're looking for us."

She gazed at the approaching figures for a moment, shielding her eyes from the already strong glare of the mounting sun, then ran forward along the shingle to meet them; I followed as rapidly as my improvised foot-wear would permit. By the time I reached them, Mr. Raven and Lorrimore were off their horses, the other members of the party had come up, and my companion in tribulation was explaining the situation. I let her talk...she was summing it all up in more concise fashion than I could have done. Her uncle listened with simple, open-mouthed astonishment; Lorrimore, when it came to mention of the Chinese element, with an obvious growing concern that seemed to be not far away from suspicion. He turned to me as Miss Raven finished.

"How many Chinese do you reckon were on board?" he asked.

"Four...including the last arrival, described as a gentleman," I answered.

"And two English?" he inquired.

"One Englishman, and one Frenchman," I said. "My belief is the Chinese have settled the other two and then possibly settled themselves, among them. There's one man somewhere in these woods. Whether he's a China-man we can't say...we couldn't make out."

He stared at me wonderingly for a moment; then turned and looked at the yawl. Evidently the blue-jackets had succeeded in checking the fire; the flame had died down, and the smoke now only hung about in wreaths; we could see figures running actively about the deck.

"There may be men on there that need medical assistance," said Lorrimore. "Where's this boat you mentioned, Middlebrook? I'm going off to that vessel. Two of you men pull me across there."

"I'll go with you," I said. "I left my boots in the cabin...I may find them and a good deal else. The boat's just along here."

The search party was a mixed lot...a couple of local policemen, some gamekeepers, two or three fishermen, one of Mr. Raven's men-servants. Two of the fishermen ran the boat into the water; Lorrimore and I sprang in.

"This is the most extraordinary affair I ever heard of," he said as he sat down at my side in the stern.

"You didn't see all these China-men? Miss Raven says that you actually suspected my man Wing to be on board!"

"Lorrimore," I said, "in ten minutes you'll probably see and learn things that you'd never have dreamed of. Whether your man Wing is on board or not I don't know...but I know that girl and I have had a marvelous escape from a nest of human devils! I can't say for myself, but...has my hair whitened?"

"Your hair hasn't whitened," he said. "You were probably safer than you knew...safe enough, if Wing was there."

"Well, I don't know," I retorted. "In future, let me avoid the sight of yellow cheeks and slit eyes...I've had enough. But tell me...how did you and your posse come this way? Didn't Mr. Raven get a wire last night?"

"Mr. Raven did get a wire," he replied; "but before he got it, he'd become anxious, and had sent out some of his men folk along the moors and cliffs in search of you. One of them, very late in the evening, came across a man who had been cutting wood somewhere hereabouts and had seen you and Miss Raven passing through the woods near the shore in company with two strangers. Mr. Raven's man returned close on midnight, with this news, and the old gentleman was, of course, thrown into a great state of alarm. He roused the whole community round Ravensdene Court, got me up, and we set out, as you see. But...the whole thing's marvelous! I can't help thinking that Wing may have been on board this vessel, and that it was due to him you got away."

"You've heard nothing of him...from London?" I suggested.

"Nothing, from anywhere," he replied. "Which is precisely why I feel sure that when he went there he came in contact with these people and has been playing some deep game."

"Deep, yes!" I said. "Deep indeed! But what game?"

He made no answer; we were now close to the yawl, and he was staring expectantly at the figures on her deck. Suddenly two of these detached themselves from the rest, turned, came to the side, looked down on us. One was a grimy-faced, alert-looking young naval officer, very much alive to his job; the other, not quite so smoke-blackened, but eminently business-like, was...Scarterfield.

"Good Heavens!" I muttered. "So...he's here!"

Scarterfield, as we pulled up to the side of the yawl, was evidently telling the young officer who we were; he turned from him to us as we prepared to clamber aboard and addressed us without ceremony, as if we had been parted from him but a few minutes since our last meeting.

"You'd better be prepared for some unpleasant sights, you two!" he said. "This is no place to bring an empty stomach to at this hour of the morning and I fancy you've no liking for horrors, Mr. Middlebrook."

"I've had plenty of them during this night, Scarterfield," I said. "I was a prisoner on board this vessel from yesterday afternoon until soon after midnight, and I've sat on yonder beach listening to a good many things that have gone on since I got away from her."

He stared at me in astonishment for a moment; so did his companion, whose sharp eyes, running me over, settled their glance on my swathed feet.

"Yes," I said, staring back at him. "Just so! I was bundled off in such a hurry that I left my boots behind me. They're in the cabin and if they aren't burned up I'll be glad of them."

I was making a move in that direction, for I saw the fire, now well under control, had been confined to the fore-part of the yawl...but Scarterfield stopped me. He was clearly as puzzled as anxious.

"Middlebrook!" he said earnestly. "I don't understand it,

at all. You say you were on this vessel...during the night? Then, in God's name, who else was on her...whom did you find here... what men?"

"I left six men on her," I answered. "Netherfield Baxter, a Frenchman, a Chinese gentleman, so described...three Chinese as well. The Frenchman and the Chinese gentleman were those fellows we heard of at Hull, Scarterfield, and one, at any rate, of the other three Chinese was Lo Chuh Fen, of whom we've also heard."

"And you got into their hands...how?" he asked.

"Kidnapped...Miss Raven and myself, by Baxter and the Frenchman, in those woods, yesterday afternoon," I answered. "We came across them by accident, at the place where they'd just dug up that monastic silver...there it is, man!" I continued, pointing to the chests, which still stood where I had last seen them. "You've got it, at last."

He threw an almost careless glance at the chests, shaking his head.

"I want something beyond that," he muttered. "But... you say there were six men altogether...six?"

"I've enumerated them." I replied. "Two Europeans and four Chinese."

He turned a quick eye on the naval officer.

"Then one of them has escaped somehow!" he exclaimed. "There's only five here and every man Jack is dead! Where's the other!"

"One did escape," I said. I, too, looked at the lieutenant. "He got off in a boat just as you and your men were approaching the bar yonder. I thought you'd see him."

"No," he answered, shaking his head. "We didn't see anybody leave. The yawl lay between us and him most likely. Where did he land?"

"Behind that spit," I replied, pointing to the place. "He vanished, from where I stood, behind those black rocks. That was just as you crossed the bar. And he can't have gone far away, for he was certainly wounded as he left the yawl...a man fired at him from the bows. He fired back."

"We heard those shots," said the lieutenant, "and we found a chap...Englishman in the bows, dying, when we boarded her. He died just afterwards. They're all dead...the others were dead then."

"Not a man alive!" I exclaimed.

Scarterfield cast a glance astern...the glance of a man who draws back the curtain from a set stage.

"Look for yourselves!" he muttered. "Too late for any of your work, doctor. But...that sixth man?"

Lorrimore and I, giving no heed just then to the detective's questioning about the escaped man, went towards the after part of the deck. Busied with their labors in getting the fire under control, the blue-jackets had up to then left the dead men where they found them...with one exception. The man whom they had found in the bows had been carried aft and laid near the entrance to the little deck-house...some hand had thrown a sheet over him. Lorrimore lifted it...we looked down. Baxter!

"That's the fellow we found right forward," said the lieutenant. "He's several slighter wounds on him, but he'd been shot through the chest...heart, perhaps just before we boarded her. That would be the shot fired by the man in the boat, I suppose...a good marksman! Was this the skipper"

"Chief spirit," I said. "He was lively enough last night. But...the rest?"

"They're all over the place," he answered. "They must have had a most desperate do of it. The vessel's more like a slaughter-house than a ship!"

He was right there, and I was thankful that Miss Raven and I for whatever reason on the part of the Chinese, had been so unceremoniously sent ashore before the fight began. As Lorrimore went about, noting its evidences, I endeavored to form some idea, more or less accurate, of the events which had led up to it. It seemed to me that either Baxter or the Frenchman, awaking from sleep sooner than the Chinese had expected, had discovered that treachery was afoot and that shooting had begun on all sides. Most of the slaughter had taken place immediately in front of the hatchway which led to the cabin in which I had seen Baxter and his two principal associates; some sort of a rough barricade had been hastily set up there; behind it the Frenchman lay dead, with a bullet through his brain; before it, here and there on the deck, lay three of the Chinese...their leader, still in his gaily colored sleeping suit, prominent amongst them; Lo Chuh Fen a little further away; the third man near the wheel, face downwards.

He, like Chuh, was a small-made, wiry fellow. And there was blood everywhere.

Scarterfield jogged my elbow as I stood staring at these unholy sights. He was keener of look than I had ever seen him.

"That fourth China-man?" he said. "I must get him, dead or alive. The rest's nothing...I want him!"

Chapter 24

I glanced round; Lorrimore, after an inspection of the dead men, had walked aside with the lieutenant and was in close conversation with him. I, too, drew the detective away to the side of the yawl.

"Scarterfield," I said in a whisper, "I've grounds for believing the fourth Chinaman is Lorrimore's servant, Wing."

"What!" he exclaimed. "The man we saw at Ravensdene Court?"

"Just so," I said, "and who went off to London, you remember, to see what he could do in the way of discovering the other China-man, Lo Chuh Fen."

"Yes...I remember that," he answered.

"There is Lo Chuh Fen," I said, pointing to one of the silent figures. "And I think that Wing not only discovered him, but came aboard this vessel with him, as part of a crew which Baxter and his French friend got together at Lime-house or Poplar. As I say, I've grounds for thinking it."

Scarterfield looked round, glanced at the shore, shook his head.

"I'm all in the dark about some things," he said.

"I got on the track of this craft...I'll tell you how, later and found she'd come up this coast, and we got the authorities to send this destroyer after her. I came with her, hell for leather, I can tell you, from Harwich. But I don't know a lot that I want to know, Baxter, now...you're sure that man lying dead there is the Baxter we heard of at Blyth and traced to Hull?"

"Certain!" I said. "Listen, and I'll give you a brief account of what's happened since yesterday, and of what I've learned since then and it will make things clear to you."

Standing there, where the beauty of the fresh morning and the charm of sky and sea made a striking contrast to the horror of our immediate surroundings, I told him, as concisely as I could, of how Miss Raven and myself had fallen into the hands of Netherfield Baxter and the Frenchman, of what had happened to me on board, and, at somewhat greater length, of Baxter's story of his own career as it related to his share in the theft of the monastic treasure from the bank at Blyth, his connection with the *Elizabeth Robinson* and his knowledge of the brothers Quick. Nor did I forget Baxter's theory about the rubies and at that Scarterfield obviously pricked his ears.

"Now there's something in that," he said, with a regretful glance at the place where Baxter's dead body lay under its sheet. "I wish that fellow had been alive, to tell more! For he's right about those rubies...quite right. The Quicks had them...two of them."

"You know that?" I exclaimed.

"I'll tell you," he answered. "After we parted, I was very busy, investigating matters still further in Devonport and in London. And through the newspapers, of course I got in touch with a man who told me a lot. He came to headquarters in London, asking for me...wouldn't tell any of our people there anything. It was a day or two before I got at close quarters with him, for when he called I was away at the time. He left an address, in Hatton Garden...a Mr. Isidore Baubenheimer, dealer, as you may conclude, in precious stones.

Well, I drove off at once to see him. He told me a queer tale. He said that he'd only just come back from Amsterdam and Paris, or he'd have been in communication with me earlier. While he'd been away, he said, he'd read the English newspapers and seen a good deal about the two murders at Saltash and Ravensdene Court, and believed he could throw some light on them, for he felt sure either Noah or Salter Quick was identical with a man with whom he had not so long ago talked over the question of the value of certain stones which the man possessed. But I'll show you Baubenheimer's own words. I got him to make a clear statement of the whole thing and had it taken down in black and white, and I have a typed copy of it in my pocket-book...glance it over for yourself."

He produced a sheet of paper, folded and endorsed and handed it to me...it ran thus:

My place of business in Hatton Garden is a few doors away from the Hatton Garden entrance to the old Mitre Tavern, which lies between that street and Ely Place. On, as far as I can remember, the seventh or eighth of March last, I went into the Mitre about half-past eleven o'clock one morning, expecting to meet a friend of mine who was often there about that time. He hadn't come in...I sat down with a drink and a cigar to wait for him. In the little room where I sat there were three other men...two of them were men that I knew, men who dealt in diamonds in a smallish way. The other was a stranger, a thick-set, middle-aged, seafaring sort of man, hard-bitten, dressed in a blue-serge suit of nautical cut; I could tell from his hands and his general appearance that he'd knocked about the world in his time.

Just then he was smoking a cigar and had a tumbler of rum and water before him, and he was watching, with a good deal of interest, the other two, who, close by, were showing each other a quantity of loose diamonds which, evidently to the seafaring man's amazement, they spread out openly, on their palms. After a bit they got up and went out, and the stranger glanced at me. Now I am, as you see, something of the nautical sort myself, bearded and bronzed and all that... I'm continually crossing the North Sea and it may be he thought I was of his own occupation...anyway, he looked at me as if wanting to talk.

"I reckon they think nothing of pulling out a fistful of them things hereabouts," he said. "No more to them than sovereigns and half-sovereigns and bank-notes is to bank clerks."

"That's about it," I said. "You'll see them shown in the open street outside."

"Trade of this part of London, isn't it?" he asked.

"Just so," I said. "I'm in it myself." He gave me a sharp inquiring look at that.

"Ah!" he remarked. "Then you'll be a gentleman as knows the valley of a thing of that sort when you sees it?"

"Well I think so," I answered. "I've been in the trade all my life. Have you got anything to dispose of? I see you're a seafaring man, and I've known sailors who brought something nice home now and then."

"Same here," he said; "but I never known a man as brought anything half as good as what I have."

"Ah!" I said. "Then you have something?"

"That's what I come into this here neighborhood for, this morning," he answered. "I have something, and a friend of mine, says he to me, 'Hatton Garden,' he says, 'is the port for you...they eats and drinks and wallers in them sort of things down that way,' he says."

"So I steers for this here; only, I don't know no fish, do you see, as I could put the question to what I wants to ask."

"Put it to me," I said, drawing out my card-case. "There's my card, and you can ask anybody within half a square mile if they don't know me for a trustworthy man. What is it you've got?" I went on, never dreaming he'd got anything at all of any great value. "I'll give you an idea of its worth in two minutes."

But he glanced round at the door and shook his head.

"Not here, mister!" he said. "I wouldn't let the light of day shine on what I got in a public place like this, not no how. But," he added, "I see you've an office and all that. I ain't undisposed to go there with you, if you like...you seem a honest man."

"Come on then," I said. "My office is just round the corner, and though I've clerks in it, we'll be private enough there."

"Right you are, mister," he answered, and he drank off his rum and we went out and round to my office.

I took him into my private room...I had a young lady clerk in there, she'd remember this man well enough and he looked at her and then at me.

"Send the girl away," he muttered. "There's a matter of undressing...in getting at what I want to show you."

I sent her out of the room, and sat down at my desk. He took off his overcoat, his coat, and his waistcoat, shoved his hand into some secret receptacle that seemed to be hidden in the band of his trousers, somewhere behind the small of his back, and after some acrobatic contortions and twisting's, lugged out a sort of canvas parcel, the folds of which he unwrapped leisurely. And suddenly, coming close to me, he laid the canvas down on my blotting-pad and I found myself staring at some dozen or so of the most magnificent pearls I ever set eyes on and a couple of rubies which I knew to be priceless. I was never more astonished in my life, but he was as cool as a cucumber.

"What do you think of that lot, mister?" he asked. "I reckon you don't see a little lot of that quality every day."

"No, my friend," I said, "nor every year, either, nor every ten years. Where on earth did you get them..."

"Away East," he said, "and I've had them some time, not being particular about selling them, but I've settled down in England now, and I think I will sell them and buy house-property with the money. What do you fix their valley at, now, mister...thereabouts, anyway?"

"Good heavens, man!" I said. "They're worth a great deal of money...a great deal."

"I'm very well aware of that," he answered. "Very well aware indeed...nobody better. I've seen, a deal of things in my time, and I ain't no fool."

"You really want to sell them?" I asked.

"If I get the full price," he said. "And that, of course, would be a big one."

"The thing to do," I said, "would be to find somebody who wants to complete a particularly fine set of pearls...some very rich woman who'd stick at nothing. The same remark applies to the rubies."

"Maybe you could come across some customer?" he suggested.

"No doubt, in a little time," I answered.

"Well," he said, "I'm going up North...I've a bit of business that way, and I reckon I'll be back here in London in a week or so I'll call in then, and if you've found anybody that's likely to deal, I'll show them the goods with pleasure."

"You" better leave them with me, and let me show them to some possible buyers," I said. But he was already folding up his canvas wrapping again.

"Guv'nor," he answered, "I can see as how you're a honest man, and I treats you as such, and so will, but I couldn't have them things out of my possession for one minute until I sells them. I've a brother," he added, "as owns a half-share in them and I holds myself responsible to him. But now that you've seen them, find a buyer or buyers and I'll shove my bows round that door of yours again this day week." And with that he restored his treasures to their hiding-place, assumed his garments once more, and remarking that he had a train to catch, hastened off, again assuring me that he would call in a week, on his return from the North. It was not until he had been gone several minutes that I remembered

209

that I had forgotten to ask his name. I certainly expected him to be back at the end of the week...but he didn't come, and just then I had to go away. Now I take him to have been the man, Salter Quick, who was murdered on the Northumberland coast...no doubt for the sake of those jewels. As for their value, I estimated it, from my cursory examination of them, to have been certainly not less than eighty thousand pounds.

I folded up the statement and restored it to Scarterfield.

"What do you think of that?" he asked.

"Salter Quick, without a doubt," I answered. "It corroborates Baxter's story of the rubies. He didn't mention any pearls. And I think now, Scarterfield, that Salter Quick's murder lies at the door of...one of those China-men who in their turn are lying dead before us!"

"Well, and that's what I think," he said. "Though however a China-man could be about this coast without the local police learning something of it at the time they were inquiring into the murder beats me. However, there it is! I feel sure of it. And I was going to tell you until I got wind of this yawl down Lime-house way. I found out that she'd been in the Thames, and her owner had enlisted a small crew of China-men and gone away with them, and I found out further that she'd been seen off the Norfolk coast, going north, so then I pitched a hot and strong story to the authorities about piracy and all manner of things, and they sent this destroyer in search of Baxter, and me on her. If we'd only been twelve hours sooner!"

Lorrimore and the lieutenant came up to us.

"My men have the fire completely beaten," said the lieutenant glancing at Scarterfield. "If you want to look round..."

We began a thorough examination of the yawl, in the endeavor to reconstruct the affair of the early morning. For there were all the elements of a strange mystery in that and curiosity about the whole thing was as strong in me as in Scarterfield. We know now many things that we had not known twenty-four hours before. One was the many affairs, dark and nefarious, of Netherfield Baxter, had nothing to do with the murders of Noah and Salter Quick; another those murders without doubt arose from the brothers possession of the pearls and rubies which Salter had shown to the Hatton

Garden diamond merchant. All things considered it seemed to me the explanation of the mystery rested in some such theory as this. The China-man, Lo Chuh Fen, doubtless knew as well as Baxter and his French friend the Quicks were in possession of the rubies stolen from the heathen temple in Southern China; no doubt he had become acquainted with that fact when the marooned party from the *Elizabeth Robinson* were on the intimate terms of men united by a common fate on the lonely island. Drifting eventually to England, Chuh had probably discovered the whereabouts of the two brothers, had somehow found the rubies were still in their possession, might possibly have been in personal touch with Salter or with Noah, had taken others of his compatriots, discovered in the Chinese quarters of the East End into his confidence, and engineered a secret conspiracy for securing the valuables.

He had probably tracked Salter to the lonely bit of shore near Ravensdene Court; associates of his had no doubt fallen upon Noah at Saltash. But how had all this led up to the attack of the Chinese on Baxter and the Frenchman? And who was the man who, leaving every other member of the yawl's company dead or dying and who had exchanged those last shots with Netherfield Baxter, had escaped to the shore and was now, no doubt, endeavoring to make a final bid for liberty?

Reckoning up everything we saw, it seemed to me, from my knowledge of the preceding incidents, the drug which the Chinese gentleman, as Baxter had been pleased to style him, had not had the effects that he desired and anticipated, and that one or other of the two men to whom it had been administered had been aroused from sleep before any attack could be made on both. I figured things in this way...Baxter, or the Frenchman, or both, had awakened and missed the China-man. One or both had turned out to seek him; had discovered that Miss Raven and I were missing; had scented danger to themselves, found the Chinese up to some game, and opened fire on them. Evidently the first fighting...as I had gathered from the revolver shots had been sharp and decisive; I formed the conclusion that when it was over there were only two men left alive, of whom one was Baxter and the other the man whom we had seen escaping in the boat.

Baxter, I believed, had put up some sort of barricade and watched his enemy from it; that he was already seriously wounded I gathered from two facts...one that his body had several superficial wounds on arms and shoulders, and that in the cabin behind the hastily-constructed barricade, sheets had been torn into strips for bandages which we found on these wounds, where, as far as he could, he had roughly twisted them. Then, according to my thinking, he had eventually seen the other survivor, who was probably in like case with himself as regards superficial wounds endeavoring to make off, and emerging from his shelter had fired on him from the side of the yawl, only to be killed himself by return fire.

There was no mistaking the effect of that last shot... chance shot or well-directed aim it had done for Netherfield Baxter, and he had crumpled up and died where he dropped. A significant exclamation from Scarterfield called me to his side...he, aided by one of the blue-jackets, was examining the body of Lo Chuh Fen.

"Look here!" he murmured as I went up to him. "This chap has been searched! After he was dead, I mean. There's a body-belt that he wore...it's been violently torn from him, his clothing ripped to get at it, and the belt itself hacked to pieces in the endeavor to find something! Whose work has that been!"

"The work of the man who got away in the boat," I said. "Of course! He's been after those rubies and pearls, Scarterfield."

"We must be after him," he said. "You say you think he was wounded in getting away?"

"He was certainly wounded," I affirmed. "I saw him fall headlong in the boat after the first shot; he recovered himself, fired the shot which no doubt finished Baxter, and must have been wounded again, for the two men again fired simultaneously, and the man in the boat swayed at that second shot. But once more he pulled himself together and rowed away."

"Well, if he's wounded, he can't get far without attracting notice," declared Scarterfield. "We'll organize a search for him presently. But first let's have a look into the quarters that these Chinamen occupied."

The smoke of the fire, which seemed to have broken out in the forecastle and had been confined to it by the efforts of the sailors from the destroyer had now almost cleared away, and we went forward to the galley.

The fire had not spread to that, and after the scenes of blood and violence astern and in the cabin the place looked refreshingly spick and span; there was, indeed, an unusual air of neatness and cleanliness about it. The various pots and pans shone gaily in the sun's glittering lights; every utensil was in its place; evidently the galley's controlling spirit had been a meticulously careful person who hated disorder as heartily as dirt. And on a shelf near the stove was laid out what I took to be the things which the vanished cook, whoever he might be, had destined for breakfast...a tempting one of kidneys and bacon, soles, eggs, a curry. I gathered from this, and pointed my conclusion out to Scarterfield, that the presiding genius of the galley had had no idea of the mutiny into which he had been plunged soon after midnight.

"Aye!" said Scarterfield. "Just so...I see your point. And you think that man of Lorrimore's, Wing, was aboard, and if so, he's the man who's escaped?"

"I've strong suspicions," I said. "Yet, they were based on a plum-cake."

"Well, and I've known of worse clues," he rejoined. "But...I wonder? Now, if only we knew..."

Just then Lorrimore came along, poking his head into the galley. He suddenly uttered a sharp exclamation and reached an arm to a black silk cap which hung from a peg on the boarding above the stove.

"That's Wing's!" he said, in emphatic tones. "I saw him make that cap himself!"

Chapter 25

The bit of head-gear which Lorrimore had taken down assumed a new interest; Scarterfield and I gazed at it as if it might speak to us. Nevertheless the detective when he presently spoke showed some incredulity.

"That's the sort of cap that any China-man wears," he remarked. "It may have belonged to any of them."

"No!" answered Lorrimore, with emphatic assurance. "That's my man's. I saw him making it...he's as deft with his fingers, at that sort of thing, as he is at cooking. And since this cap is his, and as he's not amongst the lot there on deck, he's the man that you, Middlebrook, saw escaping in the boat. And since he is that man, I know where he'd be making."

"Where, then?" demanded Scarterfield.

"To my house!" answered Lorrimore.

Scarterfield showed more doubt.

"I don't think that's likely, doctor," he said. "Presumably, he's got those jewels on him, and I should say he'd get away from this with the notion of trusting to his own craft to get unobserved on a train and lose himself in Newcastle. A China-man with valuables on him worth eighty thousand pounds? Come!"

"You don't know that he's any valuables of any sort on him," retorted Lorrimore. "That's all supposition. I say that if my man Wing was on this vessel...as I'm sure he was...he was on it for purposes of his own. He might be with this felonious lot, but he wouldn't be of them. I know him and I'm off to get on his track. Lay you anything you like...a thousand to one that I find Wing at my house!"

"I'm not taking you, Lorrimore," I said. "I don't mind laying the same."

Scarterfield looked curiously at the two of us. Apparently, his belief in Chinese virtue was not great.

"Well," he said. "I'm on his track, anyhow, and I

214

propose to get away to the beach. There's nothing more we can do here. These naval people have got this job in charge, now. Let's leave them to it. Yet," he added, as we left the galley, and with a significant glance at me, "there is one thing Middlebrook...wouldn't you like to have a look inside those two chests that we've heard so much about...you and I."

"I certainly should!" I answered.

"Then we will," he said. "I, too, have some curiosity that way. And if Master Wing has repaired to the doctor's house he's all right, and if he hasn't, he can't get very far away, being a China-man, in his native garments, and wounded."

The chests which had come aboard the yawl with Miss Raven and myself the previous afternoon...it seemed as if ages had gone by since then and still stood where they had been placed at the time; close to the gangway leading to the main cabin. Lorrimore, Scarterfield, the young naval officer and I gathered round while a couple of handy blue-jackets forced them open...no easy business, for whether the dishonest bank-manager and Netherfield Baxter had ever opened them or not, they were screwed up again in a fashion which showed business-like resolves that they should not easily be opened again. But at last the lids were off to reveal inner shells of lead. And within these, gleaming dully in the fresh sunlight lay the monastic treasures of which Scarterfield and I had read in the hotel at Blyth.

"Queer!" said the detective, as he stood staring meditatively at patens and chalices and reliquaries. "All these, I reckon, are sacred things, consecrated and all that, and yet ever since that Reformation time, they've been mixed up with robbery, and now at last with murder! Odd, isn't it? However, there they are and here," he added, pulling the parchment schedules out of his pocket which he had discovered at Baxter's old lodgings in Blyth, and handing them to the lieutenant, "here is the list of what there ought to be; you'll take all this in charge, of course...I don't know if it comes within the law of treasure trove or not, but as the original owners are dust and ashes four hundred years ago, I should say it does...anyway, the Crown solicitors will soon settle that point."

We went off from the yawl, the three of us, in the boat which had brought Lorrimore and me aboard her. The group on shore saw us making for the point where the escaping figure had landed in the early morning, and followed us along the beach. They came up to us as we stepped ashore, and while Lorrimore began giving Mr. Raven an account of what we had found on the yawl I drew his niece aside.

"You had better know the worst in a word," I said. "We were more than fortunate in getting away from the yawl as we did. Don't be upset...there isn't a man alive on that thing!"

"Baxter?" she exclaimed.

"I said...not one!" I answered. "Don't think about it...as for me, I wish I'd never seen it. But now it's a question of a living man...Wing."

"Then it was as I thought?" she asked. "Wing was there?"

"Lorrimore is sure of it...he found a cap of Wing's in the galley," I said. "And as Wing isn't amongst the dead, he's the man who escaped."

Scarterfield came up, the local policeman with him who had joined Mr. Raven's search-party as it came across country.

"Whereabouts did this man land, Middlebrook?" he asked. "You saw him, you and Miss Raven, didn't you?"

"We saw him round these rocks," I replied. "But then they hid him from us...we couldn't see exactly. Somewhere on the other side of them, anyway."

We spread ourselves out along the shore, crossing the spit of sand, now encroached on considerably by the tide, and began to search among the black rocks that jutted out of it thereabouts. Presently we came across the boat, slightly rocking in the lapping water alongside a ledge. I took a hasty glance into it and drew Miss Raven away. For on the thwarts, and on the seat in the stern, and on one of the oars, thrown carelessly aside, there was blood. A sharp cry from one of the men who had gone a little ahead brought us all hurrying to his side. He had found, amongst the rocks, a sort of pool at the sides of which there was dry, sand-strewn rock; there were marks there as if a man had knelt in the sand, and there was more blood, and there were strips of clothing...linen, silk, as if the man had torn up some of his garments as temporary bandages.

"He's been here," said Lorrimore in a low voice. "Probably washed his wounds here...salt is a styptic. Flesh wounds, most likely, but," he added, sinking his voice still

216

lower, "judging from what we've seen of the blood he's lost, he must have been weakening by the time he got here. Still, he's a man of vast strength and physique, and he'd push on. Look for marks of his footsteps."

We eventually picked up a recently made track in the sand and followed it until it came to a point at the end of the overhanging woods, where they merged into open moorland running steeply downwards to the beach. There, in the short, wiry grass of the close-knitted turf, the marks vanished.

"Just as I said," muttered Lorrimore, whom with Miss Raven and myself, was striding on a little in advance of the rest. "He's made for my place as I knew he would. I knew enough of this country to know there's a road at the head of these moors that runs parallel with the railway on one side and the coast on the other towards Ravensdene...he'd be making for that. He'd take up the side of this wood, as the nearest way to strike the road."

That he was right in this we were not long in finding out. Twice, as our party climbed the steep side of the moorland we came across evidences of the fugitive. At two points we found places where a man had recently sat down on the bank beneath the trees, to rest. And at one of them we found more...a blood-soaked bandage.

"No man can go far, losing blood in that way," whispered Lorrimore to me as we went onward. "He can't be far off."

And suddenly we came across our quarry. Coming out on the top of the moorland, and rounding the corner of the woods, we hit the road of which Lorrimore had spoken...a long, white wall-less ribbon of track that ran north and south through treeless country. There, a few yards away from us, stood an isolated cottage, some gamekeeper's or watcher's place, with a bit of unfenced garden before it. In that garden was a strange group, gathered about something that at first we did not see. Mr. Cazalette, obviously very busy, the police inspector. a horse and trap, tethered to a post close by, showed how they had come. A woman, evidently the mistress of the cottage, a child, open-mouthed wide-eyed with astonishment at these strange happenings, a dog that moved uneasily around the two-legged folk, whimpering his concern. The bystanders moved as we hurried up, and then we caught glimpses of towels and water and hastily-improvised bandages and smelt brandy, and saw, in the midst of all this Wing, propped up against a bank of earth, his eyes closed, and over his yellow face a queer gray-white pallor. His left arm and shoulder were bare, save for the bandages which Cazalette was applying... there were discarded ones on the turf which were soaked with blood. Lorrimore darted forward with a hasty exclamation, and had Cazalette's job out of the old gentleman's hands and into his own before the rest of us could speak. He motioned the whole of us away except Cazalette and the woman, and the police inspector turned to Mr. Raven and his niece, and to myself and Scarterfield.

"I think we were just about in time," he said, laconically. "I don't know what it all means, but I reckon the man was about done for. Bleeding to death, I should say."

"You found him?" I asked.

"No," he answered. "Not at first anyway. The woman there says she was out here in her garden, feeding her fowls, when she saw him stagger round the corner of the wood there, and make for her. He fell across the bank where he's lying in a dead faint, and she ran for water. Just then we came along in the trap, saw what was happening and jumped out. Fortunately, when we set off, Mr. Cazalette insisted on bringing a big flask of neat brandy, and some food...he said you never knew what you mightn't want and we gave him a stiff dose, and pulled him round sufficiently to be able to tell us where he was wounded. And he's got a skin-full...a bullet through the thick part of his left arm, another at the point of the same shoulder, and a third just underneath it. Mr. Cazalette says they're all flesh wounds...but I don't know. I know the man's fainted twice since we got to him. And look here...just before he fainted the last time, he managed to fumble among his clothing with his right hand and he pulled something out and shoved it into my hand with a word or two. 'Give it Lorrimore,' he said, in a very weak voice. 'Tell him I found it all out...was going to trap all of them...but they were too quick for me last night...all dead now.' Then he fainted again. "And...look at this!"

He drew out a piece of canvas, twisted up anyhow, and opening it before our wondering eyes, revealed a heap of magnificent pearls and a couple of wonderful rubies that shone in the sunlight like fire.

"That's what he gave me," said the inspector. "What is it? What's it mean?"

"That's what Salter Quick was murdered for," I said. "And it means that Lorrimore's man ran down the murderer."

And without waiting for any comment from him, and leaving Scarterfield to explain matters, I went across the little garden to see how the honest China-man was faring.

It was a strange, yet a plain story that Wing told his master and a select few of us a day or two later, when Lorrimore had patched him up. To anybody of a hum-drum life...such as mine had always been until these events...it was, indeed, a stirring story. The queer thing, however, at any rate, queer to me was that the narrator, as calm and suave as ever in his telling of it...did not seem to regard it as anything strange at all...he might have been explaining to us some new way of making a good cake.

At our request and suggestion, he had journeyed to London and plunged into those quarters of the East End where his fellow-countrymen are to be found. His knowledge of the district of which Lime-house Causeway forms a center soon brought him in touch with Lo Chuh Fen, who, as he quickly discovered, had remained in London during the last two or three years, assisting in the management of a Chinese eating-house. Close by, in a lodging kept by a compatriot, Wing put himself up and cultivated Chuh's acquaintance. Ere many days had passed another China-man came on the scene...this was the man whom Baxter had described as a Chinese gentleman.

He represented himself to Wing and Chuh as a countryman of theirs who had been engaged in highly successful trading operations in Europe, and was now, in company with two friends, an Englishman and a Frenchman, carrying out another which involved a trip in a small, but well-appointed yacht, across the Atlantic. He wanted these countrymen of his own to make up a crew. An introduction to Baxter and the Frenchman followed, and Wing and Chuh were taken into confidence as regards the treasure hidden on the Northumberland coast.

A share of the proceeds was promised them: they secured a third, trustworthy China-man in the person of one Ah Wong, an associate of Chuh's, and the yawl, duly equipped, left the Thames and went northward.

By this time, Wing had wormed himself completely into Chuh's confidence, and without even discovering whether Chuh was or was not the actual murderer of Salter Quick. He believed him to be Wong to be the murderer of Noah, at Saltash. He had found out Chuh was in possession of the pearls and rubies which...though Wing had no knowledge of that... Salter had exhibited to Baubenheimer.

And as the yawl neared the scene of the next operations, Wing made his own plans. He had found out that its owners, after recovering the monastic treasures, were going to call at Leith, where they were to be met by the private yacht of some American, whose name Wing never heard. Accordingly, he made up his mind to escape from the yawl as soon as it got into Leith, to go straight to the police, and there give information as to the doings of the men he was with. But here his plans were frustrated. He was taken aback by the capture of Miss Raven and myself by Baxter and the Frenchman, and though he contrived to keep out of our way, he was greatly concerned lest we should see him and conclude that he had joined the gang and was privy to its past and present doings. But that very night a much more serious development materialized. The Chinese gentleman, arriving from London, and being met by the Frenchman at Berwick, had a scheme of his own, which, after he had attempted the drugging of his two principal associates, he unfolded to his fellow-countrymen.

This was to get rid of Baxter and the Frenchman and seize the yawl and its contents for themselves, sailing with it to some port in North Russia. Wing had no option but to profess agreement...his only proviso was that Miss Raven and myself should be cleared out of the yawl. This proposition was readily assented to, and Chuh was charged with the job of sending us ashore. But almost immediately afterwards, everything went wrong with the conspirator's plans. The drug which had been administered to Baxter and the Frenchman failed to act; Baxter, waking suddenly to find the China-men advancing on the cabin with only too evident murderous intent, opened fire on them, and the situation rapidly resolved itself into a free fight, in the course of which Wing barricaded himself into the galley. Before long he saw that of all the men on board, only himself and Baxter remained alive...he saw, too, Baxter was already wounded. Baxter, evidently afraid of Wing, also barricaded himself into the cabin; for some hours the two secretly awaited each other's onslaught. At last, Wing determined to make a bid for liberty, and cautiously worming his way to the cabin he looked in and as he thought, saw Baxter lying either dead or dying. He then hastily stripped Chuh of the belt in which he knew him to carry the precious stones, and taking to the boat which lay at the side of the yawl, pushed off, only to find Baxter after him with a revolver. In the exchange of shots which followed Wing was hit twice, but a lucky reply of his laid Baxter dead.

At that he got away, weak and fainting, managed to make the shore, to bind up as much of his wounded body as he could get at, and set out as well as he was able for his master's house. The rest we knew. So that was all over, and it only remained now for the police to clear things up, for Wing to be thoroughly whitewashed in the matter of the shooting of Netherfield Baxter, and for everybody in the countryside to talk of the affair for nine days and perhaps a little more. Mr. Cazalette talked a great deal. As for Miss Raven and myself, as actors in the last act of the drama which ended in such a tragedy, we talked little: we had seen too much at close quarters. But on the first occasion on which she and I were alone again, I made a confession to her.

"I don't want you...of all people...to get any mistaken impression about me," I said. "So, I'm going to tell you something. During the whole of the time you and I were on that yawl..."

"You were?" she exclaimed. "Really frightened?"

"Quaking with fright!" I declared boldly. "Especially after you'd retired. I literally sweated with fear. There! Now it's out!"

She looked at me not at all unkindly.

"Um!" she said at last. "Then, all I have to say is that you concealed it admirably...when I was about, at any rate. And..." she lowered her voice to a pleasing whisper, "I'm sure that if you were frightened, it was entirely on my account. So..."

In that way we began a courtship which, proving highly satisfactory on both sides, is now about to come to an end or a new beginning in marriage.

The End

Printed in Great Britain
by Amazon

25815883R00126